OLAF
AND
ESSEX

PRETTY COOL LLC

www.patticalkosz.com

First edition, 2024

Cover and interior design and formatting by Jennifer Kyte
Illustrations by Xiao
Published in New York, NY
Library of Congress Control Number: 2024911863
ISBN 979-8-9901433-7-1

By
Patti Calkosz

ONE

Behind the cover of a tree, Olaf watched the humans soar through the night on their broomstick.

The baby's laughter had attracted him—distracted him from foraging for food. It sounded like the chirping of baby birds, even sweeter than blueberries.

The adult female carried the baby, and a hunk of metal which glinted in the moonlight. She was tall, taller than Olaf when he stood on his hind legs. She had a lot of unruly orange fur on top of her head. The male steered. He had a big, round belly. Like Olaf. He, too, must be storing food for the long winter.

As Olaf was a bear and had no need to sweep floors, he had never seen a broomstick before. But his best friend, Essex, was a curious red fox. She, too, was not fond of cleaning, but liked to spy on the nearby humans in the dwellings surrounding the park. She had told him of witches flying on broomsticks—at least, on the TV.

Essex had admitted to Olaf, she'd never seen a real-life witch. But she'd heard humans debating them. Some maintained that witches were merely precise gardeners, concoctors of homemade medicines, and experts on the phases of the moon. Others argued they could simply look at you and make your toes blacken and fall off, if they wanted to.

Olaf stared at the humans on their broomstick. He was only an animal, and hardly ever left the park, but he had now seen his very own pair of witches. He checked that his belly wasn't sticking out past the tree trunk, and looked down at his already-black toes. He rather liked them, and hoped if the witches *did* spot him, they wouldn't look at him funny.

The broomstick slowed, descended, and landed in the meadow. Right near the great black tupelo. Which shook its branches sadly, as if it knew what those humans were up to.

Olaf shoved a pawful of blueberries in his mouth, and kept

watching. Why were these boneheaded humans here? What boneheaded thing were they about to do? It wasn't safe for humans to be in the park after dark. Even when they weren't fighting amongst each other, the human species was in general unreasonable. Prone to violence. A human could be lurking here right now. Just waiting for other, careless humans to happen along with their precious baby. Who, even if they *could* make someone's toes fall off, would be at a massive disadvantage if caught off guard.

Good thing they'd happened by where Olaf happened to be tonight, so should something *happen*, he could protect their baby. *And them*, he added, somewhat grudgingly. He had good reason not to like—not to *trust*—humans. But the baby—like all species' babies—was weak and vulnerable.

The adult male at least had the sense to keep looking about. Probably watching out for bears ... bears like Olaf. Or other humans. Who, if they were in the park after dark, were likely up to something shady.

Essex had taught him that human expression. Olaf didn't understand what doing morally questionable things had to do with shade from a tree, which was cool and refreshing on a hot day. But then, Olaf really didn't understand humans.

They dismounted. The male slung the stick over his back by its strap and took the baby off the female. They shuffled down the woodchip footpath into the woods.

Olaf left the blueberry bush, and followed.

Harvey and Mabel hated each other. They had used to be in love. Funny, how that worked!

At this precise moment, Harvey specifically hated his wife for her plan—and himself for going along with it. Filming the baby in distress, here in the darkness of Central Park. The baby they'd stolen, the daughter of Chief Detective Damon Thomas, the head of New York's Magic Detection Unit.

"We won't actually hurt the baby," Mabel had said. "We'll just *frighten* him into believing we'll hurt it."

Harvey wasn't sure the ends justified the means. He'd grumbled, but given in. Mabel was a much more powerful witch than he, and had repeatedly threatened, over the years, to turn him into a frog. He didn't think she was actually *that*

powerful. But you never knew what was possible, and Harvey wasn't about to push his luck.

He peered into the dark between the trees, shrubs, and rock outcrops. Few ventured into the wilderness of the Ramble anymore. The park hadn't *quite* reverted to its dangerous and decrepit state of the 1970s, but it was rapidly getting there. This area was called Muggers' Woods for a reason. Anyone in the park after dark was likely up to no good.

Like, uh, him and Mabel.

A horrible noise! Harvey jumped—ready to defend himself—and the baby . . .

Eh, it was only an owl. Mabel hadn't even noticed. He cursed the owl, and silently cursed himself for even being out here. He hated being in the park at night. The eeriness, the creepy sense something from the Other Side would suddenly emerge, to punish him for all the terrible things he had done . . . and was about to do now.

The owl hooted again, angrily, as if it had understood him. Which was ridiculous. He was losing his mind.

Even Mabel glanced worriedly about. She claimed everything had sentience: the trees, the animals, even the rocks. It was best not to arouse ill will, so she and Harvey needed to act "nonchalant."

"We're just out for a nighttime stroll with our baby . . ." she loudly proclaimed. "Who we love a lot—"

"Whom."

"Oh, do shut up, Harvey." Mabel looked around furtively and softened her tone. "Heh-heh, just a little fond banter with my husband, whom I love . . ."

He glanced sidelong at her. All seven feet of her. It wasn't that she was bad-looking. He wasn't sure she was particular-ly *good*-looking, either, but she certainly was striking. Flaming, frizzy hair. A wide mouth he'd once enjoyed kissing. A nose, long and crooked, seemingly undecided whether to snub you or poke itself into your business. But over time, with so much hatred spewing from that mouth … Imagining it now, it'd be like kissing a frog.

Gross!

What if Mabel actually *could* turn him into a frog?

What if the spell backfired and turned *her* into a frog instead?

Eh, who was he kidding. It was *he* who was prone to spells backfiring. The only thing he was any good at was flying. Which was why he'd had to lug her here—all seven feet of her.

They stepped off the dirt path, over the wire fencing and into the dense undergrowth. He looked back down at the baby. The baby smiled at him, then gazed at the trees with an expression of awe and wonder, and waved to them.

He stared at the trees … through them, almost. The Delacorte Theater stood not far from here. He'd enjoyed many of the Bard's plays, in the years the theater was still hosting free SHAKESPEARE IN THE PARK. *Macbeth* was his favorite. The drama. The violence. That weak, pathetic thane, totally led around by the nose by his—hey, wait a minute …

Mabel yanked the baby out of his hands and shoved the video camera at him. She knelt before a clearing, by a trio of trees—a birch, a maple, a holly.

He waited while she propped the baby up against the trunk of the maple. It gurgled and waved its tiny hands, smiling up at him. He glanced away, too ashamed to look it in the eye. Wild eyes seemed to stare back at him through the trees. Shivering, he jerked his gaze away.

Mabel stepped back and pulled her wand from her pocket. The wind howled. Harvey set the camera to recording.

"By the might of the moon and stars …" She swirled the wand above her head. A blue ember of light glowed at the tip. "Chief Detector Thomas, you *will* release all incarcerated witches—"

"Actually," said Harvey, "Gertrude Gawfersheen hexed that poor innocent traffic cop. She *had* double-parked, and not for the first time. Now every time he cuts his beard, it grows twice as fast. Last week he tripped over it and broke his—"

"Oh, do shut up, Harvey." Mabel glowered and lowered her wand. The blue light faded.

Harvey stopped the recording and started over, grumbling. Probably in a far corner of Mabel's dark heart she *did* care about their fellow witches, and all of the other magic-competents— humans who could manipulate energy to effect change—who had been thrown in the slammer at the whim of the Chief Magic Detector. But would Mabel lift a long, scrawny finger to help anyone if she wasn't worried she'd wind up behind bars as well? Harvey wouldn't bet on it.

At any rate, the Conflict Resolution Department—especially the Magic Detection Unit—was scapegoating them all, and something *did* have to be done about it.

Mabel raised her wand. "By the might of the moon and stars …" Blue flames coiled, waiting to strike. "Chief Detector Thomas, you will release all *unfairly* incarcerated witches, end harassment of magic-competents, and dismantle the Magic Detection Unit. Or … your only child …"

"*Dum-dum-duuuuuuum …*" hummed Harvey.

Mabel shot him a dirty look before refocusing on the baby. "Will pay the price!"

The ball of blue light erupted and rushed at the baby, enveloping it with cold.

It didn't scream.

It didn't cringe.

It *laughed*.

A pleasing sound, thought Harvey. Like the chirping of his boyhood pet bird, Burt.

The ball of cold light rushed at Mabel. She screamed. (Also a pleasing sound, thought Harvey.)

Mabel flicked her wrist and deflected the spell. It dissolved into the dirt, freezing a tiny puddle of evening rain. She stared at the baby. "His offspring—it's … it's a magic-competent!"

Harvey snorted. "Didn't see *that* coming."

"But how … how can it know how to deflect a spell? At *this* age?"

"Ha! I mean, strange." Harvey hid a grin, and busied himself with pretending to delete the video footage. (He was planning to listen to that scream over and over again.)

Mabel scowled and aimed her wand, repeating the incantation to the heavens as Harvey began recording. Repeating the threats, the demands …

Shoots of blue flame spat out into the night. Onto the ground, freezing the earth as they traveled toward the baby, enveloping its tiny toes.

The baby giggled, as if the cold had merely tickled. The flames swerved and surged toward Mabel.

On guard this time, she deftly deflected them, up and

around, striking the baby from the flanks of the tree.

The baby gurgled with pleasure. The blue shoots fizzled and dissolved into the ground.

"Make it stop, Harvey, distract it in some way!"

"Sure. Start over." He began a new recording, and made funny faces at the baby as Mabel launched another spell.

The baby laughed, as if Harvey were the funniest thing it had ever seen. (As it was pretty new to this Earth, he probably was.) The cold rays melted.

"Huh. That sure worked."

"You made it laugh on purpose!"

"You said to distract it!"

"You know what I meant!"

"What does it mean, to know a thing? As Socrates said—"

"Oh, do shut up, Harvey!"

Olaf heard the humans arguing but didn't understand what about. Although he always hid from humans—so far his existence in the park had gone unnoticed—he was concerned for the baby. Clad in only a diaper, it was surely cold.

As the humans' arm-waving and foot-stomping and even a spiteful kick or two caused them to shuffle farther away, not sounding like the chirping of baby birds at all, Olaf followed, getting closer than he'd ever dared. He growled to get their attention.

Harvey froze. That did not sound like an owl. He chanced a glance back, and stumbled in fright. He grabbed onto the sleeve of Mabel's robe to stop himself from falling onto the hard ground. She tried to shrug him off but he held on, righting himself.

"What the—let *go*, Harvey!"

Obviously she hadn't seen the huge black—

"Bear!" he managed to get out, right before tripping over a rock and falling onto his face, his broomstick plunking him on the back of the head. What a boneheaded move coming here had turned out to be!

He lifted his chin off a patch of some sort of . . . animal dung?!? Gross! Just in time to see Mabel brandish her wand, and fire a blast of ice.

TWO

Olaf fell to the ground. The ball of bright light grazed his shoulder.

He was a great big bear, with a big, round belly, so he fell pretty heavily. Thankfully not on top of the baby, which would have been messy.

Another ball of blue *whooshed* at him. He rolled out of the way and looked back up.

The human male jumped onto his broomstick, grabbed the female by the scruff of her robe, and practically threw her on the stick behind him. He launched them into the air.

Something crackled behind Olaf. He turned to see the brush crystallize, right by the baby. He looked back, ready to defend himself—

But the humans were fading in the distance, barely visible between the trees.

The female yelled at her mate, "We have to go back for the baby!"

The male shouted, "If you want to be bear food, be my guest!"

The humans and their vocalizations disappeared into the night.

Olaf growled at the sky that had swallowed the careless parents—parents who were pretty dumb to boot. If the taller-than-most female and the male storing-food-for-the-winter had been paying attention (as they should here in the dangerous woods), wouldn't they have realized he was only trying to alert them their baby was cold? Honestly, if those humans were so dumb as to forget their own baby, they must have been too dumb to realize he was trying to help them.

Perhaps they *were* precise gardeners and experts on the phases of the moon, but witches didn't seem to be any smarter than normal humans, as far as Olaf could tell.

At a sharp cry, he swiveled his head. The baby waved its paws and wailed. He stopped growling, not wanting to scare it. It lay on the ground, obviously wanting its mother. Once *he'd* been a cub, wanting his mother, as huge, scary humans approached. He looked down at his paws. They were big, with claws he couldn't retract. He would have to be careful not to scare the baby.

Staying on all fours, he crept closer. And closer … Finally, he was near enough to touch it. He bent, and sniffed. It smelled like milk and wiped-up vomit, which mixed together wasn't too terrible. And the small tuft of fur on top of its head was just as pretty as a pawful of blackberries.

He gently booped his nose against the baby's. It quieted, staring up at him with wide eyes. He booped it again, and it laughed. The stars above seemed to shine even brighter.

"Hi, baby," he said.

The baby probably heard something closer to *GrrwrrWRRwrr*. But it seemed to understand. It reached out a tiny paw, and touched his furry chin.

None of Olaf's bird friends had ever allowed him to hold one of their young. As if they were afraid he would squash them. This was his chance. Sitting on his haunches, he gently picked up the human baby, cradling it in the soft inner pads of his paws, careful not to scratch it with his claws. He cooed, *GrrwrrWRRwrrr.*

The baby made tiny baby sounds. *GaaWAAwaa?*

And somehow, they understood each other.

Gently, he hugged the baby to his chest and rocked it. It sighed and snuggled against him. It was adorable, with its tiny little body and tiny—although, relatively humongous—head. Holding it was like holding his very own baby bird. He stared at the little thing. If only he could keep it. But it must miss its parents. He would have to find them, for the baby's sake. Even if they weren't the brightest crayons in the box.

Rising onto his hind legs, he moved through the dense shrubbery, the fallen branches and rocks. He stepped over the narrow wire fencing, onto the gravel path. Tucking the baby under his arm in a secure hold, he dropped to all threes.

He lumbered with it through the park, just like his mother had carried him their last night together. Except he kept to the paths, so as not to scratch it. He took the stone steps slowly, so as not to jostle it. (His mother hadn't needed to be so careful, as cubs weren't so easily crushed.)

Don't think about Mama.

As he trampled his way over grass and shrubs, birds he knew woke and tweeted hello. One even enquired, what was so important, he was carrying it so carefully? He merely waved his free front paw as his hind legs hit the earth—then, as they sprang in the air, used that paw to canter on. And to wave again, surely making a curious sight as he loped through the woods. (He knew a lot of birds.)

He had no time to stop and answer questions. He had to find the baby's parents. And Essex, his best friend who was so much smarter than him, would help.

At a *squelch*, he glanced back. Oops. He had accidentally trod on a poor frog, its tiny head and legs squashed into the dirt. Oh, well. It was an accident.

The lovely stench of exposed intestines wafted over. Normally he would shrug his shoulders and partake in some fine dining, but that wasn't important now.

The baby was important.

～ THREE ～

Holding the baby carefully against his side, just like Essex had told him football players carried their footballs, Olaf pushed branches and brambles out of the way.

He hopped the short, black iron railing, then made his way down the stone steps, stairs some humans had built, perhaps long ago. His mother had told him the cave, which the humans had long since forgotten, had been there when *her* mother was a cub and the family moved downstate. It was their safe place.

Don't think about Mama.

His mother would be so proud of him, caring for the helpless human baby.

Don't think about Mama. Think happy thoughts. Baby birds . . . slushies . . . lollipops.

"Glk," said the baby. It pointed its paw up at the sky, just as a leaf landed between its eyes.

"That's right." Olaf plucked the leaf away. "This is the time the trees say goodbye to their leaves. To give us a better view of the stars."

He smiled, before a pang in his heart brought it back— his mother had told him that.

They reached the stone landing. The mouth of the cave loomed ahead. The cold rock looked dark and uninviting. On the contrary, it had protected him and his friends for many moons.

Olaf stepped inside. Essex was curled up in a ball, asleep. Her right ear, partially torn from a fight with a cat over food scraps, perked up at his approach. She'd always been a light sleeper. Which was understandable, given a red fox's small size. Unlike Olaf, who could squash an intruder with just one paw.

Baby, the white cat who stayed with them sometimes, was already on her feet, hackles raised. "What is that, a human?" Her raspy voice was even sharper than usual. It was unfortunate she'd come by tonight, given her hatred of humans.

Essex opened her golden eyes. They settled on the baby and glinted with curiosity. She unfurled her bushy tail, stood, and stretched. Her long snout opened in a wide yawn, showing teeth almost as sharp as Olaf's. He put his paw over the baby's eyes, just in case.

Essex padded over. Olaf knelt, and the baby stretched out its paw, trying to touch her orange-and-white fur. Essex leaned closer so it could reach her, and sniffed the small tuft of fur on top of its head.

"Mmm . . ." Her screechy voice was always tempered by her gentle manner. "Smells delicious. Good work, Olaf."

Horrified, he stepped back, shielding the baby. Should he *not* have brought it here? It was about the size of a bunny, and Essex liked to eat bunnies. Meanwhile, the baby laughed and waved its paws, seemingly delighted to be someone's next meal.

Essex laughed her screechy laugh and touched his leg with her paw. "Oh, Olaf. I'm only joking."

He grunted. "Never joke about eating."

Cradling the baby, he sat on his favorite rock—which Essex had called a "boulder" but he didn't think was all that big. He regaled his friends with the tale of the parents flying through the night, like birds on crutches. How they placed their baby on the ground, shot off some fireworks to amuse it, then set to arguing, eventually forgetting all about it and strolling off. Then trying to hurt him with that ball of ice.

Essex's whiskers twitched. "Those weren't fireworks—those were spells. I saw it on *Snarky Bravewand and Her Spookalicious Buds*. Good thing the witch fired an ice spell, not fire. She could have set the whole park ablaze."

Olaf stared. "You can make fire with magic?"

"You can do almost anything with magic. At least, on the TV. Perhaps they were trying to teach their baby magic. Although, that seems rather accelerated. Its eyes are open, but ..." She peered into the baby's mouth. "It has no teeth."

Like most animals, Olaf, Essex, and Baby had learned to communicate using a mix of growls, yips and the like, as well as approximations of human vocalizations they'd learned from wary contact with that unpredictable species. Essex had honed her human language skills further, all the nights she'd peeked in human windows to watch the TV. She'd seen and evaded the notice of hundreds of humans—maybe more! Maybe she would be able to recognize the baby's parents from his description. Such as the tall, rather scary-looking female. And the male.

"The fur on his head was the color of mud. Dark mud." To be precise, it was the same color as the baby's. But a human who was so careless with his baby ought not to be compared to blackberries.

"Who would be senseless enough to forget their own baby?" He gazed at his teddy bear resting against the wall of the cave. His own mother had protected him till the end. She would never have been so careless as to lose him.

Baby huffed. "They didn't *forget* it—they *abandoned* it! Just like my humans abandoned me. Dropped me out of a moving car right in the middle of the street! 'Another mouth to feed.' They fed me hardly anything. If my Betty hadn't been able to smuggle me something every now and then, I'd be a bag of bones, I would. I had to subsist on mice. Rats. *Insects.* Pieces of dust, in a pinch! I kept their dirty dwelling free of pests, and *that* was the thanks I got." Her face contorted in hissy fury.

Olaf and Essex nodded, pretending this was the first time

they'd heard this story. Baby was always in a bad mood when she talked about her humans. Well, she was almost always in a bad mood. Except when she spoke of her little girl, Betty. Who had named Baby, and loved her.

"They were lucky I didn't eat *them*. They deserved it, they did! I *would* have, too, if they hadn't belonged to my Betty. Although, they were horrible to her, too. Once I find them, I won't just rescue her. I *will* eat them!"

Olaf reached his paw to smooth Baby's fur, as it had gotten all poofy. She was quite given to histrionics. And maybe, a bit too much hope? As much as he and Essex wished for the best, they did not truly think Baby would ever find her little girl, no matter how much she searched. New York was quite large. At least, as far as Essex had seen.

"Humans are garbage," Baby snarled. "They abandoned the baby for sure."

Olaf smiled. "Then I guess we'll have to keep it."

"What?" Baby's eyes widened. "No! We have to bring it back to the parents . . . for its own good!"

"You just said—"

"For *once* I was wrong!"

Essex shook her head. "We should give the humans the benefit of the doubt, at least."

"You can't even get into most human dwellings, you said!" Olaf hugged the baby closer. "Finding them would be a shot in the park."

"*Dark.* A shot in the dark." Essex slitted her eyes. She always got irritated whenever the others got human expressions wrong. "We'll do what we can. If we exhaust all the available windows and still haven't found them . . ."

Baby hissed. "Why don't you take it to the police station, and be done with it?"

Essex pawed a line through the dirt. "On the TV, a police officer often turns out to be the villain. And you know they model the TV on real life."

Baby sulked, and Olaf squeezed the baby just a little bit tighter. Baby looked like she wished he would squeeze the very life from it.

"So it's settled," said Essex. "If we find the parents, we return it. And if we don't ..." She looked around the cave. "Er ... we'll figure something out. In any case, the female was quite tall, you said, Olaf? Taller than you? Anything else you can remember about the male?"

He patted his belly. "Getting ready for his long winter's sleep."

"Hibernating, is what the humans call it," said Essex. "I've seen so many humans preparing, but strangely enough, no one actually doing it."

"I'm going to hibernate right now." Baby curled up in the corner. "That thing better not be here when I wake up hungry."

FOUR

Harvey peered down at the sidewalk and neighboring windows, to make sure no one happened to be looking up at the sky—or in the direction of his and Mabel's brownstone, number 5.

The coast was clear. He angled his broomstick and swooped inside. The curtain gave way, before falling back to cover the front room from view.

There was nothing Harvey could do about the incessant refrains of "You complete idiot!" and "Senseless swine!" that had emanated from his passenger seat all the way from the park. Luckily, Mabel's verbal abuse was nothing that incriminated them as witches (people who heard them on their brooms assumed their voices were coming from pedestrians out of sight around the corner). It was nothing new (most wives seemed to suddenly find fault with their spouses the minute they said "I do"). It had actually helped, over time, to ingratiate him with the neighborhood's husbands.

His broomstick lowered itself to the hardwood floor so he

and Mabel could comfortably step off—although it seemed to give a little jerk just as her center of gravity shifted. Harvey stifled a guffaw as Mabel howled and picked herself up off the floor. He gave the broomstick's bristles an affectionate pat before leaning it inside the hall closet.

"*Now* what are we going to do? We have no leverage! He has no other children, except a teenager with his first wife he doesn't even seem to care about." Mabel smoothed her robe's wrinkles, then pulled at her hair in frustration, something she would surely regret in her old age when shopping for a wig.

Harvey did his best to ignore his wife, as usual, and stepped into the kitchen to make himself a comfort-sandwich. His stomach gnawed at him for reasons other than hunger, however. The bear was surely at this moment enjoying a comfort-baby, or possibly already digesting, leaving behind a tiny skull and bones for the Conflict Resolution Department—New York's supposedly reformed police force—to find . . . and for Chief Detector Thomas to discover was his own child.

"Couldn't you for *once* do *one* little thing right?" Mabel paced through the front room, obviously without a thought for the innocent little life they had surely snuffed out.

Harvey looked at the delectable salami-and-Muenster-on-rye sitting before him, and tossed it in the trash. He had no appetite. He had no desire to be comforted. He was a monster. He was, to quote the Bard, a treacherous, kindless villain . . . unfit for any place but hell.

"Id-i-ot! Id—"

As Mabel continued her tirade, which consisted entirely of third-grade-level vocabulary, Harvey's thoughts turned back to the English language's preeminent wordsmith and his profound wisdom, in this instance given voice by the character Macbeth:

Life *was* but a walking shadow, a poor player that strutted and fretted his hour upon the stage, and then was heard no more. It *was* a tale told by an idiot … and an idiot's wife, apparently … signifying nothing at all.

Harvey sighed, imagining that little baby, so full of life and joy, now extinguished, just like a candle.

"Out, out, brief candle!" he called, staring out the kitchen window into the night.

The little candle on Mabel's kitchen altar dutifully extinguished itself.

"Not you," he said softly to the stick of wax, so kind and obedient, even to a rogue like him. He removed a match and re-lit the candle, as Mabel and her orange hair fumed by, still ranting over his shortcomings. He imagined, staring into the fire, her head going up in flames as well, and allowed himself a flash of comfort.

FIVE

The lampposts lit their way as Essex and Olaf trotted down the dirt and gravel paths through the woods. Essex couldn't help glancing over every so often, but she needn't have worried—Olaf held the baby carefully against his side, with the soft inner pad of his paw.

The moonlight peeked through the spaces between the leaves, adding a ghostly glow. They reached a clearing, where some humans still routinely played dead during the day. A grand black tupelo rose toward the sky, and seemed to urge them on.

They took another winding path, and came upon the yellow brick gorging station where humans sometimes dropped perfectly good food and, thankfully, couldn't be bothered to pick it up. They crossed to the path curving around the water, where ducks swam and bathed and avoided toy boats sent out by humans during the day. That brought them to a slight incline and a left at the road into the park.

They came out in the gap in the wall, onto the cobblestone sidewalk. Across the street, monstrous human dwellings reached up to the sky. All with windows so high up from the ground, they would be impossible to get even a glimpse through.

Essex and Olaf shared a knowing look. The baby's parents could be in any one of them, or any of the other huge dwellings that stretched across the city. They would never know. They'd be stuck with the baby.

Essex couldn't help thinking, Olaf looked rather happy about that.

Their only shots were the single-pack human dwellings stacked against each other. Essex and Olaf crossed the street and trotted north, then east, and arrived at the first stretch of rowhouses. Checking them involved precarious balancing. They took turns. Olaf held the baby while Essex leapt onto a small planter containing a tiny tree and then up onto a light fixture, and from there, a narrow ornamental ledge. Or Olaf would lumber up the steps of a stoop, climb over a sturdy stone banister, and balance on a slightly wider ledge. From there (his big belly somewhat compromising an animal's natural grace), he'd carefully toe his way to the den window. Meanwhile, Essex would hold the baby's diaper in her teeth by the ground floor window, which was invariably barred or grilled (the humans' way of marking their territory).

"We should just give up," said Olaf, after they'd exhausted another side street.

"We'll do what we can." Essex steeled her gaze and stared across the avenue. "You never know until you try."

He grunted, and they continued on.

She glanced over at her friend. He held the baby so carefully. And perhaps, a bit too possessively? But the baby was happy. Giggling. Playing with his fur. Not seeming to miss its parents at all—which seemed rather strange, given the baby was still in a dependent stage and nowhere near the age of dispersal.

Essex was just one fox of many now living in New York, and so could wander the streets more or less at will. Most humans did not give her a second glance, and only a few were so cruel as to throw rocks or the occasional glass bottle. But Olaf was an anomaly—Essex had never seen another bear in the park, nor in the entire city.

He hid behind parked cars as vehicles coughed and rumbled by—their eyes so bright, Essex had to look away. She was familiar with quite a few of the nearby humans by now. She'd used to watch them in their dwellings, to learn more about that dangerous species. But so many long stretches of time would pass with nothing interesting happening. Often the humans would just sit watching other humans—"actors"—on the TV. So she had begun going deliberately to watch along.

It was fascinating, that someone would pretend to be something they were not. She couldn't imagine being anything other than a fox. What would it be like to be a bear, for instance? Somewhat clumsy, she presumed. Or an eagle, swooping majestically through the air. Or a bunny…a terrifying existence, to be sure.

What would it be like to be a human? Or an actor, a human pretending to be another human? Or a football player, tucking a football under his arm and running as if his life depended on it, even though it clearly didn't, as the football players pursuing him obviously weren't planning to eat him.

Sometimes the humans in the dwellings pressed a magic stick and made time speed up. They skipped over whole parts of the actors' lives. Essex hoped the actors weren't too upset about that. Other times, the humans in the dwellings pressed their sticks and made the actors live moments of their lives all over again.

What would that be like, to speed through the hard times? Times when the snow was deep and it was harder to hunt, when Olaf was hibernating, and Essex was lonely.

On the other paw, she would love to relive certain moments of her life. Raising her kits, for instance. To once more experience all the joy they'd brought her. Cubby, Broccoli, Apple Core …

Her stomach grumbled. She'd often thought she ought not to have named most of her children after food.

She *would* speed through having to say goodbye to them, when they left to find their own mates. To begin their own lives. And she would relive all her moments with her mate, Bolton. Except the very last.

But if she could relive some moments, moments of her choice … she'd never want that to end. She'd never experience life *now*. She looked back up at her friend, who was carrying the baby so carefully. Even when life was difficult or confusing, it was still full of wonder.

Vroom! Another car rushed by, and she jumped away in fright. Olaf looked back to make sure she was all right. The car hadn't been close, and she was used to them by now. It was just, she'd been thinking of Bolton.

She paused to shake out her fear, and recurring thoughts resurfaced. She ought to have insisted Bolton stay home that night. They'd already enjoyed a perfectly good meal of worms and grubs; they didn't need a "dessert" of noodles or pizza crust. Venturing out to root through gorging stations' garbage was too dangerous.

She shook her head, and shook away the thought. There was no help for that now. *She* regularly left the relatively safe confines of the park to go watch the TV. Wasn't *that* dangerous?

But it wasn't the same. She no longer had a family to look after. Olaf could take care of himself. And Baby, one day, would not return to them at all.

Olaf waited as she shook herself out, then they continued on.

Her energy was flagging, and he looked ready to quit at any moment. She'd be lying if she said she hadn't thought about keeping the baby. It *was* adorable, with its tiny little body and tiny—although, relatively humongous—head. She missed her own babies. It'd be nice to have a baby around again. Perhaps she could even teach it to be a better human than most. And *then* send it back out into the human world, to help make the world a better place.

But the baby's parents must be anguished, missing it so. Essex couldn't—*wouldn't*—keep their baby from them. Not if she could help it.

She led the way up several more blocks of ginormous human dwellings marked by rectangular green umbrellas, watched over by humans wearing funny hats. She headed west. Olaf followed behind, grumbling something about finders keepers, losers weepers.

Human arguing could be heard down the street.

A loud human voice screeching, "If you'd just had the presence of mind to *grab* the baby before getting us out of there!"

And a rather gravelly voice answering. "Yeah. I should've grabbed the baby, and left *you*."

This was followed by a great din, sounding like fragile human belongings smashing. Essex and Olaf looked at each other.

"That's them," said Olaf. "I recognize the voices. And, leaving their baby? How many stupid humans can there be?"

"Probably a lot," said Essex. "In any case, we've found them! What luck!"

"Yeah," grumbled Olaf.

As they approached the brownstone, the lovely stench of human trash wafted over from ripped-open plastic bags spilling out from a garbage can lying on its side. A raccoon or something had already been through them, but Essex made a mental note to forage for any good food items, once they'd returned the baby.

She waited underneath with it, while Olaf clambered up and over the obstacles to reach the den window, which had thankfully been left slightly ajar. He peeked inside.

"That's them all right." The distaste in his voice was thick, like he'd just eaten a rotten blueberry.

Essex gently laid the baby on the ground. "Can you leave it inside without being spotted?"

A human's first instinct when encountering an animal that hadn't been tricked into becoming a "pet" was to scream and run away. Or brandish a tree branch, as if that would accomplish anything. Regardless, it wouldn't be wise to be seen inside a human dwelling. Essex had learned this once when she was young and inexperienced. Humans just couldn't understand animal vocalizations, no matter how much she tried to explain she was just there to watch the TV.

Olaf dropped to the sidewalk. The human screaming had slightly abated. "They went farther back in their den."

Essex nodded. "There are many rooms in human dwellings. Perhaps they enjoy spending time apart. Say goodbye now, and put the baby back."

He picked it up, gazing longingly. "Can't we keep it? This can't be an enriching environment for a baby."

She looked at his big, bark-colored eyes, so soft and sad. "I know you've gotten attached, Olaf. But would it really be best for a human baby to live in the woods? In a cave? It will get cold. How will we care for it? Sometimes we can barely feed ourselves. It has no teeth! And would it really be kind, to take it away from its parents?"

He cast a disapproving look at the window. The arguing emanating from inside intensified. The humans didn't seem particularly concerned about the whereabouts of their baby.

But Essex needed to stand firm. "Maybe they're just having what the humans call 'a hard day.'"

Olaf didn't even seem to hear her. He turned away from the window and gazed into the baby's eyes.

Essex shifted uneasily. "Sometimes humans don't love each other as much after they've had their babies. Like—" She caught herself before mentioning Olaf's mother and father. Olaf thought of his mother often enough on his own. "Not like Bolton and me. It doesn't mean they don't love their babies."

Olaf didn't even have to say anything; Essex knew what he

was thinking. He loved the baby more than these preoccupied humans, who ought to love it more than anyone.

How would she explain? She tried again. "It would be all kinds of shady, to keep the baby."

"Yeah." Olaf nodded. "Comfortable for us *and* the baby."

"What would you think if I still had my cubs, and those humans entered *our* dwelling? What if they heard us arguing and assumed we were bad parents? What would you think if they stole *my* cubs away?"

Olaf pouted. How was Essex so skilled at bringing forth such excellent points, and why didn't he know how to argue them effectively?

Grumbling, he carried the baby up the stoop and cradled it carefully while climbing over the banister and balancing on the ledge. Essex waited underneath, ready to be a soft landing spot should he drop it. (Of course he would not drop it!) He reached a paw through the window and raised it higher, just enough to squeeze inside. Thinking better of it, he pushed it up some more, so the baby wouldn't get squished.

He looked down. The baby was staring up at him with bright, pond-algae eyes. As terrible as he felt, he couldn't help but smile. Holding it securely, he clambered through the window. His belly had grown big and round, so it was still a tight fit. With a mighty push, he made it through ...

He fell with a great big *thump*—making sure the baby didn't hit the floor.

Freezing, he listened to the arguing voices. After he was sure they weren't coming closer, he rose and moved toward the crib on the side of the room. The scent of a cat pervaded the air. Hopefully it was sleeping. Although, what being could sleep through all this racket?

Baby supplies lay strewn on a cabinet in the corner. Diapers. Formula. Olaf was familiar with such things because humans had a habit of losing their valuable half-used possessions in the park. He lowered the baby into the crib, and stared down at it.

Unfair! The baby's parents weren't even out looking for it. Olaf and Essex would surely make much better parents for a tiny, vulnerable baby. At the very least, they wouldn't lose it!

"Hurry, Olaf!" Essex called.

The baby waved its paw at him. He reached out his own, to touch it. Then he shuffled away, unable to bear this sadness a moment longer.

The baby began to cry. It was probably hungry. Who knew when the self-absorbed parents would get around to feeding it? The bottle of formula was right there on the cabinet. It wouldn't hurt just to feed the baby before leaving. He turned back, swept the bottle into his paws—there wasn't much in it—and padded over to the crib.

The baby looked up at him and smiled. It held out its tiny paws. His heart warmed. He didn't know why. Maybe, because the baby needed someone. It needed *him*. Like he had needed his mother. And Wendy, the kind caretaker at the zoo, after his mother had been taken from him. And now, how he needed Essex. Not to survive, as he was so much bigger and stronger.

But for companionship. He would choose Essex over all his bunny friends, if it came to that. Just as she would choose him.

"Olaf! Hurry!"

But right now, he was choosing the baby. He tucked the bottle under his armpit, and carefully plucked the baby with its blanket from the crib.

"Olaf! What's taking so long?"

Claws scraped against the building's exterior as Essex jumped up and down, trying to see through the window.

Carefully pressing the baby to his chest, Olaf moved over to the cabinet and helped himself to supplies. Diapers, baby wipes, some plastic thing that looked like a combination of a ring and a lollipop…He stuffed it all and the bottle in a diaper bag sitting on top. He looped the straps over his shoulders like he'd seen the humans do, taking care not to drop the baby. Then he stepped to the window, clambered over, and dropped to the ground.

His mother would approve. She had always protected him. She would want him to protect this tiny human baby, that couldn't protect itself.

His best friend stared at the bundle in his arms. "Olaf. We can't." Essex lifted her chin, the way she did when she was sure of something.

"We have to. For its own good." He tucked the baby under his arm, and lumbered down the deserted sidewalk. Essex would follow. She always did.

The streetlamp cast its yellow light, and the moon was a perfect circle overhead, shining upon him. Making him a most conspicuous bear, if anyone were around to see. A human did stagger by just then, singing badly, and smelling badly, too.

Carrying a bark-colored glass bottle, and taking a swig. But the human didn't seem to see him, or anything at all as it stumbled and tripped over the curb.

A stray cat yowled across the street. A car rumbled by, spewing fumes, choking Olaf with its noxious smell. He stopped at the corner and glanced around, but saw no humans staring out their windows, ready to alert the authorities and report a bear stealing a human cub.

Tiny paws skittered behind him. Olaf smiled. His best friend was coming to join him.

Essex snatched the baby's diaper in her teeth and bolted. Back to the stoop, up and over the banister, and along the ledge.

She slunk underneath the window. The baby's parents were *still* arguing. She hesitated. Was Olaf perhaps right? If the parents were so self-involved, they couldn't even break off from arguing to go search for their cub …

She looked to the ground. At Olaf—the hope lighting up his eyes.

She turned back to the window and gazed into the room, then down at the baby. It giggled and reached out its tiny fingers, and grasped at her fur. Her heart melted, like a dropped slushie in the sun. But it was the right thing to do, to give the baby back. She readied herself to jump inside.

The vocalizations grew louder.

"Just like Lady Macbeth!" said the male voice. "Get ready for a slow, steady slide into insanity!"

The tall female stomped into the room. "I'm already insane with regret—for marrying *you*." She pulled at the fur on top of her head—the same shade of yellow as Essex's fur, that Olaf called "orange."

The male dashed in behind his mate. "I am sick when I do look on thee!"

"You're not even clever enough to come up with your own insults, you worthless toad!" The female withdrew her wand from the pocket of her robe and aimed it at him. "If only I were powerful enough, you know what I'd do?"

"I *do* know, because you never shut up about it! But guess what?"

Essex knew she ought to get out of there, not indulge her curiosity and find out *what*. But she seemed frozen to the windowsill. It was somehow even more fascinating to watch humans argue right in front of her than on the TV. She had never argued so vehemently—*hatefully*—with her own mate. She couldn't understand why the humans did.

The baby giggled again, louder.

"Shhhhh," hissed Essex through her molars, hoping the baby's very loud parents had taught it to be quiet.

"You're *not* powerful enough, you'll never *be* powerful enough, and—"

The female let loose a horrible rush of vocalizations Essex had never heard a human use, on or off the TV. The air itself seemed to shrink back in fear.

Essex's heart beat so frightfully fast, her paws skittered over the windowsill. She scrabbled her claws, trying to keep from falling off the edge. The baby laughed, seemingly thinking they were playing a game.

The female, her wand still pointed at her mate, turned her head. She and Essex stared at each other. The female looked down at the baby. And the baby laughed and laughed.

The air shrunk and swelled into the body of the male. His skin emanating green smoke, he froze—

And turned into a frog.

Essex turned around and leapt back down. She did not want to be a frog.

Olaf caught her, set her on the ground, and took the baby from her.

"We must hurry," was not even out of her snout before he tucked the baby under his arm, and ran.

They dashed down the street—the lamp shining brightly as they passed underneath. Flooding them in light, making them a clear target. Her heart pounded, rising into her throat, making it difficult to breathe. She could almost feel the breath of the

human female on her tail.

Many a time had she snatched up a startled frog in her strong jaws and made of it a tasty meal. Many a time had she seen Olaf clumsily step on a frog and smash it to bits, making for a messier meal.

Neither of them would last long as frogs in the big city.

~ SIX ~

Mabel lunged toward the window, firing her wand at the vermin escaping with the baby.

Her baby. *Her* prize—her bargaining chip, which had somehow, miraculously rematerialized in her primary residence.

She clambered over the sill and dropped to the sidewalk. A loud *RIIIIIIIP* signaled the ruin of yet another good robe. She gave chase, but the fox and bear scaled the park wall and disappeared.

She turned and ran home. They wouldn't get far. Once she had her broom she'd catch up. They would regret messing with her.

Her! Mabel Blackthornudder! The most powerful witch in New York City! It'd take more than a fox and bear to outsmart—

Wait a minute ...

She tripped on her way up the stoop's steps, and just barely caught herself before smashing her jaw on the stone.

A fox and ... bear. *The bear from the park.*

The thought had crossed her mind, while she was yelling

at Harvey, that the bear would eat the baby. Was the baby so powerful, it had flown back here all on its own? Without even an enchanted broom? And lured the bear and his fox friend to follow?

Harvey hopped about, horrified to suddenly find himself so much shorter than everyone and everything else. He opened his mouth to utter expletives, normally so familiar and comforting to him, and nearly fainted to hear only *r* and *b* sounds come rumbling out.

At least the baby was still alive.

Mabel's cat, which he'd never liked—and may have (accidentally) forgotten to feed ~~once or twice~~ every time she was out of town—suddenly appeared, towering above him and smirking. Possibly remembering—gulp!—the same thing.

Exit, pursued by a cat.

Mabel grabbed her broom from the corner, just as her husband hopped over her foot.

Ribbit!

She nodded. "The baby must be an amplifier. We've got to get it back!"

Ribbit!

"Of *course* to change you back, that's the most pressing issue on my mind."

Ribbit!

"*And* get all incarcerated witches released...except Gertrude Gawfersheen...I never did like her anyway..."

As Mabel straddled her broom and grabbed Harvey— ugh, disgusting, it was like plunging your hand in a bucket of slime—she couldn't help thinking through the consequences of this sudden turn of events. If she could get the baby back in her possession, it would do so much more than serve as an effective bargaining tool to end harassment of magic-competents.

In middle school, she'd once thought she'd hexed her nemesis sister Brenda so badly, Brenda's skin had turned green. But Brenda hadn't turned into a frog, and had later been diagnosed by the nurse with a plain old iron deficiency. So even though Mabel had become a formidable witch since then, she hadn't actually *expected* to turn Harvey into a frog. She'd just been so angry, she'd figured she might as well give it a shot.

However the baby had done it, its very presence had pushed her power over the edge, and allowed her to turn her husband into an amphibian. (Finally!)

She had to get it back.

~ SEVEN ~

Back in their cave, Essex peered outside to make sure the human female was not stalking them like a good predator would.

She shook out her fear. Shake-shake-shake-shake-*shake*! A little wiggle, and then—*ahh!*—she was calm again, and could breathe properly. She knew Olaf didn't need an explanation. He was just happy to still have the baby in their possession. But she related what she'd seen. He should know what they were up against.

She paced back and forth. Had they done the right thing? The baby's mother *had* seemed neglectful. Unreasonable. Violent, even. But they didn't know all the facts. Just because the female had turned her mate into a frog, didn't necessarily mean she was a bad person, or that she'd be a bad mother. Turning your mate into a frog...maybe that was something human couples did for fun.

Olaf gently placed the baby in his bed of soft leaves, arranging it just so. He plucked a leaf out of its mouth. "No, that's not food."

Baby lifted her head from where she'd been curled in a ball in the corner, and scowled. "Nothing good can come of this. What are you going to do with a human baby?"

What were they going to do with a human baby? Olaf harrumphed. "Feed it. Take care of it. *Love* it." He picked up his teddy bear and offered it to the baby. The baby grasped it and giggled.

Essex nosed about the supplies in the diaper bag. The bottle of formula rolled out. She pushed it to the edge of their little log pile. "Humans always heat up their baby's bottle."

Olaf nodded. His best friend's seasons of spying on the humans had certainly paid off, if in an unexpected way. He grabbed their lighter from the edge of the Pile of Human Garbage—all the lost treasures they'd amassed, in the corner—stuck it under his arm, and banged his paw on the button. A tiny spark flickered. He held it to the log pile, igniting the nearest twig.

"Look!" He guffawed, sure Essex would appreciate his joke. "Magic!"

The *baby* appreciated it, laughing and waving the teddy bear about.

The flame from the lighter exploded—reaching all the way to the teddy bear and setting it on fire. Olaf watched in horror as his cherished teddy, which his beloved Wendy had gifted him, went up in flames.

Essex leapt over. Snatching the teddy in her teeth, she shook it out, then dropped it on the floor of the cave and stomped on it, till the fire settled into smoke.

Olaf picked up his charred teddy bear, now missing half its tiny black felt nose. He put it and the lighter away, far from the reach of the human baby. He sat on his rock and moaned. What were they going to do with a magic baby?

"She *is* a cutie." Essex stretched to nose the baby, and tickled it under its chin.

"She's a wet, ugly, stinky thing." Baby scrunched up her nose. "Don't ask me to babysit. *Ev*er!"

Olaf took a good sniff. The baby was *indeed* wet and stinky. He'd just been so preoccupied with getting to keep it—that is, *her*—he hadn't noticed. He picked up the diaper bag and pulled out a wet wipe. After cleaning her, he removed a new diaper. It was all terribly complicated without what Essex called "opposable thumbs," but carefully, using his teeth and claws to hook into the fabric, he succeeded in wrapping her up like a burrito.

"That's not even how you do it!" screeched Baby. "Do I have to do *ev*erything around here?" She got up and moved over to them, with that slight limp she refused to acknowledge. She wedged herself between him and the baby. He and Essex stared as she undid, then correctly refastened the diaper.

"What?" Baby huffed. "I study the humans, too."

The lighter was hidden in case the baby was ready to begin crawling, the bottle heated, and the fire extinguished as quickly as possible, with everyone careful not to make the baby laugh.

Now that the cave was back to its normal, safe state, Essex couldn't resist. She tickled the tiny baby feet.

The baby giggled. Olaf gazed down at her with love in his eyes. Baby huddled in the corner, turned her back, and pretended the human interloper was but a bad dream that would evaporate in the morning.

The baby slurped away at the little formula left in the bottle. Essex tickled the little feet again, as they were just so adorable. As was the baby's laughter. It sounded just like the tinkling of tiny bells. Or, as Olaf would say, the chirping of adorable—

The baby retched and spat milk everywhere. She began to cough and cry, sounding nothing like adorable baby birds.

Essex stared at the effects of her clumsy parenting. It would not be so simple to raise a human cub, even for just a little while. "I must go and ask the trees."

As Olaf rocked the baby and Baby's hackles rose, Essex slunk away, glad to have an excuse to go.

She trotted out of the cave mouth, up the stone steps and under the iron railing. For a while she followed the convenient gravel paths, then leapt over the short wire fencing into one of the dense wooded areas thick with shrubbery. Traveling by leaps and bounds, it did not take long to reach the Three.

Many of the trees in Central Park had been planted in clusters. Groves of firs. Scores of sycamores. Bursts of cherry blossoms. Other areas abounded with different species, with seemingly "no rhyme or reason." (Essex didn't understand that human expression, as the Three often spoke poetically.) But here at this secluded spot, some human had planted a trio of different types, perhaps as a marker. A signal of sorts.

She slowed and caught her breath. It would not do to speak with the trees all in a huff. Soon she was calm and sat. There by the majestic river birch. The grand red maple (which really ought to have been named "yellow maple," in her opinion). The somewhat silly American holly. She humbly asked for guidance.

"Please, close confidants of the Everything ... if it pleases you ... may I please partake of your wisdom and understanding?"

One could never say *please* enough, when dealing with those so close to the Everything.

"The humans who left their baby tonight ..." She paused, fidgeting. How best to phrase this? She didn't relish the idea of keeping a cub from its mother, and yet she couldn't imagine abandoning one of her own. Or being careless enough to lose one.

"If we return her to them, will they take better care of her?" And not turn her into a frog when they got angry, went without saying.

Communing with the trees was not something Essex did often. Only in emergencies. It wasn't the same as communicating with other animals. Trees were a great mystery. Almost as great as the Everything. She had to get very quiet and focus, and not pay attention to all the thoughts swirling around her head.

How were they going to feed the baby? Why did humans always make life so unnecessarily complicated? What was she missing on the TV tonight?

She let go of all these worries, sat very still, and closed her eyes.

The wind blew through the holly's spiky leaves, making them sing. It tickled the birch's flaking bark. It rustled the maple's leaves like crinkly magazines, almost lulling her to sleep ...

Danger ...

A human walking by would hear nothing but the wind.

Even Essex sometimes wondered if she were merely imagining things. Only, her mother had insisted. The Three, she'd always said, were full of wisdom. She had taught Essex to go to them for guidance.

It was the Three that had advised Essex to sit under the clock outside the zoo, under the fake animals playing their fake instruments, the night Olaf had come into her life. She'd gone to ask the trees for strength. Her mate had recently been taken from her. Her kits had long since gone. She was tired, her heart was heavy, and there didn't seem to be much point anymore. Hunting and scavenging for herself. Evading the humans and hawks. Waking up alone.

Other vixens were content to take another mate, but Essex wasn't built that way. She couldn't imagine being with anyone other than Bolton.

A bear will come along, the stately birch had said. *A bear that needs you*, said the thoughtful maple. *A huge, strong bear, that hasn't a clue how powerful it is!* said the holly.

The holly was always being dramatic.

She couldn't help doubting that night. Believing she'd imagined the entire conversation. Why would a big, strong bear need a little fox? But she had gone to sit under the clock, as her mother had counseled her to always follow the Three's advice.

She'd stayed calm while the humans broke into the zoo. Calm, while the terrified animals stampeded out.

A bear had come into sight—a huge, frightened bear. Along with his human, a young woman, her hand on his shoulder. They headed south, toward the park gates. Essex ran up, and the human somehow knew. She hugged Olaf, turned, and strode away. Olaf gazed sadly after her, his teddy bear in his mouth.

The wind howled, and Essex allowed that night to drift to a far corner of her mind.

Danger, said the grave birch.

She is not their child, said the perceptive maple.

Beware! said the holly. *Stay as far away as animally possible!*

The holly was always being dramatic.

They believe the baby will enhance their magic, said the birch.

Essex opened her eyes. "Then I must guard her, as if she were my own. Until I can . . . until *we* can . . . Who are her real parents?"

We cannot know all.

Essex's tail slumped onto the earth. She had hoped this would be easier.

How boring would that be? said the holly. *If one knew everything, knew what each new morn would bring. One wouldn't need to live.*

Be vigilant, said the birch.

Stay strong, said the maple. *You will need strength—and commitment, when the time comes to give her back.*

Essex bristled. "Of course we will give her back."

Speak you for your friend? The wind blew ominously through the holly's leaves. *You must find the strength to forgive, when he betrays you.*

Essex took a step back. "He would never. He's my best friend."

But it was okay. The holly was only being dramatic.

Read the Bard's work, said the holly. *Shakespeare's plays. You will find that all things are possible.*

"I'm a fox. I can't read."

All things are possible, said the holly. *No matter. You are all playing roles, from which you will awaken.*

"I don't understand."

Souls conspire to create challenges, so they may learn and grow. Everyone is acting, without even knowing. 'All the world's a stage—'

Pay him no attention. The birch rolled its eyes—or it would, Essex corrected herself, if it had them. *He's a big diva. A troupe of actors used to rehearse in this clearing.*

"But how will we *feed* the baby? My last litter was many moons ago."

You are always guided, said the holly, philosophically.

Everything you need will be given, said the maple, optimistically.

Two witches live in a cottage in the North Woods, said the birch, practically. *Sisters. One will be only too happy to help. The other ... not so much.*

Beware! said the holly.

Essex bowed to the Three in acknowledgment of their kindness. She prepared to leave ... then realized, she had never managed to hold a conversation with a human. "How will I communicate with them?"

They are witches, said the birch. *They will understand. Go now. We will alert our brethren. Everything you need will be given.*

Essex thanked the trees with her whole heart. She thanked them for their wisdom, their assistance, their shade and protection. (She even thanked the holly, for though it had a tendency to be over-the-top, it surely meant well.)

She waited a few moments to get her bearings back.

A cloud had obscured the moon.

A mouse raced by.

An owl took off from a branch, swooped down, snatched the unfortunate creature in its talons and carried it away.

The warnings of the holly, it seemed, were applicable to everybody.

~ EIGHT ~

Inexplicably having not caught up to the fox and bear, Mabel manually, angrily searched the Ramble. This park was full of dirt!

Harvey sat perched on her shoulder. Theoretically he could be an asset, as now that he was a frog he was far-sighted, as well as blessed with superior night vision. But instead of being helpful he kept ribbiting in her ear, afraid of the owls hungrily eyeing him as Mabel moved about the underbrush.

They had happened upon the bear right around here. It must make its home in the park, perhaps having migrated over from New Jersey like any sensible being. But half an hour later, exhausted, muddy, and not having found anything other than an angry and possibly rabid raccoon, Mabel leaned against a railing overlooking a steep drop to rest and think things through.

She scrunched up her nose. Whatever had died down there stank to high heaven. She was vaguely aware of the existence of a cave right below, but due to criminal activity in the area it had been sealed off approximately a hundred years ago.

A squirrel nattered at her to go away, and leave the wood-dwellers alone. With a flick of her wand, Mabel sent it flying. Another squirrel stared at her from between the weeds, with what looked suspiciously like vengeance in its beady little eyes. Mabel sneered to indicate how truly terrified she was of its teensy-weensy wittle claws, then turned to look back over the railing.

This was a humongous waste of time. The Ramble was huge. She could've easily missed a black bear lurking in the dark. *And* she was missing the latest episode of *Snarky Bravewand and Her Spookalicious Buds.*

Snarky and her friends, though witty, were total do-gooders. But Mabel hadn't had ~~many~~ friends at school, and the show was strangely comforting. She called to her ~~frog~~ husband to end their search. They would return home, and summon the spirits to show them the baby's exact whereabouts.

~ NINE ~

Essex watched from behind a bush as the bad witch peered down at the shrubs obscuring the cave. The witch turned and huffed off. The frog hopped toward her. She gripped it with a grimace and plopped it on her shoulder. They flew off into the night.

Evidently the witch had decided not to clamber down and search the cave. This seemed an oversight, as Essex was used to humans on the TV who took logical steps to solve their problems. But this was real life, where humans often acted irrationally. Essex and her friends and the baby were safe.

The water oaks watched the witches depart.

Danger ... The bad witches are searching ...

Via an underground network of mycorrhizal fungi—hair-like filaments that stretched to the roots of each neighboring tree—the warning advanced.

Back, all the way to the birch, the maple, the holly—the originators of the warning. And forward, following the witches' path. Back to their lair. Back to the callery pear that hovered outside their window, that waited, ready to sound the alarm.

Essex trotted down the stone steps. She entered the cave and smiled. While she'd been out, Olaf had pawed through the Pile of Human Garbage, looking for suitable outerwear for the baby. It could get freezingly cold at night, especially for a tiny, delicate human. In the absence of an appropriately-sized hat, Olaf had stuck a cardboard takeout container on her head.

Essex's belly grumbled. There had still been noodles inside the container the night she'd scored it from a trash receptacle.

Since neither she nor Olaf had ever found a lost little jacket on the ground, he'd wrapped the baby in the next best thing: a trash bag, gently used, that he'd pilfered from a bin early one morning. And it turned out that human mittens made for lovely booties, with plenty of room for growing baby toes.

The baby gurgled, obviously pleased with her new provisions.

"The humans didn't lose the baby. They abandoned her. She isn't theirs."

Olaf stared in disbelief. "Why would anyone abandon a little baby? Even if she wasn't their own?" He picked up the baby and nestled her against his chest, the trash bag rustling.

"Told you, I did. Humans are garbage! And this one will grow up to be just like them." Baby hissed at the trash bag. "Garbage!"

"Our baby will *not* grow up to be garbage. We'll teach her to be a *good* human. Like your Betty. And my Wen—"

"No human will *ever* be like my Betty." Baby's expression turned horrified. "Don't tell me you plan on keeping her long enough to try."

Olaf's eyes darkened. "We'll keep her as long as she needs us."

Baby snarled. "You won't be seeing *me* for a while, then."

They glared at each other, then looked pointedly at Essex.

Essex ignored her friends' latest disagreement and stared at the baby, barely visible underneath her hat and trash bag.

Humans could not *be* garbage. They had all been babies once, as pure and innocent as this baby. Something, or someone—more likely, many somethings and someones—had taught them to *act* garbagey, most likely over a period of many moons.

"A pair of *good* witches live here in the park. Sisters. The trees said they will help us." She did not think it wise to mention that apparently only one of the sisters would *want* to help. Baby was already in a terrible mood. "If they are like normal humans, they'll be asleep now. I will go to them tomorrow."

The baby began to cry. Olaf looked at the empty bottle. "It was already half-empty when I took it."

Essex smiled. "You mean half-full." She had learned a little bit of wisdom from the humans, after all.

"I'm half-mad already," said Baby. "Wake the witches right now!"

"They might not *want* to help if they're tired," said Essex. "They would think us rude."

Olaf grunted. "But it's an emergency. Which calls for emergency procedures."

Essex looked at Olaf. His eyes glinted with knowing. They both turned and stared at the Pile of Human Garbage.

"We always said we'd try it in an emergency." Olaf reached into the pile and pulled out a floppy hat. He set it on his head. He drew out a floofy scarf, which he wrapped around his neck. Next, shiny silver eyeglasses that showed you your snout when you looked at them. A face mask Essex had found on the ground. A coat they'd taken off a human body they'd found frozen overnight on a park bench.

(They wouldn't have disturbed it, except the spirit had urged them on. *Go ahead. I won't be needing it anymore.*)

Legwarmers. Mismatched boots, now bursting at the seams as Olaf stuck his big feet inside. A fuzzy mitten. A black glove with limp fingers that hung empty off Olaf's paw as he smushed it into the palm. Like a bunny with multiple droopy ears.

Mmm. Essex licked her muzzle. *Bunnies.*

Olaf looked exactly like a human. Albeit, no human she'd ever seen—a human with a huge left palm and no fingers, getting ready to hibernate.

Hopefully no one would notice.

He held open the diaper bag, which was large enough to hold Essex, formula, diapers, and perhaps a few more items the baby would absolutely need.

Essex looked imploringly at Baby.

Baby glanced over, scowling, already curled around the crying baby. "I'll babysit, I will! But only so you can steal milk and stop her crying. And hurry up—before *I* get hungry and eat her."

Essex jumped into the diaper bag.

Olaf slung it over his shoulders. As they left the cave, he whispered, "She's not *really* going to eat her, right?"

"Of course not."

He grunted with relief.

Essex stuck her muzzle out of the bag. "But let us hurry, just in case."

~ TEN ~

On the way to the unnaturally-bright-all-day-and-all-night food palace, Essex told Olaf the trees had warned her that one sister would decidedly *not* be enthused about helping them. Olaf promptly dubbed that one the "Mean One," and her sister, the "Nice One."

"Perhaps the not-so-happy-to-help sister isn't mean at all, just misguided." Essex had learned a lot from the trees and the TV. What was perceived as "mean" was often just a being in pain, reaching out for healing.

Olaf grumbled something about *to-may-to, to-mah-to*, and for a moment they reminisced about a ripe, juicy tomato Essex had once scored from a farmers' market. But they had to hurry. The baby was hungry.

It was perfectly dark, the only light the moon and stars, and the occasional streetlamp. Essex twitched her whiskers—from nervousness, but also, excitement. They were pretending to be someone they were not. They were acting! Just like the actors on the TV. And the acting troupe in the clearing.

They neared the entrance. They'd never been inside the food palace, as they'd never been desperate enough to try. But they'd watched as humans entered, and knew what to expect. At a great big *whoosh*, Olaf slipped through doors that slid open at their approach. Essex ducked her head inside the diaper bag so no one would see her.

As he confidently strode forward, she peeked out again. A lone human female teenager sat behind a checkout counter strewn with last-minute unwanted items, filing her nails and looking bored.

The rest of the food palace seemed deserted. Olaf hurried into an aisle before the checkout teenager could look up.

Pulling the diaper bag off his shoulders so Essex could see where he was going, he lumbered down the next few aisles, and soon they came upon one with pictures of baby faces on the products.

He stopped in front of the diapers, picked up the smallest bundle, and dropped it into the bag. "How much can a tiny human go?"

"A *lot*. All the grown-up humans complain about it. Get a bigger size."

She immediately regretted saying this, as Olaf skipped right past the medium and large sizes and grabbed the hugest stack. He wedged it inside the bag, flattening her against the side.

"Ooh, and she'll need this, and that pretty purple thing— whatever it is—and this looks interesting …" Olaf stuffed package after package into the bag, apparently forgetting Essex was even there. She gasped for air.

"Olaf! This is not a *magic* bag."

"Oops. Sorry about that."

The bag opened wider, and she breathed in deeply. He shifted the products around, with all their weird angles, to fit everything more efficiently.

"Still, Olaf. There's hardly any room left. We need formula— the thing we came for, remember? From now on just get the bare necessities."

"These are *human* necessities."

As Essex sighed and tried to make herself more comfortable, Olaf methodically trod down each aisle. He slowed, staring at packages of brightly-colored candies bulging from the shelves. On the other side of the aisle hung costumes humans routinely wore this time of season, to make them look like pirates, or superheroes, or ...

Witches.

As Olaf oohed and ahhed over the candy, Essex inched her head a few more whisker-breadths out of the bag. A human female stood at the end of the aisle, trying on a pointy black hat. A witch's hat. A long case like musicians sometimes carried lay at her feet, along with a basket filled with eggs, milk, and a big bag of something lumpy.

The human was well-insulated, had long hair the color of night, and a long, bulbous nose with warts jockeying for position. She sported cute sneakers like all "the kids" were wearing, and a sparkly, sequined tracksuit. Tilting the hat this way and that, she checked her reflection in the glass containing the cold drinks.

Essex stared at her. Her face radiated love and joy, even without smiling. Perhaps it was something in the eyes. Essex stared at those eyes through the reflection in the glass . . .

When one of those eyes turned toward her, and winked.

Essex ducked back into the bag. Her experiences with humans had taught her, they did not like animals they didn't own being in spaces they *felt* they owned, even if the animals had been there first. Heart pounding, she trembled, dreading the human alerting the bored teenager to Essex's presence.

But nothing happened.

No red lights shone down on her and Olaf. No alarms blared from above. A disembodied human voice alerted shoppers to a special on baked beans in Aisle Ten.

She peeked out. The human was gone. Dumbfounded, she sank back into the bag.

Olaf hadn't noticed anything amiss. He stuffed another package of candy into the last remaining pocket of air in the bag, cutting off Essex's breathing.

"Just let me rearrange some things—"

His big paws with their glove and mitten shuffled things about, and miraculously she could breathe again. And somehow an empty space *still* opened up. For formula, hopefully. The one thing they'd come for.

Finally, on their second trip through the baby things aisle, they found the formula they'd overlooked in this sea of products. Olaf stopped short, and stared at a container featuring a picture of a mama bear and a baby bear. Or, a baby bear and . . . Olaf's eyes lit up . . . a *papa* bear.

He tucked it into the diaper bag. Along with bottled water. And a bowl to mix it all in. And a spoon to mix it all with. With everything else inside, it was a snug fit, but Essex somehow managed to make herself even smaller, squeezing into the last remaining space. Human babies sure needed a lot of stuff!

Olaf closed the flap over her head and slung the bag over his shoulders. All they had to do now was get past the bored checkout teenager. Essex sighed, relieved, just as two more products the baby would "absolutely need"—but which she suspected had just caught Olaf's fancy—were somehow squeezed into the bag with her.

Perhaps it was a magic bag after all.

Olaf made his way to the exit, more confident this time. The food palace was deserted now, but that one human who'd been in the candy aisle had believed he was a normal human, just like her.

He peeked around the corner of the aisle that held all the tools humans used for grooming their fur. The bored teenager brushed hers over her shoulder—it was the same shade of blackberry as the baby's—and began painting her nails. He didn't think she'd looked up once so far. If she did now, hopefully she wouldn't notice his diaper bag bursting at the seams. Or if she did, perhaps she'd assume it had been that way when he came in.

He hurried to the exit. The doors slid open—

"I see you, y'know."

Olaf froze.

He was a great big bear. He could run faster than any human. So why was he suddenly unable to move? His heart pounded. Had he remembered to hide his tail, or was it sticking out of the slit in the coat?

But nothing happened. No animals swarmed about in terror. No zookeepers ran around in a panic. He could see the bored teenager out of the corner of his eye. She hadn't even looked up from her nails, yet somehow she knew.

"They just don't pay me enough to care."

Olaf let that sink in a moment. He couldn't imagine choosing to be somewhere and not caring. Even at the zoo, where he had not chosen to be, he had cared about Wendy. And the other animals, even though he'd never met them. Though he'd seen them just once, in all the confusion.

Essex trembled against his side. Something in him released. He lumbered through the sliding doors and rounded the corner. Which smelled pleasant, as if someone or something had relieved itself there. He sniffed. Someone they knew? No . . . some strange animal . . . or perhaps a human.

He dropped to all fours and let the diaper bag slide to the ground. Essex slipped out. They shook out their fear.

"Let's not do that again."

"Agreed." Essex wedged herself back into the bag. "From now on, the witches will help us . . ." Her voice wavered slightly. "I hope."

~ ELEVEN ~

C'mon . . . c'mon . . . Where is that baby?

Mabel gazed impatiently at the black mirror on her altar, the only lights the candles on either side—as well as the mugwort incense sticks that were supposed to assist with divination, but instead got up her nose and provoked coughing fits.

Vague images filled the mirror. A forest . . . trees talking to each other, what else was new. Something orange . . .

She squinted. Was that . . . a *fox* the trees were talking to? No, it couldn't be. Of course, trees could talk to animals, but most animals—like most humans—were too dumb to decipher whispers that sounded just like the wind. Well. No matter. What were the trees going to tell the fox and bear, that Mabel was looking for them? Of *course* she was looking for them. And she *would* find them. There was no hole she would not crawl through, no structure she wouldn't break into to get that baby back. If the fox thought it was cleverer than Mabel, it was in for a big surprise.

A hard, incessant *knocking* downstairs made her jump. The visions in the mirror faded. She jumped up and peered through the window at the stoop below.

Cops! Darn cops. Technically, "Conflict Resolution Professionals" was what they were called now. In ugly mustard-yellow uniforms. Yellow! The color of cowards.

She had made sure to pay off all her outstanding parking tickets, so what were they doing calling on her, especially this late at night? Had someone spotted her and Harvey with the baby? Seen the news reports? Put two and two together, and tipped off the CRPs that Mabel had stolen Chief Detector Thomas's baby?

Or had someone seen them flying and reported them as witches? Mabel shook her head. Even Harvey, for all his faults,

was exceedingly careful to stay out of sight—flying only at night, or high above the clouds, landing only when the streets were deserted, the windows unattended.

The Professional on the right was tall, black, and handsome. He projected confidence. *Un*cowardliness. *Courageousness.* Mabel sighed. She was married. To a frog, yes. Still.

To his right stood a white man, thin as her wand and nearly as short. Didn't they have any height regulations at the Conflict Resolution Academy? He wore an apologetic, over-friendly expression. He would be easy to fool. She would do her best to shoo them away. But just in case—

Mabel dashed through the house, yanking down and hiding anything that might clue them in that she was a witch. Incantations hanging on the walls, statues of the goddesses, a scroll she'd neglected to put away . . . A pointy black hat on the dresser, which she'd never be caught dead wearing (at least in this lifetime), but for nostalgia reasons couldn't bear to throw away . . .

She tucked her amulet under her dress. Quick—anything in the baby's room? Not that she knew of—

More impatient *KNOCKING.*

"I'm coming!" She shoved everything on her bureau into a drawer and shut it again. "Get in there, you."

KNOCKING—

"Coming! Keep your ugly yellow hat on!"

She rushed to the foyer and smoothed down her hair. She would, as Lady Macbeth had advised, "look like th' innocent flower, but be the serpent under't." She opened the door. "Why, good evening, officers."

The confident one looked up at her with surprise. (She was, admittedly, rather tall for a normal human being, which of course she was not.) He quickly masked his expression.

She continued, "How may I be of assistance this fine evening?"

His eyes narrowed. Perhaps she had come off *too* flowery. She had better tone it down. "What the hell do you want?"

Oops. Now she may have erred on the side of serpentdom, for there was surprise again.

"Heh-heh, just a little joke, there." She smiled her friendliest smile (which even Harvey had once thought genuine).

The confident CRP tipped his hat. "Evening, ma'am. I'm Professional Jackson, and this is my partner, Professional Gardner." They flashed their badges. "We've had a report of a baby stolen from these premises. May we come in?"

The wandlike one smiled. "A colleague of ours picked up an inebriated citizen, who swore he saw a bear carrying a baby drop from your window. Saw it rush down the street."

"A bear? In my house? I think I would have noticed such a thing." Mabel laughed. Actually, she wouldn't have noticed the fox had her argument with Harvey not migrated into the baby's room. Who knew what else she'd missed tonight. The fox and bear could've hosted a party for all their four-legged friends, for all she knew.

The confident, pushy one—Jackson, had he said?—stepped over the threshold, uninvited. "CCTV cameras corroborate it. At least, a large animal, carrying something small under its leg. Er, arm. Mind if we look around?"

Mabel shrugged, turned, and led the way down the hall. Arguing would just encourage suspicion.

They entered the baby's room. The crib was empty, as she and Harvey had left it. But the supplies were haphazardly strewn across the cabinet, as if someone—or some*thing*—had hurriedly gone through them. It looked like a crime scene. She had to pretend to be sad. Quick—what was she sad about?

Nothing! She was *glad* Harvey was now easily accidentally-step-on-able, *intrigued* that the baby was apparently so in tune with nature, the bear not only hadn't eaten it, it had come here to steal it back.

She couldn't think of a single moment in her life when she'd been sad. Mad, yes. *Angry.* Justifiably angry. Especially at Brenda. Brenda, who *would* be very sad right about now. Quick—what would Brenda do?

Mabel whirled around, wringing her hands. "Woe is me! Woe is me!"

Jackson—*Professional* Jackson—looked suspicious. He was smart. She had a grudging respect for him. Was "woe" a bit much? She unclasped her hands.

"Let's just get down to what happened. What time, would you say, did you last see your baby?"

"I only put it down for a moment, while I . . . er, took a quick shower."

Jackson gazed at her obviously dry hair.

She reached up and touched a curl. "Shower cap."

"Riiiiight. What time would you say this was?"

It must have been an hour since she'd turned Harvey into a frog. Too bad she hadn't been able to turn him into a toad—toads were even more loathsome. "An hour ago? Perhaps?"

Jackson nodded, glancing at the crib, then over at the messy cabinet. "May we have a description of your baby?"

Mabel drew a blank. It was a baby. It looked like all babies. Small, loud, oozing all sorts of disgusting goo. Still, the CRPs might find it and bring it back...or maybe send in Animal Control.

Jackson pulled out a notebook. "Physical appearance, identifying marks, clothing he or she was wearing?"

"Sheeeee..." Yes. Mabel was at least sure of that. "Was small. Baby-sized. Browwwwwwn—blackish?—hair. Wearing..." A diaper. On this chilly fall night. Would that seem negligent? Probably. Didn't non-magical people typically swaddle their female progeny in pink? "A pink onesie."

Jackson nodded and wrote this down. "May we have a recent photograph?"

Shoot. Typical parents did take pictures of their brood, didn't they. Mabel wouldn't look like a loving parent if she couldn't produce at least one. "Of course. Hold on a moment."

She pretended to rummage through the top drawer of the cabinet. "Wouldn't you know it? The bear took those, too."

Jackson grunted and wrote in his notebook. Mabel craned her neck, but couldn't make out anything upside down, or in such scrawly handwriting.

"May we see your driver's license?"

Was this standard procedure? Or did he suspect something?

"Or other photo ID?"

She should have prepared for this. She had an old ID in her bureau, with her real name on it. She'd always used magic to update the expiration date, but never futzed with the name. She was proud of her name. Honoring her ancestors and whatnot. But now it could prove to be a liability.

She strode to the bedroom, looking over her shoulder to

make sure the CRPs weren't following. She grabbed the laminated card from the top dresser drawer. What should she change it to? Jones? Yes, Jones was good. She'd heard that name thrown around a lot, that was believable. Or Smith. That was common, too. Either one would work.

On the other hand, if Chief Detector Thomas thought to review reports of all recent baby abductions and ran the addresses through the department's database, Mabel's innumerable traffic violations would surely surface. He'd connect her with her sister and know she'd used a fake name. He'd probably suspect her anyway, but that would clinch it.

She returned to the baby's room, and held out the ID.

Jackson took it. "Mabel Blackthorn"—he squinted—"udder? Unusual name."

Mabel scowled at this rude, attractive man. "What, you think it's funny, do you?"

He coolly handed her card back. "Ma'am, when you've been on the job as long as I have, not much amuses you anymore."

"I can understand that." She took her ID and tucked it into her pocket.

"It's just …" The wandlike one turned from where he was taking pictures of the cabinet. "You'd think it would be Blackthorn*adder*. More witch-like. That one letter makes it seem a bit ludicr—" He met his partner's glare and quickly turned back to his pictures.

"Witch-like? Why, I never!" Mabel laughed. A shrill, high-pitched laugh that sounded suspicious, even to her. "As *if* I would be caught dead associating with witches."

Jackson frowned. "Doesn't matter if you do. It's a huge waste of departmental resources, in my opinion, harassing these

★ 75 ❋

chanting, deluded arm-wavers, when there are *real* criminals on the streets."

This one was a sensible man. At least, regarding who the real criminals were. But, deluded? Arm-wavers? Obviously he'd been raised to underestimate humans with unusual gifts. He'd been blinded to the hidden truths of life. The great mysteries. Such as, how did the Earth know to orbit the Sun at the exact precise distance to sustain life? Why, when you were thinking nasty thoughts about your mother-in-law, did she always call? How was Mabel going to ~~turn Harvey~~ get the baby back?

The phone in the hallway rang. She ignored it. "So. A bear. How are you going to find my baby?"

The wandlike one turned again, from where he was now examining the window, which was open a foot more than she'd left it. Just wide enough for a bear. He glanced out the doorway. "Aren't you going to get that?"

"Eh." She waved a dismissive hand. "That's just my mother-in-law. So. About my baby?"

"Don't worry, ma'am. We're on the case." The wandlike one returned his attention to the window, and removed a pair of tweezers from his shirt pocket.

Mabel wished he would just go away, and leave her alone with Jackson. Then an interrogation might turn heated, and suppressed desires would be unleashed. Jackson might confide he was a widower, passion would override sense and they would stride toward each other, arms outstretched (his looked very strong). Someone might accidentally step on Harvey ... which would be sad, but not for long.

Perhaps she could magically point the wandlike one's shoes

toward the door and give him a subtle kick to propel him on his way. With her mind wandering to the Bard (she'd read a few more plays in Harvey's collection—Shakespeare's insults were actually very creative), she focused on the wandlike one and subtly flicked her fingers. *Away, you three-inch fool!*

He stumbled over seemingly thin air, caught himself on the windowsill, and gave his partner an embarrassed grin. But he stayed in the room, and used his tweezers to lift from the sill a tiny, velvety torn piece of fabric.

A piece of Mabel's robe, where she'd ripped it.

Jackson disinterestedly watched his partner perform what must be routine procedure. He turned back to her. "You live here alone?"

A soft *thumping* in the hallway grew louder. Mabel suppressed her inclination to curse as Harvey, her "dearest partner of greatness" (not!) hopped into the room.

Jackson looked at Harvey with an expression that radiated, *Ugh. Amphibians running loose.* Mabel agreed with him.

"Don't mind *him*." She waved a second dismissive hand. "That's just Harvey."

"My son has a snake. I suppose it's a nice enough creature, but when I'm home I insist it stay in its cage."

"A cage. Huh. Interesting idea."

Harvey hopped onto her foot, ribbiting angrily. Annoyingly. Mabel reached for her broom, which she'd propped up in the corner after that last flight. Now there was an even more enjoyable use for her broom. She swept Harvey and his annoying ribbiting out of the room.

Jackson looked on rather approvingly, she thought. "So, you're a single parent?"

"Yes. Well. I had a husband, but he croaked."

"Sorry to hear that."

"Thank you. Yes. I'm extremely broken up about it."

The wandlike one turned, to butt in yet again. She felt the urge to wave a third dismissive hand, a hand that would stretch out on a very long arm, wrap around his throat and throttle him. But she wasn't that powerful. Yet.

The wandlike one merely gave Jackson a thumbs-up.

Jackson nodded. "We're done here, ma'am. We'll contact you when we have anything concrete to go on. Um, very sorry for your loss ..."

"But we always get our man!" chimed in the wandlike one. "Or, in this case, our *bear*." He giggled.

Mabel and Jackson exchanged a look over the absurdity of his partner. She was sorry he was stuck with him.

Huh. She couldn't remember ever feeling sorry for someone. She shoved that feeling down, deep into her unconscious. It would only be a distraction.

Jackson strode toward the door.

"I like your robe," said the wandlike one. "It's so shiny and velvety-looking."

Jackson turned to her, and took a good look. He glanced at his partner, who still held the plastic baggie into which he'd carefully transferred the piece of her robe. The wandlike one followed his partner's gaze.

Drat! How could she have forgotten about her robe? "What, this old thing?" She laughed, taking care not to sound so self-conscious this time. "It's a regular old, ratty bathrobe you'd find in any department store. They're available to purchase anywhere. Everywhere. Everyone's wearing them nowadays.

Even outside the house."

She cleared her throat, hoping she did not sound too shifty around the subject of her robe, which, she had to admit, did not look like any department store bathrobe she'd ever seen. What with its crescent moons and glittering stars that moved across the fabric's midnight sky all on their—

Stop that, she thought sharply. The stars immediately obeyed. She was looking suspicious enough without fidgety stars giving her away.

Jackson's face turned blank, like he was about to bluff through a poker hand against a bunch of equally untrustworthy witches. "Right. Like I said, ma'am. We're done. Thanks very much for your time. We'll do our best to find your baby and contact you as soon as possible."

"Yes, you do that. Woe is m—er, I'm very, very sad about my baby." She escorted them through the hallway, weighing her options. Were they going off to obtain a search warrant? To confiscate her robe? And, if she were to burn it while they were gone, arrest her on probable cause?

If she had that baby in her possession, she could turn them into a real-life Frog and Toad. Now she would have to cast a freeze spell, and hack them up into tiny icicles. Or dispose of them without magic. Perhaps with her broom. Although, that could get messy. And the neighbors might hear screaming. Then she'd have to dispose of the neighbors. And . . .

She'd be sliding further and further down the slippery slope on which Lady Macbeth had crashed and burned.

Her momentary hesitation cost her. The CRPs left.

Was she overreacting? Of *course* a piece of snagged fabric on the windowsill would belong to her. She could have ripped her robe while raising the window to wash it, or to let in fresh air, or while leaning outside to ~~catch butterflies for potions~~ admire butterflies and other wildlife.

But the seeds of suspicion had surely been planted.

Mabel stared out the window, and suppressed a sigh at the sight of a set of broad shoulders sauntering away, next to a set of narrow shoulders in close proximity to the ground.

They weren't heading toward their car. Instead, they were climbing the stoop to the neighbors, the wandlike one talking into his radio. Was he alerting headquarters something was afoot?

She let the curtain fall away and slumped onto the couch to think this problem through. Out of the corner of her eye, she noticed a dark mark on the fabric that had never been there before. Dirt, or something. She brushed it away.

"Out, damn'd spot! Out, I say!"

Ribbit!

"Oops. Sorry, Harvey. Didn't realize that was you." Mabel giggled to herself.

A subtle movement caught her eye. "Fluffy, stop leering at Harvey, he's not a real frog. He's some kind of frog/human hybrid, he probably tastes terrible."

Well. No rest for the ~~wicked~~ well-meaning. Back to scrying! She jumped up and ran to the attic.

She sat up straight in front of the black mirror, with all her energy centers aligned, and began all over. Starting with the long, drawn-out process of letting go of the usual nagging thoughts . . .

Brenda would pay . . . Why were all the good men taken . . . . Why-oh-why had she ever married Harvey

… … …Couldn't she have foreseen what a frog he'd turn out to be … …not literally, of course …

She refocused on the mirror and said a prayer to her helping spirits. The mirror filled with fuzzy images. Witches wearing pointy hats. Searching for a place to hide. Casting spells to remove the bricks that had sealed off the cave in the Ramble.

Brews bubbling in cauldrons. Chanting. Naked dancing. (Mabel rolled her eyes. What with heat and cold, flies and mosquitoes, continuing certain outdoor traditions just wasn't worth it.)

A witch rolling a small boulder into the cave, no doubt for use in some strange ritual. Or doing crunches. Witches dying of old age. Or spells gone wrong.

A bear family discovering the cave. Bear cubs growing up and leaving, all except one. The old bear dying. The remaining female giving birth.

A long absence.

A fox and bear.

Mabel hopped excitedly on her chair. Her two nemeses! (Other than Brenda and Harvey. And the Chief Magic Detector. And her next-door neighbor. And the surly checkout girl at the all-night food market. And—oh, *everybody* infuriated her!) Surely there couldn't be that many bears in the city. Foxes had become commonplace, but they were reckless and constantly getting run over.

An injured white cat. Being cared for by the fox and bear.

And …

A baby.

The mirror clattered to the floor, as Mabel jumped for joy and hit her head on the low-hanging chandelier.

Harvey hopped by, followed by Fluffy, who was really only toying with Harvey at this point. Mabel scooped up her husband—ugh, disgusting, she would never get used to that sticky sliminess—and set him on her shoulder. Throwing open the window, she mounted her broom and set out.

Momentarily, she hovered in the fog and filthy air. If New York *wasn't* the greatest city in the world, it certainly was the stinkiest.

She leaned forward, urging her broom onward—

CRACK!

She'd been shot, she realized as she fell to the ground, before all went dark.

"Perfect shot, Carney," Chief Detector Thomas commended his best sharpshooter. He strode to the prone body on the sidewalk, mentally cursing the tranquilizer darts that had been foisted upon his department. Real bullets would save the city a whole lot of money.

The body was turned over and loaded into the paddy wagon. Chief Detector Thomas took off his hat and scratched his hairless head. That was—if he wasn't mistaken—his estranged second wife's estranged sister.

And he was never mistaken.

Harvey hopped toward the Conflict Resolution car and jumped onto the grille. The engine started up and the vehicle moved into the avenue, where it picked up speed, heading downtown.

As cars and trucks rattled on all sides, Harvey hung on for dear life, lest he fall and become a mere splotch on the pavement, like in that '80s video game he'd played as a youth with no sense of compassion for frogs whatsoever.

On he clung, not so much out of loyalty to Mabel as desperation, as what other magic-competent in New York City might be able to change him back into a human? There was Helga Hagglebottom, of course, who was highly skilled, perhaps the most powerful witch in all the five boroughs. She would never turn down a request for help.

But that might bring him into contact with Helga's sister, Hilda, who would probably enjoy nothing more than to squash him under her shoe.

The callery pear, which had been planted in the neighbors' tiny courtyard many moons ago, had grown to reach the witch's window. It had seen the witch depart more times than it could count. But this time was different. Her visage had not just reflected purpose, but knowing—a mad glint in her eye, the frog trembling on her shoulder.

And now the witch had been apprehended by the humans in yellow, themselves quite a harmful bunch. The trees had conferred over the yellow humans often.

The frog—the witch's husband—had followed, clinging to the yellow humans' vehicle.

Something was abranch.

The callery pear sent the warning—across its limbs, through its leaves—to its neighbor, the silver linden. Their branches intertwined; their leaves followed.

The silver linden sent the warning deep, under the grate in the sidewalk, down to its roots, where it was picked up by the mycorrhizal fungi.

The fungi sent the warning on, to the tips of the roots of the nearest tree, the ginkgo biloba. Which sent it on ...

All the way to the correctional facility, where the body was heaved up the stairs and inside the heavy double doors.

The sweetgum out on the sidewalk watched—and waited.

~ TWELVE ~

Had he still been human, Harvey would have let out a sigh of relief when the CRP car finally slowed and rolled to a stop in front of a large concrete building. Alas, he was but a frog, and as such managed only a soft, tired *ribbit.*

This was Conflict Resolution Headquarters, no doubt. And, prison.

He scrambled to get down, his fragile frog fingers and toe pads smarting from clinging onto the grille. But that was of no consequence, for he had a plan. Small enough to slip into the station unnoticed, he would hide, steal the keys from a sleeping guard—hours spent watching break-out-of-the-clink films and television would prove productive after all—and slip them to Mabel between the bars.

They would escape. She would be so grateful, not only would she immediately turn him back into a man upon recovering the magic baby, she would never again harp on his faults, real or imagined.

That last was definitely delusional. But at least he would be human again.

He hopped furiously to follow the CRPs as they climbed up the concrete steps, three of them carrying Mabel's limp, extra-tall frame. No one looked down and marked him, a small, albeit moving, speck in the dark. Adrenaline surged as he pushed himself to make it through the heavy metal doors before they banged shut—

Meowwwwwrrrr!

Harvey's tiny frog heart exploded, panic rendering his little frog legs more suitable for delectable consumption than mobile function, making him stumble and fall short of the slamming doors. The sound of claws on concrete followed him as he composed himself to hop over the banister and down to the sidewalk.

Mrrr mrrr mwwwwrrrrrrooow!

As he bounded toward the closest CRP car, the nearest bastion of safety, he swiveled a bulging frog eye to take in the sight of a huge orange tabby cat, its collar tag jangling. Obviously belonging to the CRP station—and taking its mission of keeping Headquarters free of intruders pathologically seriously—it raced after Harvey to the car.

He jumped onto the grille and climbed up, scrambled over the hood and to the side, and used his sticky toe pads to scale the window pane. Thankfully it had been left slightly ajar, just wide enough for a frog to slip inside. He dropped down onto the passenger seat and allowed himself a smirk at the glass, as the cat's glowering face appeared at the height of its jump, then disappeared on its way to the ground.

Ribbit, ribbit ribbit ribbit! Too bad the cat was illiterate and could not appreciate Harvey's vast knowledge of the Bard's work. ("A cat, to scratch a man to death!")

Not today, pal! *Ribbit ribbit, ribbit!* This the cat understood, its furious face appearing then vanishing every other second, its yowling the only sound disturbing the night. Harvey allowed himself a moment to relax against the comfortable leather and figure out his next move.

A distinctly non-feline *growwwwwwwl* emanated from the back. Harvey looked up. Slobbery jowls and a spiked collar poked over the edge of the passenger seat, along with a set of pointy black ears.

BARK BARK BARK BARK BARK BARK

As Harvey leapt throughout the car's interior—trying to stay away from the fangs of an angry Doberman Pinscher while the spitting cat's visage loomed out the window with every other lunge—he willed his thoughts to stay with the Bard—"the cat will mew, and dog will have his day"—so his mind wouldn't wander where it naturally wanted to stray, to an image of his mangled frog body, sliding down a slimy gullet.

The driver's side door opened, and a Conflict Resolution Professional stepped inside.

"All right, all *right*, Sweet Pea, I'm here. Let's go home."

As Harvey dove into a rear seat organizer, the CRP drove one-handed while trying to settle down her dog, which she'd clearly named following a severe fall and head contusion.

"What are you after there in the back, huh? I've got the beef-and-turkey treats right here."

Harvey briefly fantasized about a more serene life, perhaps in Central Park's Hallett Nature Sanctuary, where dogs were not allowed. But the words of Macbeth brought his focus back.

"Tomorrow, and tomorrow, and tomorrow." Harvey would persevere. Tomorrow he would find a way to return, alive, to the station, and again attempt to spring Mabel.

After all, marriage vows were sacred. For better, or for frog.

~ THIRTEEN ~

Upon their return to the cave, Essex and Olaf found, to their immense relief, the baby. Uneaten.

Baby flicked her tail. "I'm still digesting a full meal of rodents. If I ate her, I'd only get a bellyache."

The baby cried out and grasped a pawful of her fur. Baby's hackles rose, but she didn't bat her away. Essex smiled. Baby was warming up to the baby. If only in her grumpy way.

Olaf prepared the formula—while absolutely nobody made the baby laugh—and soon she was contentedly sucking it down. As they waited for her to finish before they could go to sleep, Essex mentioned it might be wise to think up a name. To use while the baby was in their care.

"Just for now, you understand." Essex directed this at Olaf. "For our convenience."

Baby huffed. "So we don't confuse her with the next baby Olaf brings us?"

Essex ignored her disgruntled friend. "We won't keep her

long enough that she'll get used to it."

"Right." Olaf seemed to hide a smile.

This did not reassure Essex. Still, she and Olaf bounced around ideas. He felt they should name the baby after a street, like Essex's mother had named *her* cubs. Essex thought of all the street names she'd heard humans say to each other. They could call the baby something short and snappy, like Madison or Park. Or something grand and sophisticated, like Franklin D. Roosevelt East River Drive.

Or—she screeched with delight—*Sesame.*

On the other paw, Bolton's mother had named him after a lovely Christmas tune she'd heard emanating from a car.

Olaf whispered, couldn't they name the baby, Baby? And call Baby something more fitting? Like, Grumpy? Or, Hissy? Or, Surprisingly Antagonistic for Such a Small Creature?

By now the baby had finished her bottle, and Olaf watched while she played with his teddy bear. Wendy, the kind caretaker at the zoo, had given it to him. Its name was Bearington. Olaf had said she'd shown him the tag, but of course, he couldn't read.

Maybe they should name the baby after a teddy bear or a doll? Olaf dug into the Pile of Human Garbage. He pulled out a frog doll, a cowboy doll, a little girl doll the color of bark, a little girl doll the color of cooked spaghetti, and realized, he didn't know what any of them were called, because he didn't know how to read.

Olaf sat on his rock and moaned. How were they going to teach the baby to read?

Essex gently suggested, that was a problem for another day.

Even Baby was helpful and suggested ideas. But Essex felt

Tiny Ungodly Unit of Mayhem and Destruction was rather long and unwieldy.

*

The baby slept through the night. Or at least, she did not cry out and wake them.

Essex rose early. She would have to wait till a reasonable human hour to visit the witches, but in case that expedition took longer than expected she needed to fill her belly.

She nuzzled with Olaf before leaving, as one never knew if one would make it home again. (Baby was never demonstrative, but she did flick her tail goodbye.) He'd wanted to come, but humans were afraid of bears. What if the good witches also fired their wands at him?

Essex bounded up the steps and sniffed, on the alert for leftover human food or living prey, and looking to not *become* prey.

A mouse scampered away. A bunny munched on a leaf. The shouts of human teenage males disturbed the quiet, and the bunny stilled.

A memory surfaced, of human teenage males throwing stones at a bunny and laughing. Essex cringed. She would never torture smaller animals for fun. She just needed to eat, like every other being ever.

And she made clean kills. Her prey didn't suffer. They went off to again be One with the Everything. To a better existence. One not filled with hunger and danger. With worry and pain. With grief.

She would not be sorry, when it was her time to go. She

would again be with Bolton. Surely he was patiently waiting.

The shouts faded. The bunny resumed munching. Essex steadied her tail and skulked forward.

The bunny sensed her and ran off.

She turned and stalked silently through the shrubbery. Soon she homed in on a chipmunk.

The grass sang sweetly. The dragonflies buzzed busily. A crow cawed overhead.

Essex slunk low to the ground, moving almost imperceptibly. Swiftly, she said a short prayer, thanking the Everything. And the spirit of the chipmunk.

She quickly calculated the right angle, and sprang.

The chipmunk did not suffer.

She ate.

The grass sang sweetly. The dragonflies buzzed continuously. Life went on for almost everybody. Hopefully the chipmunk had not had a family depending on it.

Essex finished her meal, and looked up to gauge the sun's position in the sky.

*

At the northern end of the park, Essex poked her nose through a prickly rose bush at the edge of the fenced-off woods. In a clearing with a well-kept garden stood the witches' tiny cottage.

It appeared to have been simply built. Yellow wooden planks made up the walls, rising to a yellow thatched straw roof, where a yellow brick chimney spewed smoke into the sky. (Olaf had once told her, not everything she thought was yellow, was actually yellow.) The cottage looked straight out of a picture book.

Tiny, frosted windows stared back at her, framed by inviting curtains of white and . . . yellow.

Her tummy rumbled, and she breathed in deeply. The chipmunk had not sated her, and whatever was cooking didn't smell totally terrible. Perhaps the Nice One would answer and be inclined to share.

Warily, Essex approached the door. She reached out a paw and gently tapped.

She waited. A few long moments, and then, when no one answered, she knocked harder.

Heavy footsteps approached. The door creaked open. A string of warts attached to a long, bulbous nose paraded through the crack. A long, puffy face featuring an annoyed frown followed. "What? Who's there?"

The witch looked eerily like the human in the food palace

who had tried on the pointy hat. Every feature was roughly the same size and shape. Perhaps the nose was a little longer, the warts a tad more numerous.

The frown turned into an expression of confusion. The door opened wider and the rest of the body followed, well insulated, clothed in a robe as dark as the night sky. Finally the witch looked down. She saw Essex and scowled. "What do *you* want, fox?"

Essex stepped back in surprise. The trees had said the witches would be able to understand her, but not that they would *expect* to talk to a woodland creature they encountered. "I . . . I wanted to ask . . ."

Tentatively, Essex stepped forward. First one paw, then the other . . . over the threshold. (She had watched humans get what they wanted by being assertive.) She wound around the witch's leg, the witch staring down at her like her bulging eyes couldn't believe a being could be so rude.

Essex got a good look into the tiny room. A large black cauldron sat over a fire in the fireplace, full of murky liquid judging from the burbling sounds and the occasional shooting bubble.

"The trees said you might help—"

"Help? I don't help anyone. If you're not selling Girl Scout cookies you stole from actual Girl Scouts at a deep discount, I'm not interested. Buh-bye!" The witch stepped back and moved to close the door.

Except Essex stood in the way. The door banged against her side and sprang back. She cried out, "*Please*. My friend and I need help caring for a human baby we rescued from *bad* witches—not like you, of course—and the trees said—"

"Trees, schmees! Annoying creatures. And you. Can't you see I'm busy brewing a potion? Go away, and don't come back."

The door slammed against Essex once more, but she almost didn't feel it this time, entranced by the sight—visible under the witch's armpit, which was particularly smelly—of a small TV on a cupboard in the corner. It was Snarky and her spooka-licious buds! Maybe Essex could use their shared fascination with humans pretending to be other humans to bond.

"I watch *Snarky*, too! Maybe we could watch togeth—"

"Rude. Scram. Shoo!" This was followed by several unintel-ligible syllables, a flash of yellow light, and the door closed with such force Essex was knocked all the way across the garden.

For a moment she lay on the cold ground, dazed. She picked herself up, jumped over the fencing, and hid behind the prickly rose bush. The witch would have to leave the cottage some-time. Perhaps to bathe. Essex was used to all kinds of smells, but ... *phew!*

Olaf popped out from behind a tree. "No luck with the Mean One?"

"What are you doing here? I told you not to come."

"I thought you might need help."

Poking their noses through the prickly rose bush, they peered at the cottage. The well-kept garden. The yellow wooden planks. ("Brown," said Olaf.) The yellow thatched straw roof. ("Yellow," agreed Olaf.) The yellow brick chimney. ("Red," said Olaf.)

Essex gazed at the front door. "Perhaps the more helpful sister is home and is sleeping."

The door opened. They leaned forward. Hopefully it would

be the *nice* sister.

The not-so-helpful sister emerged, carrying garden shears and a watering can. She approached the first plant in the first column in the first row of the garden, and knelt, knees cracking. She lovingly tended to her garden, going from plant to plant, watering each and pulling up weeds. Speaking to her plants in a soft, gentle voice, so very opposite her manner with Essex.

The witch stood. Essex and Olaf tensed, ready to run—but she merely turned and walked off, stepping over the fencing into the woods.

This was their chance. Except . . .

"If we go in uninvited, we'll be invading the sisters' privacy." Not something that had ever mattered to Essex before, considering all the human dwellings she'd breached. But they were hoping for assistance from these humans, and trespassing was considered rude.

"We'd have to go back to the food palace, wouldn't we," said Olaf, his shoulders slumping.

"The nice sister probably isn't home anyway. Humans don't generally lie about all day."

"I think the checkout teenager is a witch, too."

"On the other paw, like foxes and bears, most human siblings don't live together after the age of dispersal."

"The way she made me freeze. Maybe she was pointing a magic stick at me under the counter."

"What if the Nice One is living in the cottage against her will?" Essex's heart leapt at this possibility.

Olaf straightened, his eyes lighting up. "Tied up, captive, a prisoner of the Mean One?"

"It's our duty to help!"

Essex raced across the garden, with Olaf lumbering behind. She ran around the front door to the open back window. She coiled into a ball, sprang inside, and landed with a soft *plunk*.

Just as a loud *CRASH!* indicated that Olaf had banged through the front door. Essex peeked through the entranceway. The door lay off its hinges on the floor.

"Oops." He looked glum for a moment, then brightened. "Maybe they won't notice."

"Maybe the Mean One won't rip off my whiskers and sprinkle them in her potion. Well, we're here now. Let's look around."

Essex glanced about. Snarky had finished her latest escapade. Successfully, one would imagine. The potion brewed in the fireplace, the stirring stick stirring *all on its own*.

A noise outside the cottage startled her, and she wrenched her gaze away from the stick. They didn't have much time. She scanned the tidy little room. The living space doubled as a kitchen, with a too-small-to-be-holding-a-human-body-captive refrigerator in the corner. Quickly they searched the rest of the cottage. A bathroom. Two tiny bedrooms, with neat, made-up beds. No nice sister sleeping, or tied up. They checked the two closets, Essex rising up on her hind legs, grasping and turning one doorknob with her paws, while Olaf was hopefully carefully—

CRACK!

"Oops."

Essex sighed, and looked inside her closet. It contained black robes. Black, non-pointy shoes. Black jeans. Black blouses. But no pointy black hats.

A dark shape appeared in the doorway, too short to be Olaf.

Essex sprang up onto the sill and scrabbled at the base with her paws, as this window was shut. As she struggled trying to raise it, footsteps approached. Olaf could do this so easily, but he was not *here* when she *needed* him—

"Why, hello there. Isn't this a pleasant surprise. I usually get birds and squirrels visiting me, but—" A hand gently descended on Essex's head and floofed her fur. "Welcome! Welcome!"

Essex gazed in surprise at a long, bulbous nose—complete with warts—and a radiant smile. It was the human from the food palace who had tried on the pointy hat!

But where was the pointy hat now? Not the toy one she had tried on in front of Essex, but her *real* witch's hat. Didn't all witches wear them?

True, the Mean One hadn't. And Snarky and her friends didn't, either. But they were young, modern witches. Essex had seen enough TV shows to know the Mean One and her sister belonged to the "Old Guard."

"Are you hungry? Were you not able to find any breakfast? I'm sure I have something here ..."

The helpful witch turned and strode into the kitchen. Which only took her four strides, the cottage was so tiny (at least for a human dwelling). She opened a cupboard and rummaged through it.

Olaf nodded so vigorously, one would think he hadn't eaten since the new moon. "Yes, please, Nice One."

The helpful witch chuckled, and pulled open the top of a small, circular tin. She spooned the contents into a bowl and set it by Olaf, who gobbled it down.

Essex salivated, as whatever it was smelled delicious. "Thank you, that's very kind. But we really came to ask if you'd help us, somehow—in whatever way would be most convenient for you—procure milk for a baby we rescued from ...um ..."

The witch seemed to be listening with kind interest, so Essex continued, "Bad witches."

Essex cowered and, just in case, backed up toward the door. Perhaps any witch, even a nice one, would take offense at the idea that any of her kind could be "bad." Humans were unpredictable, but they could pretty much always be counted upon to take things personally.

"Bad witches. Ah. Might you be talking about the husband and wife who live on the outskirts of the park, on the East Side? Or Gertrude Gawfersheen? Oh no, that can't be, she's been locked up awhile now. Or the threesome who live on the banks of the Hudson? Or any of the many bad witches in Queens?" She watched Olaf lick the bowl clean and rummaged in the cupboard for another tin. "Yes, for some reason bad witches like to congregate in Queens."

As the helpful witch rattled off descriptions of witches and their locations in the city, and Olaf devoured the extra food, Essex wondered at how many witches were running around New York in plain sight.

"Let's just put this back." The Nice One took out her magic wand and waved it at the door lying on the floor. She chanted. The door ascended. It danced in time to her singing and attached itself to its hinges.

Essex stared, much less used to real-life magic than Snarky's daily accomplishments. "So, you'll help us?"

"Of course. I'd be happy to."

"You'll make milk for our baby?" Olaf jumped with excitement and landed with a *crash*, causing the leftover food to jump for joy, too.

Essex couldn't resist, and took a nibble.

The front door lurched open, and the Mean One stormed in with an armload of firewood. "*No*, she can't *help* you. Look at her honking huge nose!" She waved an angry hand at her sister. "Look at those warts! She couldn't deny being a witch if she tried. The last thing either of us need is to be seen conversing with the likes of you."

Essex stood dazed, stunned that any being could be so unkind toward its own sibling. And she couldn't help thinking ... "You look almost exactly the same."

The Mean One turned to her. "Exactly! We fit the stupid stereotype *exactly*. All we need is green skin to look completely like the stereotypical picture of witches that stupid people have in their big dumb heads!"

Essex pointed a tentative paw. "Um ... you do look kind of yellow. Which might be green. Did you eat something—"

"Gaah!" The Mean One threw up her hands. The firewood fell to the floor. She turned to her sister, who stood calmly at the counter, opening up another tin.

Olaf rose onto his hind legs, the stance he used when he wanted to intimidate someone. "Were you ... leavesdropping on us?"

The Mean One whirled back with no fear at all, as though a gigantic bear with huge fangs and claws standing in her kitchen were an everyday occurrence. "It's 'eavesdropping,' you nitwit. And I didn't need to, you were gabbing so loud I could hear you all the way across the clearing! I could've heard you if I'd plugged my ears with pillows!"

"She does that a lot," said the Nice One, setting another

bowl of food in front of Essex.

The Mean One turned on her sister. "Neither of us can afford to go around helping a bunch of silly woodland creatures who took on more than they could chew. 'Rescuing' a human baby, how ridiculous! It's even ridiculous in stories, let alone real life. 'Sly as a fox,' ha! More like stupid as a fox and its dumb bear friend! And you want to be seen with them? What if someone spied you talking to them? Only magic-competents can understand animals—everyone knows that!"

Olaf growled. "I know I'm not the brightest tool in the box, but no one had better insult my best friend."

"Brightest bulb," said Essex.

"Or what?" the Mean One sneered. "You'll sit on me?"

"Actually," said the Nice One, "he would probably break every bone in your—"

"Oh, for crying out loud! Go away, and leave the two of us in peace."

"Now, Hilda, I *want* to help them. And honestly, who really would notice if we—"

"Oh, you *want* to help them, do you? How incredibly nice, sweet, and *stupid* of you, after all we've been through!" The Mean One turned away from her sister and glared at Essex and Olaf. "Fantastic. Helga wants to help you two fools. Go ahead and take her to do whatever harebrained scheme some nosy trees stuck into your tiny brains. And while you're at it, do me a favor—don't bring her back."

She huffed, whirled around, and stormed out the way she'd come—her black robe billowing behind her. The front door slammed, catching a piece of robe, which poked out between the door and the jamb.

There was a muffled "Gaah!" The door separated from the jamb, the robe was pulled away, and the door and jamb melded together once more. Angry footsteps stomped off.

Essex turned to the Nice One. That is, Helga. "Please excuse us. We didn't mean to cause trouble between you and your sister."

Helga smiled and waved a dismissive hand. The teacups hanging on the kitchen wall trembled.

"Oops. Heh-heh. Let me just …" She hurried over and caressed the cups till they quieted again. "Don't mind her, dear. She purposely rolls out of the wrong side of the bed in the morning. I'm just worried about her blood pressure. Now. About your milk. I'm happy to help—except, I'll need to ask the trees for leaves and bark."

A cat meowed outside. Loudly. Complainingly.

"I come, Graymalkin!" Helga seemed to radiate tenderness through the wall. She turned to Essex and Olaf. "I already borrowed from them today. Trees are so kind and generous, but I hate to impose. How have you been feeding the baby?"

"Er … by borrowing formula." Essex figured, since Helga couldn't actually return leaves and bark she'd used from a tree, technically taking formula for the baby also counted as borrowing. "From the food palace. Where we saw you in the candy aisle."

Helga smiled. "Could you come back tomorrow?" When Essex nodded, she added, "And bring that baby, won't you? I'm keen to see it."

Essex thanked Helga profusely, while Olaf stifled a grunt. He obviously wasn't at all worried about the Mean One's—that is, Hilda's—blood pressure, whatever that meant. But Essex was sorry to make trouble for Helga. Who was perfectly lovely, never mind what her mean sister said about her nose. And her warts.

*

They took their leave, and trotted through the northern woods and fields. Presently they heard the vocalizations of excited human teenage males.

They crept warily along the bushes, and took a peek. The human teenage males in the clearing were tossing around a football and putting together teams.

The competition began. One teenage male grabbed the football, "faked," and handed it to another . . .

Who tucked it under his arm, and ran.

Essex and Olaf looked at each other.

*

Football laughed and waved her tiny fingers. (The lighter had been safely tucked away.)

"Wonderful, you like your new name." Essex nuzzled the baby's belly, which made her laugh harder, while Olaf did a celebratory dance.

Baby turned her back, and went back to sleep.

~ FOURTEEN ~

After reassuring Graymalkin that he was her One & Only Darling and Number One Woogawagamuffin, Helga entered the cottage to find Hilda brewing a potion. Her sister was always brewing potions, whether to make money, keep herself busy, or deal with stress.

She placed a tentative hand on her dear-but-grumpy sister's shoulder, then thinking better of it, removed it. "I was just thinking ..."

"Of course you were." Hilda stirred her potion. "You big buttinski."

"That I could ask the fox if *I* might have the baby—"

Hilda whirled around, her wooden spoon spraying potion, forcing Helga to jump away. "You want a *baby* now?"

"I'll leave it in front of the fire station. So *they* can return it to the real parents."

A look appeared on Hilda's face as if Helga had suggested they light a fire by the station's fire pole and tie each other to it. Reminiscent of days of yore …

Helga smiled. "They put them *out*, you know."

"I *know* what fire people do. You're nuts if you think they don't share their surveillance footage with the cops."

"The Conflict Resolution Pro—"

"Whatever!"

Helga reached out a hand to calm her sister. "I could wear sunglasses and a face mask. Some people still—"

"With *our* nose? Masks are useless!" Hilda batted her hand away. "Are you forgetting we almost got thrown in the slammer in Philadelphia? We've barely gotten settled here and you want to endanger—"

"I was only thinking how anguished the baby's real parents must be."

"Suffering builds character." Hilda turned back to her potion. "I should know."

"*I'll* bring the baby. You don't have to get involved."

Hilda threw up her hands, which caused potion batter to fly off her spoon and stick to the ceiling. Which was one of the many reasons they did not get back their rental deposit in Philadelphia. Magic goo could be difficult to clean, even with magic.

"We look almost exactly the same! Of course I'd get involved!"

"Surely it couldn't hurt if we—"

"It could. Very much. Ruin our lives, is what it could do."

"Or I could bring it to Child Protective Serv—"

"Street cams! Witch-hunts! Drowning! Or in this day and age, prison! Orange is not our color. Need I remind you it brings out the green in our complexion?"

Helga sighed. It was hard to reason with her neurotic sister, who carried each slight and wound close to her heart, as if they would protect her from whatever new awful thing life was planning to throw at her.

"We could disable a surveillance camera or two—"

"And there'd be a dozen more to capture us doing it. They're all over the city now."

"Perhaps if we—"

"Did nothing, all would be well. I agree." Hilda turned her back and grabbed a poor bat from her bag of ingredients. "End of discussion. Now, if you'll excuuuuse me, I've got some eyes to gouge out."

Helga sighed, went to her room, and sat on her bed. She stared blankly out the window, drained of energy suddenly.

A bird flew onto the sill and helped itself to the seeds she'd left out. Even though humans weren't supposed to feed wildlife in the park. Because that was interfering.

She and her sister had magically cleared a space for their cottage in these fenced-off woods. Along with the Conservancy's *Help Us Protect This Landscape—Please Keep Out* signs, the sisters had added their own fake warnings of rat poison and pesticides, as well as generous real plantings of poison ivy. *Also* interfering. And they routinely helped the sick. Definitely interfering.

Central Park, though designed to look natural, was almost completely man-made. Swamps had been drained, lined with cement and gravel, laid with drainage pipes and flooded to form the lake, ponds, and reservoir. Bedrock had been blasted, smaller rocks artfully placed. Soil had been trucked in, trees and shrubs planted and carefully maintained. Per "eminent domain," scores of poor residents had been displaced. Wasn't that interfering? Who was to judge what was *good* interfering and what wasn't?

She lay down and rested her head on her comfortable memory foam pillow. The trick was to know when and how to interfere, wasn't it? But then, everything one did rippled out into the world and affected others exponentially. There was no way to be sure what would be helpful in the long run. Only the One knew all. All humans could do was muddle through as well they could and hope for the best. And apologize when things invariably went wrong, and try to set them right.

It was so complicated to be a human. Not for the first time did she wonder, why after each "perfect" lifetime (her guide's words, not hers—she would never be so arrogant as to think that of herself), hadn't she ever taken the offer to become a guide herself? Or to remain immersed in Oneness, in the eternal bliss? She'd always felt she could do more for her fellow human beings living as one of them, but she was no longer sure.

The bird sang a beautiful, lilting song, before flying away to continue its day.

Helga smiled, and got up to continue hers.

FIFTEEN

Mabel sat handcuffed to an uncomfortable chair, the lower half of her face encased in an electronic contraption it must have taken years for money-grubbing engineers to secretly develop.

She had woken from a drugged sleep with this atrocity attached to her jaws, in a tiny cell with bright lights and bass-heavy "music" blaring from overhead speakers. Despite this, she'd managed to fall back asleep thanks to years of intense training in meditation and breathwork. Only to be woken yet again by frustrated Conflict Resolution ~~Professionals~~ goons. Try as she might to utter well-earned threats, no sound escaped into the ether.

She stared at the wall opposite. Inlaid was a mirror she'd watched enough cop shows to know was one-way glass.

On the other side of the glass, Chief Detector Thomas watched Detector Cook fiddle with levers and dials, then shifted his gaze to the witch.

She had most certainly kidnapped his infant daughter and was surely holding her for ransom somewhere, possibly with the aid of an accomplice. Said infant daughter was, at best, an inconvenience. Still, the witch could've stolen a counterfeit nickel from a no-good bum, and he would still stop at nothing to put her away forever.

They *all* ought to be locked up. Or better yet, done away with altogether. Save the law-abiding taxpayers money. If one of *his* daughters turned out to be a witch ... He shuddered, not wanting to complete the thought; it was too terrible. Was that really what was in his heart?

He didn't hate his unexpected daughter, exactly. She *had* tied him forever to a person he couldn't remember why he'd married. Now he had to extricate himself from said person, but would never be able to fully. There would always be child support payments, even though Brenda's monthly income surpassed his by an almost obscene amount.

Meanwhile, his elder daughter had developed a "mind of her own" (her words). She had refused his offer to pay her way through college if, upon graduation, she applied to the Conflict Resolution Academy. She was now slumming it at the local food market, saving up tuition money.

She and the majority of citizens believed what the department called "witches" were merely delusional, harmless old ladies practicing a similarly old, washed-up religion. Along with their fellow "magic-competents," they encouraged the ill to look for the "root causes" of their problems and to consume or apply concoctions made from plants, instead of taking scientifically-developed pharmaceuticals like a sensible person in the modern world.

Furthermore, most voters blamed the roots of crime on years of unbalanced resources. Hogwash! You couldn't blame your troubles—nor actions—on others who just happened to have been born with more. Life was inherently unfair, and that was no excuse for deviant behavior.

The recent social uprising could directly be traced to those sneaky witches. Subtly influencing society from the shadows. "Healing" people with "energy" and those dumb plants. Decrying the use of force. It had resulted in the dismantling of his beloved crimefighting unit, turning it into a shell of its former mighty self.

But now this witch had inadvertently gifted him with the means to turn the hearts and minds of the entire city against her and her kind.

Detector Cook handed him an electronic tablet. "It deciphers the signals from the Vocal Cord Negator."

"Excellent," said Chief Detector Thomas. "I'm going in."

Mabel watched, her heartbeat steady, as Chief Detector Thomas—the vile, power-hungry creep her estranged sister had married (most likely in the midst of a mid-life crisis)—entered the room, the harsh overhead lighting glinting off his bald dome like a flashlight beam off a bug.

"Sooooo," hummed ~~the bug~~ Chief Detector Thomas smugly. "Out for a nightly jaunt to steal more babies?"

"*Steal babies?*" mouthed Mabel. Her words marched digitally across the screen he held. *"I was on my way to find MINE, which was stolen from me by—"*

"Silence, witch! We know you're a …" The smugness dissolved into awareness of redundancy. "Er, witch."

"What if I am?" Mabel sneered. Or tried to, with that thing across her face. *"It's no crime, being a magic-competent."*

"Not yet."

Chief Detector Thomas slowly strutted around the table, like a bug oblivious it was about to get squished. By the time he made the turn back to the twelve o'clock position, Mabel had thought up twelve variations of torture spells she would try on him for pure amusement, once she got ahold of her wand. None of them involving harm to that baby, of course.

"Rather a coincidence that a certain someone's baby was recently kidnapped, no?"

"I don't believe in coincidences."

"Neither do I."

He turned suddenly and got right in her face with those beady little eyes, his breath reeking of garlic as if he'd expected to capture a vampire. "Tell me where my baby is, and I'll consider putting in a good word with the judge."

"What judge? You mean you'll treat me like a regular citizen instead of another of your scapegoats?"

He frowned, as if actually offended. "No one's in here who doesn't deserve to be."

"You'll release me right now, if you know what's good for you. If I'm not back soon, my assistant will alert reporters yet another magic-competent has been held without due process."

Actually, her assistant was currently cowering in an air shaft high on the left side of the room. But Mabel was impressed that Harvey had made it this far through the station without getting stomped on.

Her super-sharp witch hearing allowed her to discern a low ribbit of outrage, that translated into, *Assistant?!?*

Chief Detector Thomas sneered. "I think we'd have heard by now if somebody missed you."

That stung. But only briefly. Visionary leaders were always misunderstood in their time. Mabel was going to do great things for the world. Starting with New York City. Once she got her hands on that baby, she would turn the whole Conflict Resolution Department into an army of frogs.

A knot of toads! A surfeit of skunks! A mob of emus! Animals couldn't fire guns. They couldn't launch missiles. Mabel could dismantle entire governments. She would make the world a better place. Wanting to enhance her power was not *just* personal ambition, which had been Lady Macbeth's undoing. Mabel had a mission. A divine purpose.

"We have ways of making you talk." Chief Detector Thomas smiled sadistically.

"Oh?" It was Mabel's turn to smile, albeit under the gag. *"I thought you had ways of making floors sparkle, Mr. Clean."*

The smile vanished, if not the sadism. Obviously the Chief Detector was not one of those inwardly confident men who wore his shortness well.

"Detector Kinney!" he barked. "Get the *room* ready."

SIXTEEN

Essex woke to find Baby sitting, waiting patiently. She had brought them a rat and mouse, and tidied up. Her corner of the cave looked like she'd never been there at all.

Baby stretched out fully, then pulled herself together. "Well, I'm off. I may see you again in a moon or two."

Olaf grunted. "But you just got here."

Baby licked her armpit clean before turning back to them. "I've rested long enough. It's time to go find my Betty."

Essex watched in dismay as Baby stalked to the mouth of the cave. Even though she was grumpy, when she was gone they missed her. Even Olaf, though he wouldn't admit it. (Although he continued to grunt unhappily.)

"But..." Essex's first instinct was to appeal to whatever sliver of sympathy for the baby that Baby might have developed these last two nights. But that was probably truly tiny. So instead, she appealed to their friendship. "We need you. Especially now that we have the baby."

"You don't need me now. You have a witch to help you. My

Betty is all alone. She needs me more than you do."

Essex could not argue with that. She cringed a little, needing to make one last request. "Would you mind terribly, while you're looking for your Betty, keeping an eye out for the baby's parents?"

Baby bristled. "How would I have the faintest clue who they are?"

"Just try to narrow it down. Humans who are sad."

"They all are."

"I mean, unhappy."

"Fine. If I notice any humans who are pathetic *and* unhappy, I'll be sure to make a note of it."

"Thank you, Baby."

She left them.

Essex lay down and tucked her muzzle between her paws. "She's never going to find her."

Olaf said nothing. He just picked up the baby, and hugged her to his chest.

*

The cave felt heavy with Baby's absence. Outside, the sky pelted rain. Even the clouds were sorry she had left them.

Breakfast was a solemn affair, punctuated by Football's belching. After Olaf changed her diaper and adjusted her trash bag, he and Essex ran with her toward the North Woods—ducking under whatever trees they could on the way. Essex had snuck through enough windows on rainy nights to know humans could smell wet fur, and they didn't find the scent particularly pleasant. (She was sure wet flowers did not elicit the same reaction of, "*Ugh, what is that stink?*")

Up above, something flashed, dark and fast.

Essex leapt away. Outstretched talons just missed her. She raced to the nearest hollowed-out tree and hunkered down to wait out the hawk. Birds did not usually fly in rain, but the sight of Essex must have been too tempting.

The hawk circled once...twice...Unrelenting, even as Olaf flashed his fangs and batted at the sky. Finally the hawk gave up and flew off to find shelter, and perhaps an easier meal.

Warily, Essex emerged. She and Olaf ran off, keeping a careful watch.

They reached the witches' cottage. Black smoke spewed from the chimney. Confidently this time, but still softly and politely, Essex tapped at the door.

They waited.

And waited.

And—

Olaf harrumphed and banged a paw, causing the door to shake. Essex hid her eyes behind her paws. Then, thinking better of it—in case the not-so-helpful witch appeared—placed them on the ground, ready to run, duck under a spell, or perhaps sneak inside while the witch and Olaf traded insults.

Footsteps approached. The door opened, and—

Essex tensed as Hilda looked down at them with a scowl and a scrunch of her big, warty nose.

"What do you want, fox?" She glanced over at Olaf. "And you, dumb-dumb?"

At least she didn't slam the door in their faces. As Olaf growled, Essex pawed nervously at the mud. "Your sister...she said she'd help—"

"She's out. Come back later."

The rain pattered and splattered. A familiar voice said something snarky. Essex looked over at the TV playing on the counter. It was Snarky and her spookalicious buds! Essex hadn't been able to go out to watch the TV since the baby had come into their lives. And the room was warm and dry. And the hawk might still be out there. Yes, this sister was unpleasant. But all things considered ...

"Would you mind terribly if we wait inside?" She cowered a little, half-expecting another barrage of synonyms for *go*.

Hilda looked over Essex at the falling rain. Leaving the door open, she shrugged and moved to the fireplace to tend to her bubbling cauldron.

"Suit yourself."

Football reached behind Olaf and babbled, wanting something. Olaf looked back, then said to Essex, "I'll wait with her under the tree."

With a last growl and death stare at the Mean One, he lumbered away. Football grunted and reached for Essex, wanting her to follow.

Essex placed her paw over her heart, to communicate they wouldn't be separated for long. She turned back to the witch.

Hilda grabbed a towel off the mantel and wiped off some condensation. The towel fell to the floor.

"Darn it." She picked it up and tossed it toward Essex. "You might as well use that to dry off, seeing how it's already dirty."

Essex hesitantly padded closer, picked up the towel with her teeth, then retreated over to the door. She did not want to get too close to that cauldron, having seen and heard plenty of stories about wicked witches. Perhaps the trees had been mistaken about one of the sisters not being happy to help. Perhaps this sister would be only *too* happy...to help herself to Essex's eyeballs.

At a *buzzing*, the TV screen went blank. Hilda seemed not to notice. An awkward silence fell, as Essex rolled around on the towel to dry off while keeping an eye on the witch. A silence broken only by the bubbling liquid and gasps of dying insects. Hilda threw tiny body part after tiny body part into the smoking brew, apparently not caring she was snuffing out tiny little lives.

Essex kept control of her emotions. *She* ate smaller living beings. She shouldn't judge the witch just because she didn't understand her. In fact, it would behoove her to make friends. What might be a good topic of conversation?

She had so many questions about real-life humans. What did she most want to know, now that she had the opportunity to ask one who could actually understand her?

"When are you and Helga going to hibernate?"

"Hiber—" Hilda glanced over at her. "What are you talking about? Humans don't hibernate."

Essex pointed a paw at Hilda's belly, which was almost as round as Olaf's. "Why are you storing up all that food, then?"

Hilda paused in tearing an ear off a bat, tore off the head instead, and threw it into the cauldron. Potion splashed so far, Essex had to jump away.

"Think you're a funny one, don't you?"

Essex's confusion must have reflected in her eyes, because Hilda's expression softened somewhat.

"I'm not deliberately storing it. I just like to eat. Sue me, why don't you."

Essex had heard humans tell each other to sue them, but had never seen them do anything that indicated what it meant. "What does that mean, sue you?"

"It's an expression."

"Oh." Essex knew a lot of expressions, both from the TV and from spying on real-life humans. How relieved she'd been to discover that "throw the baby out with the bathwater" was just an expression. Otherwise she and Olaf would have found themselves with a human baby long before now.

"It means I don't care what you think."

Essex tilted her head. "Why would I think anything about you liking to eat? I like to eat. Everyone likes to eat. Everyone *needs* to eat."

Hilda threw up her hands, like humans often did when they were frustrated. Potion gunk flew off her ladle onto the ceiling, where half of it stuck and the other half dripped slowly down. "I don't *need* to eat cake and cookies. I don't *need* to eat potato chips. I actually need to eat a salad every once in a while, for health reasons. But I'm unhappy, so I like to eat things I know are bad for me, that make me feel good."

How wonderful it must be, not to need to eat whatever was available. But Hilda's unhappiness was even more troubling. "Why are you unhappy?"

"You're just a fox, you wouldn't understand."

Essex thought of Bolton. Of her kits, who hardly ever came to visit. Of Baby, who one day might never return. She thought ahead to when she and Olaf would find Football's parents and give her back. And miss her.

"I know what it's like to feel unhappy. I don't want you to be unhappy. Maybe I can help."

"You can't help me." But Hilda smiled slightly, which she hadn't done before in Essex's presence. So maybe Essex had helped a little, after all.

But she wanted to understand further. "Your sister is also hiber—I mean ..."

"Fat. The word is *fat*." The smile was gone.

Essex pawed at the floor, shifting the straw around. "She doesn't seem unhappy."

Hilda stirred her potion so hard, out flew what looked like tiny tongues. "She's not. She's always happy, for no reason at all, the fool. She just likes to eat. The two are not mutually exclusive."

"Why do you hate her so?"

Hilda threw up her hands. A frog leg flew off her ladle and stuck to the ceiling, where it dangled precariously, looking like it was just waiting for the right moment to drop. "I don't *hate* her. I just abuse those closest to me, like almost every human ever. Don't you know *anything*?"

Essex thought of all the humans she'd studied on the TV. She had thought she knew a lot. Although, she'd never understood why so many humans were so terrible to each other. True, she and Olaf and Baby killed smaller animals, but not out of anger. Out of need. The humans who killed other humans on the TV—or did other horrifying things—didn't seem to be all that hungry.

But sometimes, they—or their territory or mate—had been threatened, and Essex understood this only too well. And the humans often had backstories that attempted to explain why they were acting so horribly now.

"Well," said Essex, staring at this human who surely had a

difficult backstory, too. And had let her wait inside. And had given her a towel. And had smiled earlier, which made her look quite a bit like Helga. "I think you're beautiful, just as you are."

Hilda harrumphed. "Your nose just grew."

Essex touched it with her paw. It had *not*.

Hilda pointed her dripping ladle at Essex. Essex hoped Hilda would have at least *some* potion left, after her visit.

"Just so you know, almost everyone does something they shouldn't to cope with their unhappiness. I just like to eat things totally devoid of the nutrients needed to sustain life. Other people drink too much alcohol, or watch too much TV—"

How could one watch too much TV? How many more things Essex would understand about the human species, if only she had more time to watch the TV.

"—or suck on cancer sticks like a fool—"

Essex shook, what with having so many questions. "What are cancer sticks?"

"You don't want to know."

"I do."

"*No*, you—"

"How will I learn to navigate the world, with all the humans in it, if I don't adequately understand all there is to know about—"

"Gaah!" Hilda threw open a cabinet above her head and reached up to pull out a large cardboard carton, leaning forward so the frog leg just missed her as it fell. She ripped the carton open. It was filled with smaller cardboard boxes. She drew out a small box and tore that open, too. "*These* are cancer sticks. *I'm* the fool. Happy now?"

Shoving five of the small sticks inside into her mouth, she

lit them with her wand, and drew in a breath as long and deep as the reservoir.

Essex had never been more confused. But she recognized these "cancer sticks." They looked and smelled just like the stubs she had found littered all over the ground. In the park, outside the park ... everywhere, strewn about. They smelled awful, and she wondered why humans seemed so fond of them.

Hilda pulled the sticks out of her mouth, breathing out smoke and sighing deeply. "Ahhhh, I needed that. You two are driving me nuts."

"Your sister's not even *here*."

"The very thought of her, is enough. Just like the song." Hilda hummed a beautiful tune, which Essex was absolutely sure was not about nose growing, or maligning one's sibling, or anything other than pure love.

"How does magic work?"

"Nobody truly knows. Everyone's just winging it till they learn what works for them, and then they do more of that. Anyone who tells you different is trying to sell you something."

"I'm a fox. I have no money. Except a few coins in the Pile of—"

"Just an expression."

"So magic is ..."

"A great mystery. Nobody knows all. Which is as it should be. Otherwise life would be not only frustrating, but boring, too."

"That's what the trees said."

"Trees. Exasperating creatures. So stingy with their bark and leaves."

"Your sister said they're so *generous* with—"

"Well she's a regular Pollyanna, isn't she."

"What's a Pollyanna?"

"All these questions! Sneak in a library. Read a book."

"I can't read."

"Not my fault you haven't tried."

Essex pondered this. The holly had also believed she could learn to read if she put in the effort. Maybe the newspapers she'd been collecting for their log pile—the ones she'd found just before Olaf had come upon the baby—could provide a clue as to the real parents.

To think she had almost left the baby with the *unlov-ing*, fake parents. With that awful human female, who had somehow … "How is it a witch could turn another human into a frog?"

Hilda whirled toward her with such excitement in her eyes, Essex worried for Helga's safety. "You *saw* this?"

"NoooOo …" Essex tried to keep the quaver out of her voice—or at least, hoped Hilda wouldn't notice. "I just meant … hypothetically."

"Oh." Hilda's face fell. "Well, it was a lovely thought." She turned back to her cauldron and stirred her potion rather more forcefully than was necessary, in Essex's opinion.

"So … no?"

Hilda shrugged. "I suppose it's possible. One would have to be very powerful, to accomplish it. Word knows I've tried." She stopped stirring. "Or, if one had an amplifier …"

She turned back to Essex, suspicion in her eyes. "You sure you haven't actually seen this done?"

Essex trembled. She quickly masked any show of nervousness and shook her head.

Hilda sighed and turned back to her potion. "Not an actual frog, mind you. You can't just erase a person's consciousness. It would still be the same human consciousness, just trapped in the body of a frog. The body is really an illusion, when you get down to the deepest level."

Essex understood so little of that, she couldn't decide what question to ask first. So she went with another burning inquiry.

"Where's your hat?"

"I'm indoors. Why would I need a hat?"

Essex pawed at the floor. Hopefully Hilda would not think her rude. "I mean, your witch's hat."

Hilda threw Essex a dirty look. "Real-life witches don't wear pointy hats. What are you, stupid?"

Essex ignored this insult and dug in. "Why?"

"Why are you stupid? How should I know?"

"I mean, why can't you wear a pointy hat?"

"Because non-magical people would *know*. It's enough with the warts and nose, without the hat and robe and pointy-toed shoes. Right now my sister and I can *just* get by masquerading as two otherwise perfectly normal, aesthetically-challenged middle-aged ladies. We put on any of the stereotypical accoutrements, it's like we're calling the Conflict Resolution Professionals ourselves."

"Are witches not allowed?"

"Just barely. At least for now. That doesn't stop people blaming us because their cow's dried up—or, in more modern terms, the battery of their car's died. It doesn't stop people from siccing the authorities on us for any reason at all."

Essex thought this over as Hilda continued to pull off wings, gouge out eyes, and yank out tongues. Finally she couldn't hold back any longer. She didn't want to be rude, but—

"Can't you at least put them out of their misery first?"

Hilda startled. She did not, however, "go through the roof," as the humans liked to say. Thankfully, as the roof was all sticky. Instead, her expression softened somewhat.

"I don't do it to be cruel. But once something's dead, the life force is gone. I need their life force for my potions to work."

"Oh." What Essex really meant to say was, why were the lives of the little sentient beings less important than Hilda's potions?

"I use the potions for good." Hilda seemed to read Essex's mind. "Mostly. To heal sick people. People who come crawling to me after acknowledging that Western medicine has failed them. You have to take the good with the bad. You have to break a few eggs to make an omelette."

Essex's stomach grumbled at the mention of food.

"Just an expression."

Essex had recently eaten. She wasn't really hungry. It was just, her stomach was used to being empty.

Hilda stood a moment, as if deliberating. Then she moved to the refrigerator, took out a handful of eggs and a stick of butter, and began cooking the eggs on the stove.

"Talking about food makes me hungry. I always make too much. I guess my eyes are bigger than my stomach."

She scowled and turned to Essex, whose eyes had surely gone wide. "Again, just an expression."

Essex thought back on what Hilda had said the first time they'd met. "May I ask ..."

Hilda shrugged and turned back to her eggs. "Not like I can shut you up or anything."

"You *do* help people."

Hilda glanced over at her. "Sure. If they pay me enough."

Somehow this did not sound like true helping. On the other paw, Essex, Olaf, and Baby all helped each other. Even Baby didn't just take shelter in their cave and eat their bunnies, fish, and berries. She killed rats and mice for them. She had even deigned to look after the baby so they could go to the food palace *for* the baby. Maybe humans paying Hilda to help them worked the same way.

She came out of her musing to realize Hilda had been talking all this time.

"—just because my manner is sometimes a bit brusque. And I'm not falling all over myself to help people without a thought for myself, like certain people who can't keep their big noses out of other people's bus—"

She stared at the plate of eggs she'd just set in front of Essex, and scowled. "*Don't* thank me. I don't want it to go to waste, is all."

Essex gratefully gobbled down part of the omelette. Leaving half for Olaf, she moseyed back to the door and peeked outside. He and the baby had moved under a bush. He was introducing her to roses, and just barely stopped her as she tried to eat a thorn. The Nice One—er, Helga—was still nowhere in sight.

The sisters were both pretty nice, to be honest.

The rain had stopped, but the floor had gotten wet. Essex politely nosed the door shut.

The door banged open, hurling Essex across the cottage and into the wall.

Hilda laughed—*not* not unkindly—as her sister rushed up to Essex.

"Oh my, my little dear!" Helga peeled Essex off the floor. "Are you hurt?"

"Perhaps a little." Essex rubbed her muzzle with her paw. She looked up at Hilda, who was still smirking. She *was* a Mean One after all.

Helga placed her palms on either side of Essex's muzzle and whispered some strange words. Essex's whole snout buzzed, like it had suddenly been beset by a swarm of fizzy bees. Then the buzzing vanished as if it had never been . . . and the pain along with it.

She gazed up at Helga in astonishment. "How did you do that?"

"I just vibrated some energy back the way it was meant to go."

Something still alive in her sister's bubbling brew groaned, then made a noise that sounded suspiciously like drowning. Hilda continued to nonchalantly add small, sentient ingredients to her potion for healing people for money.

Suddenly she began to cough as if *she* were drowning. She spat the sticks out of her mouth and ground them out on the floor, glaring at her sister. "Don't"—*cough cough WHEEZE*— "say a word."

Indeed, Helga said nothing, although she seemed to hide a smile. Then she gave Essex her full attention.

"Why don't we go outside? The rain kindly left when I—I mean, has stopped all on its own—and I've set up my cauldron out back. It's time to make some milk."

They left the tiny cottage, Hilda mumbling behind them, "I *really* gotta quit these things."

SEVENTEEN

On a dry patch of grass behind the cottage lay a bed of bark and leaves. A crackling fire blazed underneath a black cauldron, which shot occasional water bubbles toward the sky. A makeshift platform of wooden planks stretched over the cauldron, supported on each side by a tower of cement blocks arranged like a series of steps.

Helga took up a position by the cauldron and stretched, perhaps in preparation for upcoming vigorous activity. She hummed, her eyeballs rolling up in their sockets.

Essex didn't want to interrupt. But once Helga sighed and stilled, and her eyeballs resumed their normal positions . . .

"May I ask you a question?"

"Of course, dear."

"Why are you fat?"

Helga looked like she'd never been asked that. "It's very simple. I love to cook. I love to bake. I love to eat what I cook and bake, as well as share with others."

Essex thought back to what Hilda had said. "Should I sue you, then?"

"You've been speaking with my sister." Helga chuckled, then turned thoughtful. "It could be something from our past lives that's keeping us fat in this one. Fat helps you float—and we certainly needed to in some of those lives. Perhaps our bodies hold on to the fat because they fear we might still need it."

"Oh." Essex didn't really understand that part. She opened her jaws to ask again.

"And I figure, anyone who doesn't like me because of my size, shape, nose, warts, or anything else about my appearance isn't someone I want to spend time with, anyway."

"What's wrong with how you look? I think you look very beautiful." Even if humans didn't hibernate, they could live for several moons on all that stored food, if times got tough. And the insulation! Essex shivered, thinking of all those nights out in the snow, trying to focus on stalking her prey. She would love to be a fatter fox, if only food were more reliable.

"Well," said Helga. "I think you're very sweet."

"Why is your sister angry all the time?"

"She hasn't learned not to take things personally. She'll get over it. Someday . . . Some life."

Essex pawed at the ground. Perhaps she shouldn't sow the seeds of more discontent between the sisters, but wasn't it important to warn Helga? "I asked her how a witch could turn someone into a frog, and she got all excited. It was almost like . . ."

"She wanted to turn *me* into a frog?" Helga laughed. "I wouldn't worry about it."

Essex tried to understand how one could see this as anything other than a worrisome proposition.

"I can turn someone into a frog." Helga said this nonchalantly, as if Essex were a witch too, and they were comparing notes. "It's not that hard, if you've been diligently practicing for hundreds of years."

"You've been alive hundreds of years?!?"

"Did I say that out loud?" Helga smiled sheepishly. "I mean, my past lives. I remember them so vividly, it feels like one long life, you know?"

Essex did not know. Her expression must have reflected this, because Helga added, "I feel my spirit having these continuous experiences, where the bodies wear out and change, and the personalities somewhat, too. But it's always me. The *real* me."

Essex stared at her, fascinated. She'd always thought when life was over, you went off to be One with the Everything, and again be with all your loved ones who'd gone before, forevermore.

"Have you always been a witch?"

"Not in the pointy hat sense—although I've worn plenty of those. But yes, I usually do some type of healing work. Working with energy, plants, other green things . . . frogs, for instance." Helga chuckled. "Not that I ever would, of course. Turn someone into a frog, I mean. Although there's something to be said for knowing you could if you absolutely had to. And please don't tell my sister. I'd never hear the end of it."

Essex would never. She shuddered to think what the Mean One would do if she could somehow persuade her sister to teach her how to harness such power. "Have you always been sisters?"

"Not always. But we've always been close. Now, if you would please climb up onto the platform. That's a good dear."

Essex padded up the cement blocks and onto the wooden planks, which were already warm. Perhaps a nervous joke was in order? "You're not going to burn me alive? Accidentally, of course ..." (Snarky and her friends had once almost been burned at the stake. But they had prevailed, thanks to Snarky's quick thinking.)

"Don't worry—it's only ever happened once, I think." Helga smiled, also joking. At least, Essex hoped.

Helga took out her wand and pointed it at the cauldron. "Double, double toil and troub—Oops! Had a little flashback there."

She stilled and focused on the water. Soon mysterious syllables filled the air, similar to those she'd uttered while healing Essex's pained muzzle. The vapor ascended. A buzzy, fizzy feeling filled Essex's belly. She had felt this numerous times—whenever she'd carried kits. Her milk was flowing!

"You can come down now," said Helga. "Don't want to burn your paws after all."

Essex bounded onto the grass. She stared at Helga. "How did you do that?"

"Everything's part of the One energy. Yet everything vibrates at a slightly different speed. I just coaxed your cells to vibrate at a frequency they're familiar with, to produce milk."

She shrugged. "It's probably not as flashy as my sister with her potions, or Snarky Bravewand with her zombie slaying ... or whatever it is Snarky does ... I don't really have time to watch TV."

How could one not make time to watch the TV? It was so educational.

The cat meowed in the distance. Loudly. Complainingly.

"I love you best, Graymalkin!"

A contented little *meep*, then all was quiet again.

"If you can do this …" Essex glanced over at the window, and lowered her voice just in case Hilda was eavesdropping. "Won't your sister realize you're more powerful than you've let on? Maybe she'll suspect you *can* turn someone into a frog?"

"She can do all this, too. And anyway, I think she already suspects. She just doesn't want to come out and say it."

Olaf ambled around the corner, tickling the baby under her trash bag. She squealed with laughter. The flames under the cauldron shot up twice as high, crackling menacingly.

Hilda stuck her head out the window, stared at the flames and then at Football. "That baby's an amplifier!"

Essex quivered. *Had* Hilda been eavesdropping? "What is an amplifier?"

Helga nodded toward Football. "She can enhance another user's magic. No wonder someone stole her."

"It was probably Gertrude Gawfersheen." Hilda scowled. "I never did like her."

"It couldn't have been. She's in prison."

Hilda nodded. "As she *should* be."

Essex chimed in. "It was a rather tall female, with orange fur on her head."

"Blackthornudder!" Hilda spat. "I never liked *her*, either."

Helga sighed. "You don't like *anybody*."

Hilda threw up her hands. "Is it *my* fault the collective character has gone down the toilet?"

Helga turned to Essex. "Now you can feed the baby all on your own. You won't have to rely on anyone."

"Thank you," said Essex. She and Olaf turned and padded

through the clearing toward the woods. The baby gurgled and reached for the roses, and Olaf paused to let her smell—and not eat—them again.

Before leaping over the fencing, Essex looked back. "You *are* going to help us find the parents, right?"

"Of course—" said the sisters together—

"—not!" finished Hilda.

*

"It's magic!" said Olaf, as Football attached herself to Essex's belly and began to nurse. "It's unbelievable!"

"It's wonderful." Essex sighed, relaxing into the profound feelings of love and connection that coursed through her, as she nurtured this tiny being that totally depended on . . .

Her gaze fell on the Pile of Human Garbage. On the cold cave wall.

No. It would not do to become attached. They had to find the parents, as soon as animally possible.

~ EIGHTEEN ~

Chief Detector Thomas sat at his desk, seething. All traditional, *efficient* forms of torture had been banned. He'd been forced to get creative.

Mabel regained consciousness. As her fogginess faded, the walls of another interrogation room came into focus.

She was still wearing that doggone gag. Stretched on a rack, her feet bare—wrists shackled at the top, ankles at the bottom. Were they going to stretch her past her mortal body's limits, like in that film with the adorable stable boy turned dread pirate? Or—not so nostalgically—as in days of yore, like in that past life where she was stretched to death, refusing to confess she was a witch?

Think, Mabel! She had turned Harvey into a somewhat stretchable frog, yes—but through the baby's amplification. She probably wasn't powerful enough to minutely stretch herself in time to the stretching of the rack—to fool her captors she was in terrible pain, but just too tough a nut to crack.

Metal *clanged*, the door slid open, and Chief Detector Thomas entered.

Mabel squared her shoulders, bracing for action. Perhaps they planned to affix electrodes to her tongue or pull out some teeth, in which case they would have to remove her gag. She would be too fast for them and immediately chant her most powerful spell (any witch worth her salt could cast even without a wand). She would blow them against the walls with such force, hurricanes would be envious. Then she would chant the ancient spell for removing all bonds, break free of the rack, steal the Chief Detector's huge set of keys, ~~find Harvey if time permitted,~~ and skedaddle.

"Sooooo …" drawled Chief Detector Thomas, followed by two of his goons, who were carrying paintbrushes and leading inside two (admittedly) adorable goats. "Tell us, Ms. Blackthornudder, are you familiar with tickle torture?" He looked down at the portable screen he carried to read her speech.

"Duh! Anyone who managed to stay awake in high school History knows all about those sadistic Romans."

Mabel kept up a brave front, but even were the CRPs not *quite* as sadistic as the Romans, she was in for a world of hurt.

"Good luck, then. Unless you want to confess right now you stole my baby?"

"My lawyer will hear about this."

"How so? When you can't even talk?"

His two heavies and their bleating goats approached on either side. The goons dipped their brushes into a bucket filled with what was presumably salt water and applied the solution to the soles of Mabel's feet.

She would have to rely on her powers of persuasion. She was a witch! She could talk to animals—even though her vocal cords were sadly compromised at the moment. She would communicate with her energy—her aura. Establish a bond, her being a magical human quite like them in their noble, animalistic state. Help them see the CRPs—their captors—were the *real* villains here. She closed her eyes . . . breathed in deeply . . . and emitted chill vibes of love and peace . . .

"I remember a past life," said one goat to the other, "where I was a donkey, and she rode me and continuously kicked me in the ribs."

Uh-oh.

The goats lunged forward—and were unleashed.

They lapped at her feet, over and over. At first it was like taking a rollercoaster ride, naked, through a down pillow factory...except even worse. Hysterical laughter escaped her—possibly showing up on the Chief Detector's screen written something similar to *hahahhahawwrrrrrgghh-hhhhhaaluuuuuulooooooooo* and falsely giving the impression this was an enjoyable experience. Mabel knew with the goats' abrasive, sandpapery tongues, the sensation would soon spiral into one similar to that past life when she'd been shaving her legs in the shower and the magnitude 8.4 earthquake started.

It was all right, they wouldn't actually *kill* her, she attempted to reason with herself, as her vision went red and inner alarm bells rang in her head. Well, maybe the goats would, but the CRPs wouldn't let it get that far. They *were* trying to get information out of her, after all. Breathe, Mabel, b-r-e-a-t-h-e ...

She relaxed. Ha! If they thought *this* was torture, they didn't know what torture *was*! Lightweights! In past lives she'd been drowned, hanged, set on fire, squashed to death with metal weights ...

One such life presented itself in her awareness even now—with her, an old English crone, attempting to flail her bound arms in Crummock Water, and ...was that *Harvey*, on the banks of the lake, watching her? Not feeling any remorse for falsely accusing her. *Interesting*. Of course, in that life his name had been ...Oh, what was it? Edward? No ...Edwin? No ...

The goats were yanked away, bleating hysterically for more, while Mabel wheezed and tried to catch her breath.

"Anything you'd like to tell us, Ms. Blackthornudder?"

"Egbert!"

Wouldn't Harvey be mortified to discover his past self had been saddled with such a nerdy name?

"Round Two then," seethed His Baldness.

Mabel refocused on her husband in his ridiculous 19th century get-up, and smiled.

NINETEEN

The rain began again.

Baby dashed across the street, evading honking vehicles. She hid underneath two bicycles locked to a pipe, their plastic-wrapped seats forming an adequate umbrella for her slight frame, and peered into the night. Feet and legs encased in vibrant colors plodded by. It was that craziest night of the four seasons, when humans acted even more irrationally than usual. Dressing up in wild costumes, pretending to be other humans, even humanoids who didn't exist in real life. Zombies. Vampires. Supermen ... As if!

But it was a good night for Baby to search. More humans running amok meant more humans going in and out. She was able to enter many more human dwellings on this night than usual.

Her stakeout of the neighborhood school had yielded no results. So many excited children, so much anticipation in her heart. But it was always a letdown.

The next dwelling on her mental map—the next "apartment building"—stood right across, sandwiched between a gorging station and a gorging takeout. She peered through the pelting rain and focused on the entrance. She had an advantage Essex didn't—she could enter multi-human dwellings because she didn't have to make absolutely sure she wasn't seen. Most humans regarded urban foxes as pests (oh, the irony). But humans didn't think twice about a cat darting through a door behind them. They assumed the cat belonged there, belonged to the neighbors.

Neighbors. Betty's family had had a few neighbors. All of them frightful creatures.

She slunk out from underneath the bikes and ran a quick reconnaissance mission—the apartments wrapped around the corner—checking the locations of the fire escapes and all the open windows. This was subject to change, especially during a rainstorm. But it was better than going in completely blind.

She returned to her shelter and resumed her lookout. No human was turning into the entrance. But a shadow loomed within. Someone was on their way out.

Baby emerged—and swerved between little legs that suddenly ran up the sidewalk. Legs too tiny to be Betty's. She just barely darted through the doorway in the moment before the glass and metal clanged shut.

She shook out the rain, here in the empty, dingy lobby. She caught her breath and took a look around. A closed door, on which notices were posted. Obviously an "office." Another room, open, where humans washed their clothes. (To no avail. Humans just naturally stunk.)

She trotted farther down the hallway and came upon

another closed door. Probably a trash room, where, honestly, all humans except Betty belonged. Then another shut door, with a large green sign Olaf would argue was "red," but he would be wrong. The green sign indicated an exit.

She turned, made her way back to the stairs, and bounded up, up, up, listening all the while. At the midpoint, she stopped on the landing, and waited.

Humans getting ready to go out often jangled keys. Or pulled on a boot and lost their balance (humans grew too far from the ground), landing hard against the wall. A dog might bark, for joy it was finally getting walked, or anguished because its human was leaving it behind.

Poor, misguided dog.

But often, all Baby would hear was—

A door, opening somewhere above.

She raced up the stairs, leaping two at a time. One floor, then another—she jumped onto the uppermost landing just as a human was exiting. With a final burst of speed, she dashed inside.

The door banged shut, nearly missing slamming her tail in the jamb.

She pulled it to her, curled it around her body, and took in her surroundings. The foyer was empty. A TV blared from one of the back rooms.

She had only been able to get a glimpse of the human who'd left. A male, not Betty's father. But he could have been a visitor. (Why anyone would want to visit Betty's parents, she couldn't fathom, but very little about human behavior made sense.)

It was also possible that one of Betty's parents had finally realized the other was horrible (it was much easier to see others' shortcomings than one's own) and had thrown the other out. And was now living with a different, still horrible, human. (They were pretty interchangeable.)

She crept closer and peeked around the corner. A human female—not Betty's mother—sat watching "the news."

Baby had used to watch the news, hoping her Betty would appear with clues to her whereabouts, perhaps in a segment on one of those school events where they interviewed the children. Because Baby had begun to despair upon discovering how far the city actually stretched.

She quickly took in the rest of the apartment, just to make sure. Perhaps Betty had been able to rescue herself and find better parents. But no, Betty was not here.

A small window in the kitchen led to a fire escape. Baby jumped up and onto the balcony. The rain had stopped, but the metal was wet and slippery. She had to be careful not to let her paws slip off the slick, narrow slats. She took extra care with her injured leg so it wouldn't be a liability.

Her modus operandi—even Essex, she bet, had not yet learned that phrase—was to get on the first available fire escape and exhaust all the open windows. The apartments with closed windows were the riskiest. More than once had Baby been trapped inside all night, hiding under a bed, yet delighting when a human continuously sneezed and couldn't figure out why. (Allergies were wonderful things.)

From the fire escape she leapt onto the next window ledge and toed her way across, making a mental note, where she'd been, and where she had left to go. Carefully she hopped up onto a narrow ornamental ledge and down onto the next sill—just barely making it—and from there, the railing of the neighboring balcony. Then it was a short, precise hop down to the landing and a few paces to the next open window.

A cat dwelled inside; she could smell it. Cats and dogs were a risky business. Would they be friendly? Or hostile, overly protective of their food providers?

She jumped onto the sill and into the dark room. She slunk down the hallway. Chanting emanated from the far room. She peeked inside. A human female wearing a dark robe was in the midst of casting a spell, having surrounded herself with various stones, feathers, and other totems of "elemental" magic. Baby watched awhile, to see if she could pick up anything useful. When you lived in a world full of garbage, you had to learn how to deal with garbage.

She'd practiced a few of the techniques she'd witnessed over the seasons, back in the safety of the cave. She'd tried "scrying," asking the spirits where her Betty was. She'd stared at a puddle of water for so long, an image had started to form. But it turned out to be an animal shelter, which had to be wrong. Betty would never go to a shelter intending to replace her.

A low *hiss*, and Baby met the yellow eyes of a black cat lurking in the corner. Baby turned up her nose. Whatever. She had seen all she needed to see.

*

Six apartments later, and another drenching rain, she had still not found her Betty. She had witnessed countless examples of humans being horrible. She'd exhausted all the fire escapes and open windows, as window after window had shut against the rain. She sat patiently, waiting for the deluge to end.

It was late, and she could reasonably give up and seek food and shelter. But still she sat, as she hadn't ruled out enough apartments. She hadn't accomplished enough.

She had plenty of time to think. To think about Betty.

Baby had never had to sit out in the rain when she had her Betty. Betty had kept her warm and dry.

It had rained the night Baby had been dumped out of the moving car. She'd been hit by the next, which hadn't even bothered to stop. She'd crawled to the side of the road, not yet feeling the physical pain. So full of rage and anguish she couldn't run after the car and get back to Betty.

That's when she'd met Essex.

Essex hadn't even seemed to see a cat—normally an enemy to foxes. Perhaps Baby had reminded her of her fallen mate. She sat with Baby and licked her wounds. Helped her hobble to the cave where she and Olaf sheltered.

As soon as Baby could move with just a slight limp, she'd left them.

Finding the right apartment building took time. Getting inside did not. For three days she sat in front of the family's door. Heard neighbors whisper a new word, "evicted." Seen the posted notice. Of course, she couldn't read. Finally, when the new family moved in, she understood.

The rain tired, and finally stopped altogether.

Not too long after, a *thud* sounded from above. She carefully made her way up the slick metal steps. Under the open window, she sniffed. As usual, the overpowering odor of humanity permeated the air within, in sharp contrast to the sweetness outside, freshened by the rain.

She hopped inside. Soft singing rang out from a room at

the back. She padded down the hall and craned her neck to spy around the corner. A human female was changing her baby's diaper.

Baby shuddered. Human babies were grotesque, with their tiny little bodies and humongous heads. Of course, Betty must once have been a baby . . . but no one was perfect.

She turned and trotted back, checking the open doors. She made her way to the open window and outside.

It was possible that Betty's parents had propagated yet again. Kindhearted Betty would not want to leave her sibling behind. Baby had figured this out long ago and realized she should at least learn about infants, for Betty's sake. She'd paid attention when humans took care of their babies.

So far this knowledge had just resulted in caring for the abomination back at the cave—which, she conceded, *did* provide comfort to Olaf, so wasn't totally horrible and could be tolerated yet a while longer.

She thought back to Essex's request, and huffed. Look for the baby's parents? She had not enough time, and had no way to access those apartments. The baby had come to them plump, well-tended-to, and probably—*sigh*—delicious. The parents doubtless lived in one of those buildings guarded by self-important humans wearing funny hats. (Or one of the fancy rowhouses, which Essex could check herself.) Baby targeted the shabby buildings, the only dwellings likely to admit Betty's parents. And even those stretched endlessly throughout the city. Baby might exhaust all nine of her lives, before she'd searched them all.

It was late, and the humans in the last apartment had turned off their lights and gone to bed. Which was just as well. Baby did not want to go out onto the inner landing this late at night. She had unfortunately learned, not all humans who left at dark could be counted upon to come back before the sun. She couldn't risk getting stuck in the building overnight.

Her tail drooped, and she could no longer ignore her growling stomach. It was time to seek shelter for the night. Rather than take refuge in an unfamiliar spot, she needed a safe place to rest and recharge.

She carefully pawed her way down each ladder till she reached the landing closest to the ground. A last ladder hung from the platform another dozen cat-lengths. She turned and backed down. Hanging onto the top rung with both front paws, clamping her legs around the bottom, letting go of the top and falling and scrabbling to hang on. One by one, she methodically and slowly dropped down each rung.

She fell to the pavement below, landed, and waited for the shock to absorb through her paws, evenly through the rest of her body. She ran across the street and under the arch, the whooshing, rattling, and vrooming of vehicles resounding above.

Turning left, she ran parallel to the bridge. A bus coming from across the river rolled off the ramp, and she pushed herself to catch up. She jumped onto the rear bumper. She let it take her a few blocks west, to the underground train headed south. From there a bus would carry her crosstown, the rest of the way to Jack's house.

*

The bus approached the subway station. Baby leapt off the bumper and bounded toward it. She rushed down the stairs, around the stinky corner, down another set of steps and under a turnstile. Small groups of humans, many wearing costumes, waited for the oncoming train as it rattled farther down the dark tunnel.

She trotted down the dirty floor and scrunched up her nose at the awful stench. Some humans had relieved themselves in the corner. Not to mark their territory. Not even because they were dirty. Because they lived in a world full of horrible humans, and they couldn't hack it.

Baby couldn't blame them.

A huge rat scurried down the platform, hugging the wall, like a large piece of moving dirt. Baby liked to eat rats. But she also liked to hear humans scream. So, the rat would live to see another day.

The train shot into the station, screeching as it slowed. Baby waited as the doors opened and humans shuffled in and out. She darted inside a moment before the doors slid shut.

Inside the subway car, the humans stood and sat, some alone, some with companions. It was late and therefore not crowded. Baby trotted down the sticky floor to the empty two-seater in the corner. She hopped up and curled into a ball. Judging from her past trips, the ride would last approximately ten stops. She only needed to be left alone for ten stops.

A human female sat across from her, dressed in a tacky witch costume, complete with pointy shoes and hat. The human female looked up from pawing through one of those huge sacks "trick-or-treaters" used for hauling their loot, and smiled at her. Baby snarled in return.

The fake witch merely laughed. "What a brave kitty! Taking the train all by yourself."

Baby hissed. The fake witch chuckled and pulled a cell phone from the pocket of her costume. She turned it toward Baby and took her picture—without even asking! Baby would eat her, except she had to focus on getting to Jack's before her energy flagged completely. The rude female would live to see another day.

Brakes screamed as the train slowed, entering the next station. The doors opened. Humans filed in and out. Pushing and shoving ensued, needlessly, as there was plenty of room for each of the horrible humans, and then some. The smell of alcohol permeated the air. The females in the car—all except the fake witch—seemed to make themselves small. An overhead voice warned the doors would be closing. They did, and the train lurched forward.

Baby endured. Seven stops . . . six . . . five . . . Two humans approached her seat, but Baby flashed her fangs and they slunk away.

The doors closed and the train pitched forward. Baby relaxed somewhat. She would soon be at Jack's.

The car scuttled into the next station and slowed. It stopped and the doors slid open. In burst two humans dressed in yellow. They strode to the corner, to the fake witch.

"All right, lady. We got you on camera." One of the yellow humans stood over her, his fists on his hips. "Selling medicine without a license."

"Aha! So you *admit* plants are medicine."

"Enough funny stuff." The other yellow human grabbed her arm and hauled her up. "Let's go."

"All right, *all right*—hands off the merchandise." She pulled her arm out of his grasp. "*And* my bag, thank you very much." She swiped the trick-or-treating sack out of his reach.

They hustled her off the train. The fake witch flashed Baby a grin before disappearing from sight.

The doors began to slide shut. There was a flash of green light, and an odd sort of *quacking*—as if one of the yellow humans had been turned into a duck. Baby shook her head. That was clearly impossible.

*

The lights were out in the green brick rowhouse at the end of the quiet side street. The American beech in the sidewalk grate hovered protectively by a window.

Baby wearily climbed the stoop, scratched at the door, and waited, shaking herself out. A few moments later, the knob turned. She headbutted the door open and slunk through the narrow space.

"I sensed you might be by, Baby." Jack nudged the door closed with his big, wet nose. He nuzzled her. "How did it go tonight?"

"How do you think it went?" she snapped. She was cold, wet, and hungry. "If I had found my Betty, would I come here?"

"Right, of course. Sorry." Jack shook his shaggy frame. "Are you hungry? I saved you some food."

Jack, being a Golden Retriever and therefore constantly, irrationally happy, was not one of the smarter dogs Baby had met. But he was thoughtful and kind, and that mattered more, in her opinion.

She followed him into the warm kitchen. Earl must have arrived shortly before, as he was crawling over the ridge of Jack's food bowl.

Earl's antennae twitched in acknowledgement. "Hi Baby, Baby. Baby." He scuttled slightly to the side to make room for her, as though he took up any at all.

Earl was an insect—specifically, a roach—and Baby's first instinct, upon making his acquaintance, had been to pounce. To bat. To play. And perhaps, afterward, to eat. Jack had quickly interjected; Earl had been all over the city and could provide intel about the humans—which might help Baby find her little girl.

The problem was, to Earl, all humans looked pretty much the same. "Very tall, tall. Big feet, big." He flexed his wings. "Thankfully I'm springy, springy, springy."

As Earl rattled on over the seismic force of a human shoe, Baby's mind had wandered, envisioning her paws around his tiny, enticing frame. Batting and playing. And then, eating. But soon they were getting along splendidly. Jack happened to mention Baby's slovenly former family, and Earl waved his antennae in solidarity.

"Humans, slovenly, slovenly . . ."

It was easy to make friends with someone who agreed with you.

"How wonderful, wonderful."

At least, on some things.

And one didn't bat around a friend. Or eat them. Eating would be reserved for Betty's horrible family.

Baby stuck her head into the bowl next to Earl and finished off her portion of the food Jack had so kindly left them.

He nudged his water bowl over, and she drank. He reached and pulled down a kitchen towel for her to roll on and dry herself. His humans would of course assume, in the morning, he'd dirtied the towel himself, but the most they ever did was roll their eyes. Or laugh and take a "shaming" photo, using an agreeable Jack to prop up a sign stating his supposed crime.

Jack was entirely too agreeable, in Baby's opinion.

"My humans went to another meeting last night."

Jack's humans took him everywhere. Perhaps they wouldn't, if they knew he understood them.

"More humans are protesting against the yellow humans. They're having a meeting here next moon. Some of the rebels will bring their dogs. It's a perfect time to have *our* first meeting. I'm going to call us, *Guard Dogs of New York. Watching You Like Hawks.*" He hung his tongue out and drooled.

"Why hawks? You're not birds, you're canines."

"It sounds good."

"It's stupid."

"My friends shall come too, too." Earl waved his antennae. "Many, many, many friends."

Jack wagged his tail. "You should come, Baby."

"Perhaps I will. Unless, of course, I find my Betty."

Jack and Earl looked at each other but didn't say anything. Jack turned to Baby and smiled.

One could never tell if Earl was smiling or not.

After drying off, Baby padded into the den and stretched out on a corner of Jack's bed, making sure to leave him enough room. In one of the human dwellings she'd once been in, she'd seen a teenager watching cat videos. (Humans obviously recognized the superiority of animals and aspired to be like them.) One showed a cat taking up the center of a huge dog's bed, forcing him to squash into her tiny one. Rude! Baby would never do that to a friend.

She squeezed her eyes shut and welcomed sleep. Earl settled down next to her. She opened her eyes to make sure his wings weren't getting squished.

Jack padded to the mahogany cabinet in the corner. (A poor tree had died, because two humans couldn't keep their things tidy in a corner!) He fiddled with an electronic device sitting on top, pressing buttons with his nose. A human female—undoubtedly an awful person, because all humans were, except for Betty—began to sing about a house that Jack built. It was Jack's favorite song.

The human female sang it over and over and over again—softly, so as not to wake Jack's humans in the next room.

He played that song every night Baby stayed over—and probably every night of his life. As her eyelids grew heavy, she imagined Jack building a new, better house over the ruins of this one. Once he had kicked out his only-good-for-food-and-walks humans. Or eaten them.

Baby had suggested that once. Jack had merely laughed, as if she'd been joking.

He lay down next to her, his flank warm and comforting. Earl had already fallen asleep on Baby's other side, his wing cool and refreshing.

All was not right with the world, because she still hadn't found her Betty. But it was all right, for tonight.

In the morning, Jack accompanied his humans on their jog. After they went upstairs to splash around in the water, he called to his friends to come out of hiding and share his breakfast.

"Well, I'm off," said Baby.

He patted her shoulder in farewell, and started. "What've you got there?" He pawed at a tiny, square-shaped protrusion under her fur.

She shrugged. "Some horrible human mad scientist put it there, before I was rescued by my Betty."

Jack nodded. Some misguided human mad scientist had once put a plastic cone around his neck, so he couldn't lick himself. And then, once the cone was finally removed, he'd discovered . . .

He shuddered. It was too awful to think about. His friends at the park had told him he'd been fixed, but Jack knew better. His humans always told him he was perfect.

Baby trotted to the door. "See you at your meeting, maybe."

"I'll be here whenever you need me, Baby." He reached up to paw open the lock, turn the doorknob, and pull.

She left, with Earl calling out, "Goodbye, goodbye, goodbye, Baby."

Jack softly nosed the door shut behind her, and turned back to his tiny friend. "She's never going to find her."

For once, his eternal optimism had left him.

"Never," said Earl, his antennae drooping. "Never, ever, ever."

TWENTY

Now that the problem of feeding the baby had been solved, Essex turned her attention to the next—how she would find Football's parents.

If only she'd paid more attention to "the news" when she'd gone to watch the TV, she might have seen a report of a stolen baby. And possibly remembered, once Football entered their lives.

She didn't like to watch the news. It was full of humans doing terrible things to each other. True, the dramas on the TV were just as full of violence and sorrow, if not more so. But at least there was character development. You could somewhat understand what had driven the desperate humans to do what they did, and root for them to become better people.

Thankfully, Essex had the newspapers she'd collected to add to their log pile, ones from right before Olaf found the baby. One of the articles might lead to information.

The trees and Hilda believed she could learn to read if she put in the effort. But that would take time. And Olaf was already too attached to the baby. And Football seemed to get more attached to him and Essex every day.

So the next morning, after she'd nursed Football and Olaf returned from foraging, they shared a meal of grubs and berries. ("Sorry," he said. "Dim pickings today." "*Slim*. Slim pickings," she said.) Then she shook her head—all those bunnies he'd probably let scamper by!—nuzzled with him and the baby, grabbed a jawful of newspapers from the Pile of Human Garbage, and ran to the cottage.

She tapped at the door. It opened. Helga smiled down at her.

Essex dropped the newspapers by her feet. "They're from right before Olaf found the baby. Maybe they contain clues for where she belongs."

"Oh!" Helga beamed. "Wouldn't that be an easy solution."

Essex looked over Helga's shoulder. The cauldron bubbled in the fireplace. Hilda must be nearby.

"Let's see here." Helga ushered Essex inside and closed the door. She sat on the floor, arranged the papers in a neat pile, picked them up—"Don't freak out, now"—and stuck her head inside.

"Nice One!" cried Essex. Helga's head was not tearing the paper and coming out the other side. It was just, not *there* anymore. It was like Helga now had a newspaper for a head. Had she sacrificed herself to help Essex and the baby? Surely that was going above and beyond. Real-life humans could not *live* without heads. "You're being *too* nice!"

Helga pulled her head out again, calmly, as if nothing out of the ordinary had happened.

Essex caught her breath, her heart racing. Even Snarky couldn't fuse with inanimate objects, and Snarky could do almost anything.

"No lost or kidnapped babies. Sorry, dear."

"How did you—" Essex glanced at the cauldron, making sure Hilda hadn't snuck into the room. She lowered her voice. "How does your sister not know you can turn people into frogs, if you can do *that*?"

"Pshaw." Helga waved a dismissive hand at the newspapers, which fluttered without her even touching them. "*She* taught me that. She refused to read to me when we were children. Insisted I had to learn for myself."

"How did you know you could stick your head inside?"

"I didn't. She said an invocation and shoved my head through a board book." Helga stood and slid the papers into a plastic bin in the corner. "Don't worry, dear. My sister and I talked it over last night, and she had a change of heart—"

"That mangy fox here again?" Hilda banged into the room, plucked a fly from the air, and held it over her potion. "Go away and let me concentrate, will you?"

"Well, maybe only a change of socks. If that."

Essex trembled. Had Hilda overheard her talking about turning people into frogs?

No. If she had, her excitement would be evident. She was just being her normal, unfriendly, uncooperative self.

"At any rate," said Helga, "we've agreed on a compromise. We'll help you find the baby's parents, and once we do, you'll return it yourselves. Of course, that might alert the authorities there's a bear running around the city, but we'll cross that tunnel when we come to it."

She pulled the curtains shut, darkening the little room. She beckoned Essex to a small folding table in the corner, and onto one of two mismatched wooden chairs. Essex stared at her own reflection in a picture frame.

"It's for scrying," said Helga.

"What is—"

"Staring into a dark mirror till your eyeballs fuse to your skull," said Hilda.

Helga smiled. "It's divination. Allowing in information your normal, everyday five senses can't perceive. The glass on the back is painted black."

She sat at an angle to the mirror. "I scryed last night, to see if I could find the parents for you. I saw things that couldn't be true. Sometimes I'm off. So let's give it another try."

She gazed at the mirror, uttering strange syllables. Then she stilled and slowed her breathing.

Essex sat quietly, so as not to disturb her. Hilda made no such concessions, throwing ingredients into her potion and muttering to herself.

Finally Helga thanked the mirror and her helping spirits, sighed, and pushed back her chair. "I must be having trouble clearing my mind, because the mirror keeps showing me the Chief Magic Detector. And Mabel Blackthornudder, except she's shorter somehow ..."

She turned to Essex. "Let's give *you* a turn, shall we? You're closer to all this. Maybe the spirits would rather speak to you."

"I'm a fox. I can't do magic."

Helga smiled. "Why shouldn't you be able to do magic? You're part of the One, and nothing's impossible for the One." She reached over and angled the mirror so Essex could still see the dark glass, but not her own reflection. "One of my best students, you'd never know from looking at her that she's a witch. What with her background . . . present occupation . . . her normal, some might say 'surly' demeanor . . ."

Essex slowed her breathing like she'd seen Helga do. She stared into the darkness and silently asked, *Who are the baby's parents?* Once, twice, three times. Her mind quieted. Everything stilled.

"I see something!"

"Wonderful," whispered Helga, while Hilda snorted in the corner. "Just let go. Don't force anything."

"I see mice, and—*mmm*—bunnies, and—"

"Gaah, this is pointless!" Hilda stomped over. "You're going about it all wrong! Automatic writing, that's the ticket." She reached for a few sheets of paper and a fountain pen lying on the table. She licked the pen nib and started scribbling. "See, you write, and write, and don't stop, and write all this garbage about mice and bunnies and whatnot and get it out of your system. That lets the mind empty to receive real answers."

Essex stared as Hilda continued to write. Finally she couldn't wait any longer. "Does it say who the parents are?"

Hilda quit writing and peered at her marks. "Yes. Yes it does. It says the parents are complete morons, not properly locking their house. *No* it doesn't say who the parents are! Because I don't care!" She slammed the pen down, crumpled the top sheet of paper, and threw it into the bin. She grumped off to her potion. "Why would that information come to me? It has no connection to me."

"We're all connected," said Helga. "We're all a part of each other's story."

Hilda ignored her. Essex turned to Helga. "Can *you* teach me how to do that?"

Helga sighed and glanced at her sister. "I wouldn't be the best person. I have dyslexia."

"What is dyslexia?"

"The letters swim around in my vision, and won't stay still long enough for me to read them."

"You can't use magic to make them stay?"

"It's not the fault of the words. It's something about the way my brain is wired. Magic doesn't work on consciousness."

"Oh." Essex pawed sadly at the paper. At least Olaf would be happy. Now they would get to keep the baby longer. At least until she figured out what to do next.

Helga looked at her sister imploringly. Essex did the same. There was an awkward silence, except for the bubbling and swishing of the potion as Hilda stirred even harder.

"*No,* I won't teach you," she finally said, as if she had eyes in the back of her head. She held her ladle to her lips and took a tiny taste. "Hmm, could use a little something . . ." She turned to Essex. "Unless you're willing to trade for an eyeball? You'll see just as well with just the one . . . almost."

Hilda was surely joking. At least, Essex hoped. She just had to stand firm. Helga believed her sister would help. And the trees had said *both* sisters would. What could Essex say, to get Hilda to agree?

"The sooner I can return the baby to her parents, the sooner I won't need to come here anymore."

Hilda let a long snort reverberate through her nostrils. "Fine. But reciprocation is important in any relationship. Even teacher-student."

She snatched another fly in mid-flight and threw it into the bubbling brew. Its dying sizzle did not bode well for their burgeoning teacher-student relationship.

"I'm a fox. I have no—"

"I don't want your measly coins from your pile of whatever." Hilda scowled. "I just want peace. If I help you, will you swear never to bug me ever again?"

This must be another human expression. Essex had certainly never groomed and defleaed Hilda. "Yes." She wagged her tail and nosed the pen toward her.

"Oh, no. I'm not going to do the work *for* you. You've got to learn to read and write for yourself."

"But it would be faster if—"

"Give a person a fish, they'll eat for a day. Teach a person to fish, they won't bother you ever again. Hopefully."

Essex's tail flagged, but only momentarily. Learning would take longer but in the end certainly prove more useful.

Hilda held her stirrer, chanted strange syllables, and waved her wand. She let go, and the stick continued to stir the brew on its own. As Essex stared, still unused to real-life magic, Hilda moved to the far corner of the room (which was not very far) and surveyed the books on the shelf. "Now, let's see …"

Essex perked up. She had been in enough human dwellings to know how human children learned to read. With lovely picture books, filled with colorful drawings of apples, and bananas, and—

"Here you go." A huge tome as thick as Essex's entire body fell with a thud from Hilda's palms, sending dust cascading from its yellowed pages. "If you're going to learn to read, you may as well learn from the classics."

Essex warily nosed the book open. It emitted a musty smell and sent dust bunnies up her nostrils. She sneezed, but that served only to send a new cloud of dust billowing through the air.

She leapt down to the floor. "Can't I learn using pictures? Like the children do?"

Hilda's usual frown turned stern as she set her fists on her hips. "Who's teaching, me or you?"

Was this a trick question? "You."

"Remember that." Hilda turned the crinkly pages toward the midsection of the book. "Teachers don't get paid squat. Power is the only perk we have."

Helga had been watching, looking positively pleased. Now she selected a smaller book from the shelf, set it on the table, and opened the cover. "If you two don't need me, I'm going to go lose myself in a good book."

"Yes," said Hilda. "Please do."

Helga lifted a leg and stepped inside the cover. Her other leg followed, then her torso, next her head and arms. A hand was the last Essex saw of her as it pulled the cover shut.

"How does she *do* that?"

"Speed-reading. Now. Ready for your first lesson?"

She licked her fingers and flipped a few pages in her book. "Here we are. Now. The prevailing wisdom, is to start with the letter A. This is a mistake. The most important letter in the English language—as well as the most important word—is 'I.' Everything in human life revolves around I. Or me. Everything's all about me. Me, me, me."

"Is that a criticism?"

Hilda scowled. "Think you're funny, do you?"

"Not at all," Essex rushed to reassure her. "I just meant, you told me you don't help anyone."

Hilda snapped the book shut with such force, the dust bunnies had dust bunny babies. "And yet I let you stink up my cottage so you didn't have to wait in the cold and rain, didn't I? I'm here teaching you now, aren't I? If you don't want my help—"

"I *do*. I'm sorry. Please, go on."

Essex meant, for Hilda to go on, and teach her.

"Just because my sister is so disgustingly cheery about helping anyone and everyone—"

Apparently Hilda had misunderstood.

"—and I'm naturally a bit more abrasive than most people are comfortable with—"

Essex watched the shadows on the floor move as Hilda continued her diatribe.

Finally, she stopped and took a breath. "Now. Do you want to learn, or what?"

Essex's stomach grumbled. The dust bunnies did not look appetizing. But she knew better than to complain. On with the lesson!

*

By the time the sun had gone down, Essex could swiftly and accurately identify the letters I and M—which Hilda declared the *second* most important letter, as M was for magic—as well as the squiggly little line called the "apostrophe." Placed between an I and an M, it created the contraction I'M. ("See? Not so important *now*, A, hmmm?")

"I can read!" Essex jumped up and down. "I can read words! *A* word." Hilda would surely congratulate her, say something inspiring and motivating, like—

"Don't let the first flush of success derail you." Hilda scowled. "Let's keep going."

TWENTY ONE

Police departments all over the country had been utilizing psychics, clairvoyants, mediums and the like for years. To find hidden bodies, track down serial killers, discern the winning Powerball combinations . . . But it was only recently they'd publicly acknowledged the existence of witches. Humans who could not only sense energy that normal people couldn't, but manipulate it to effect change in the physical world.

The wise, believed Chief Detector Thomas, realized the dangers these magic-competents presented to society. Magic was an amazing tool . . . just like guns. But like any tool, it could be utilized for good or for evil. And who would not be tempted to take advantage of having such power at one's fingertips? Even those magic-competents who professed to be on the side of good were not to be trusted.

Take away their ability to work with energy, however, and they were subject to the same weaknesses as the unskilled. Chief Detector Thomas had never failed to extract a confession. But this witch was strong. Perhaps utilizing self-hypnosis to disengage from physiological distress.

The solution was simple. Make it easy for her to escape—but not *too* easy, so as not to arouse suspicion. Let her lead them straight to his baby.

TWENTY TWO

The moon waned and waxed, and Baby returned to them. But something was wrong. She said nothing, just brought them a dead mouse, curled up in a ball in the corner of the cave, and went to sleep.

She did not get up early to hunt. She did not complain about the baby. She ate very little of the fish Olaf brought her, or the berries for dessert, returning to the corner. Returning to sleep.

Essex worried, but knew better than to pry.

"Something must have happened," whispered Olaf that night.

Essex rested her muzzle between her paws. "She's been searching so long, and still hasn't found her little girl. Maybe she's starting to think she never will."

Olaf gazed at the baby, lying in the crib he'd fashioned out of glossy magazines and small, smooth rocks. Wearing his disguise, he'd ventured farther into the city than ever before, and "borrowed" a onesie from a baby store. But their manmade crib didn't fit inside the diaper bag. The rocks and magazines would have to do for now.

Football whimpered. Olaf reached for his teddy bear and handed it to her, making reassuring sounds. She grasped the teddy, gurgled and stuck its nose in her mouth.

He sighed, perhaps sensing the inevitable, inexorable destruction of his teddy, and turned back to Essex. "Maybe, if we get to keep Football awhile . . . maybe she can take that little girl's place in Baby's heart."

Essex stared at Baby sleeping in the corner, at the rhythmic rise and fall of her fur. "No one ever takes anyone's place. No one will ever take Bolton's place, or . . ."

She did not want to say anything more. She did not want to remind Olaf of his mother.

Olaf's mother tucked him under her arm, and ran.

She'd brought him to the clearing to give him an unobstructed view of the stars. As she dashed along on all threes, her arm keeping him close and safe, her body kept shifting, every other heartbeat showing him the twinkling lights. It started raining, but only slightly. It was all very ticklish and pleasant.

Except, they were going much faster than usual. Faster than when she'd carry him home after a full day of playing and foraging, and he was tuckered out.

"Everything's . . . all right . . . darling," his mother woofed, in between gasps for air. "We're just going … fast to … get home sooner …"

Olaf thought of the cozy cave that awaited them, how nice it would be to get out of the rain and shake himself dry. His mother would get even wetter, laugh and hug him to her.

Across the field she carried him, the pounding of her paws shocking him over and over. He stopped thinking of their cave. Despite what she'd said, her terror was evident, radiating through her.

"Mama," he cried, but she just lovingly cooed to him without breaking stride.

A loud *CRACK!* reverberated through the air. His mother stumbled. She righted herself and kept running, reassuring him everything was fine.

Olaf's heart raced. Everything was *not* fine. But it would be, once they got back to their—

CRACK!

They fell.

"Mama?"

His mother did not move again.

Olaf could hardly breathe, her heavy body covering him, her arm cradling him close. He tried to wiggle away, so he could lick her face to wake her …

Heavy footsteps approached. He stayed very still, as his mother had taught him. Rough hands grasped him and pulled him out from under his mother, but still he played dead.

"Olaf! Olaf!"

Strange. These humans knew his name. He'd thought it was Wendy who'd named him.

"Wake up, Olaf!"

Something wet and warm rubbed against his muzzle.

"You're dreaming, you're dreaming. You're all right, Olaf. It was only a dream."

He opened his eyes. The wall of the cave stared back at him. Essex was licking him. "You're safe, Olaf. You're home."

Baby had wrapped herself around his leg, and was softly headbutting him. Not even upset he'd woken her.

He pulled them both closer, into a tight hug. "You're my best friends."

He would never see his mother again. He would always miss her. He would always love her. But he had Essex, and Football, and—

"You're killing me!" screeched Baby.

She and Essex released strangled breaths as Olaf relaxed his hold. After a lot of panting, they each lay down and settled in again for sleep.

"Essex?" whispered Olaf.

"Mmm?"

"Why can't I ever see my mother? I mean … out there? Wherever *there* is? Like that spirit who let us take the coat."

"I don't know, Olaf." Essex stretched out a paw, and gently patted his leg. "I wish I could see Bolton again. And my mother and father, and—"

"It's because you want it so much." Baby stretched out, then curled into a tight ball. "Try not wanting to. You'll see them all the time."

Olaf couldn't imagine not wanting to see his mother. To hear her kind voice. Feel her gentle touch. He was sure she'd named him something different. He just couldn't remember, given that she always called him "darling" or "sweetheart." As much as he loved and missed Wendy, and as familiar as "Olaf" felt . . . he just wanted to know. Then it might feel like his mother wasn't that far away after all.

He looked over at Baby, at her side rising and falling. At Essex's paw gently tapping and slowing . . . till her eyes fully shut and she started softly snoring. Meanwhile, Football slept on in her crib, with what was now her teddy bear clutched in her tiny paw.

And Olaf knew, he was all right.

Even if he never could dream of his mother, without dreaming of the end.

Essex watched as Olaf's mother caressed his muzzle with her paw. Essex knew it was merely a dream. Still, it was a lovely dream, and she didn't really care to wake.

Olaf's mother turned to her, shimmering in the fuzzy early morning light. *He can't hear me*, she said. *He can barely feel me, and when he does, he thinks I'm a—*

Olaf brushed her paw away, as if she were a flea, or a fly. He shifted on his bed of moss and leaves, and seemed to settle further into sleep.

Berry. Berry, it's me. It's Mama.

But Olaf couldn't hear her, even as she tried again. This time, *Olaf. Olaf, I'm here. Mama's here.*

He could only dream. Like Essex was dreaming now.

I love you. I am always with you, and one day you will know.

Essex stretched out her paws and scratched them lightly in the dirt. If only she could remember when she woke, she would tell Olaf. Maybe she'd tell him it had been real. That she'd seen the spirit of his mother. That his mother was always watching over him. That would comfort him.

The light in the cave brightened as the sun rose higher. The stone walls came into sharper focus. Olaf's mother faded away.

Essex's stomach grumbled. It would soon be time to scavenge and hunt.

She startled, rising onto her paws. *Had* she been awake all this time? *Had* it been real?

Olaf stretched a paw and yawned. His eyes opened, and he looked to the baby. Reassured that she was safe and sleeping, he closed them again …

"Olaf! Wake up!"

He opened his eyes and gazed at Essex.

"Your mother, Olaf! I saw her! She was right here, touching you. Saying she loves you, and she's always with you, and—"

Olaf smiled, sadly, and closed his eyes.

And Essex knew, he did not believe her.

TWENTY THREE

Alarms blared. The front plate of Mabel's electronic gag *pinged* and rolled open. So did the cell door.

The shouts of ecstatic prisoners and frenzied guards filled the air. Mabel jumped off her cot and ran to the door. She peeked around the corner—always better not to run blindly into any uncertain situation. A guard bopped Gertrude Gawfersheen on the noggin with his baton and knocked her out cold. Good.

Mabel slunk down the hallway, in the opposite direction of the yowling and caterwauling and rude references to other people's mothers, and scampered down the metal stairs. Just barely missing stomping on Harvey as he gamely hopped up in a too-little-too-late attempt to rescue her.

She grabbed him. Ugh, disgusting, she would never get used to that sticky—eh, frogs didn't live that long anyway. She stuck him on her shoulder and headed down a series of corridors, searching for the exit.

Glancing through an open door to the right, she spotted her wand and broom lying on a table, in front of a pile of other prisoners' belongings. She ran inside, grabbed them, peeked out to make sure the coast was still clear, and emerged back into the hall.

Easy. Too easy. Her personal effects just left out like that. No guard stationed inside the evidence room. Electronics malfunctioning system-wide. Her having been moved to the cell at the end of the block for her "protection." Hmm. The authorities probably didn't mind taking a chance on a few ne'er-do-wells getting loose, so she could lead them right to that baby. Well, nothing doing!

She felt up the broom handle. She found nothing, so next dug into the bristles, and pulled out—a bug.

"Here, Harvey." She slipped it to him. He grimaced, but ate it, hungry after not eating for several days, probably. She felt inside the bristles once more and this time found what she was looking for—an electronic bug. A tiny combination-tracking/listening device, attached by a small strip of Velcro.

She ran down the last few hallways to the deserted foyer and—with everyone busy quelling the uprising upstairs—out the front doors. She stared through the falling snow. This was the old correctional facility downtown. The park wasn't far away.

She mounted her broom and flew into the snowy night. She grabbed a startled pigeon going the other way, attached the tracker to its leg, and let go. The bird squawked away. Let the cops follow *that* on a wild-goose—wild-*pigeon*—chase.

TWENTY FOUR

*D*anger... *The bad witches are coming...*

Hilda groaned and rolled over in bed. Those annoying trees had woken her yet again.

There was a *POUNDING* at her door. She plugged her ears with her thumbs. The magic "do not disturb" spell she nightly cast could only withstand so much. She resisted the urge to launch a more powerful spell incinerating the door, as well as the person behind it.

It could only be one person.

The door banged open and Helga rushed in, carrying her broom, waving her arms like a lunatic. So, as usual.

"Nnn nnn nnnnnes nnn nnnning! Nnn nnn nnnnnes nnn nnnning!"

Hilda sighed and unplugged her ears. "What now?"

"The bad witches are coming! The bad witches are coming!"

Her sister had been exactly this annoying when the Redcoats were coming.

"Please get up—the bad witches are coming for the baby!

The fox and bear. We have to help them!"

"This is why I don't help anyone who can't pay me." Hilda turned to face the wall, to not look upon her sister and perhaps give in to the temptation to fire that spell after all. "They always come back needing more help."

"Please, dear sister. They need our help to escape."

"Your problem, not mine. Now leave me alone. I need my ugly sleep." Hilda grabbed her pillows and stuffed one in each ear. Ah. Much better.

The pillows were rudely plucked away, along with a few ear hairs. "If you care about me at all, you'll help me help them."

"Can't you put up some kind of barrier spell and leave me in peace?"

"I did—I called in the clouds and bats, and the trees were already helping. But they won't be able to fend off the bad witches forever. I *need* you, Hilda. *Please.*"

Obviously there would be no sleep until this matter was successfully resolved. Hilda hauled herself up from bed and reached for her broom, and her robe to pull over her Philadelphia Phillies pajamas. (Those sucky Mets could suck it! Hilda wasn't throwing away her loyalties just because certain people couldn't stop minding other people's business.) "But *you're* carrying the bear."

Her sister did not look at all put out by this assertion. She never looked put out about anything. She was always good and kind to everyone, whether they deserved it or not.

Helga led the way outside and mounted her broom. "Come, Graymalkin!"

That darn cat ran up from nowhere, hopped expectantly onto the back of Helga's broom, and stared at Hilda with its eerie yellow eyes.

Helga shot her a smile over her shoulder, and launched into the air.

Hilda seethed, and followed. Cheery, helpful Helga, a walking Richard Scarry book.

Essex woke.

She heard a terrible *whooshing*, like a gale tearing through the trees. Leaving Olaf, Baby, and Football sleeping peacefully, she crept to the mouth of the cave …

And sprang aside just in time, as Helga and her cat flew in on their broom—with Hilda just behind.

"The bad witches are coming!" Helga managed to get out, in between panting and dismounting. "The bad witches are coming!"

"The bad witch." Hilda shook snow off her robe. "And the frog."

Olaf shot up from his bed of leaves. He bounded to the Pile of Human Garbage and started grabbing disguises and baby things and stuffing them into the diaper bag.

"We don't have time for all that!" snapped Hilda. "Let's move!"

Olaf ignored her, and Hilda turned on Essex, who was gathering up the newspapers she'd collected last night.

"Are you deaf? I just said—"

Essex opened her jaws, dropping the papers. "I need them to find the baby's parents!"

She hadn't meant for Olaf to find out she was actively searching. She looked over at him, her head bowed. "So *we* can find the parents. Right?"

Olaf stood holding the diaper bag, staring at it as if he'd only just realized they really were going to give the baby back. That he couldn't keep her forever.

"Oh, for crying out loud!" Hilda ripped the bag away, turned it upside down, and dumped out its contents. Toys, diapers, that purple thing no one had yet figured out the use of, the shiny silver eyeglasses that showed you your snout when you looked at them, the floppy hat and floofy scarf . . .

Hilda grabbed the stack of newspapers and shoved them in the bag. Next she snatched up too-shocked-to-even-squeak

Baby and stuffed *her* inside as well. Hilda whirled around and reached out a hand—

Everything turned black.

Baby's whiskers brushed against Essex as they both struggled to find purchase inside the canvas. Baby pulled herself up, screeching with outrage and indignation, hurting Essex's sensitive ears.

Attempting to follow, Essex was promptly jostled and thrown to the bottom again, presumably by Hilda throwing the bag over her shoulders.

Essex regained her footing—her stomach dropped—and *whoosh*! They were off!

She finally managed to poke her head out the top. The last thing she saw of their cave, where she'd spent so many happy moments, was Olaf's unhappy face. Then trees, black sky and falling snow, and stars.

Hilda turned and headed north.

Essex blinked. Not too far behind rode the bad witch. With a dark speck—the frog?—hanging onto her shoulder.

Olaf stared at all his treasures.

"I don't mean to hurry you," said the Nice One gently. "But hop on."

He carefully picked up Football, who'd slept through all

this excitement snuggled with her teddy bear. Throwing a leg over the Nice One's broom—keeping one eye on the cat sitting staring at him—he scooped up the diapers (those were very important) and the pretty purple thing whose purpose he had yet to discover. The shiny silver eyeglasses that showed you your snout when you looked at them—those he set on his face. The floppy hat he pulled over his head, and the floofy scarf around his neck. He laid the coat over his lap. He might never come across another dead human body with such a gentle spirit.

The Nice One turned her head to see what was taking so long, and—

"Oh, my goodness, my nose really *is* big."

She turned back, uttered some vocalizations, including, "I knew it was big, just not *that* big. Of course, I haven't looked in a mirror lately, at least not in a decade or so—except for the glass at the food market, which doesn't make for the best mirror—and I know they say your ears and nose keep growing but—"

They lifted off.

The broomstick sagged slightly, as if it had not been expecting Olaf to weigh quite so much. It determinedly righted itself and lurched forward.

Olaf held on and shifted ever so slightly, gazing at the mouth of the cave as they left it farther and farther behind. He might never see it again. His cave, which held so many happy memories of his mother . . .

Then there were just trees, and snow, and stars—and the bad witch on her broom, gaining on them, a frog slipping and sliding around on her shoulder.

"I'll get you, my pretty. And your little fox friend, too!"

Olaf turned his back on the Even Meaner One and stared straight ahead. Past the Nice One's shoulder, to his friends.

One, who was staring past him with a frightened expression, and when she realized he was watching smiled with reassurance.

One, who was screeching her head off.

And one—for she *was* a friend now, if a mostly mean one—who was determinedly steering them to safety.

Or so, he hoped.

Essex hung on for dear life as Hilda skidded and swirled and barrel-rolled, dodging blasts of ice.

"We don't have to be on opposite sides on this, Hagglebottoms!" The bad witch's voice could barely be heard above the wind. "That baby belongs to Chief Detector Thomas! Just think of the possibilities! We can use it to get all incarcerated witches released!"

Hilda shot the bad witch a contemptuous look. "That's the stupidest plan I've ever heard!"

"I mean, excepting Gertrude Gawfersheen!"

Hilda looked over at her sister. "Sounds like an okay plan to me!"

"No!" Helga shook her head. "The ends do not justify the means!"

Ribbit!

"Oh, do shut up, Harvey!"

Hilda spat into the wind, and Essex had to dodge to evade the spittle. "You only want that baby for yourself, anyway!"

"Not *only!*"

"You don't even *need* it!" Helga shot past her sister and Essex, with Olaf clutching the baby tightly, his other arm corralling his human treasures. "Everything you *truly* need is already within you!"

"Someone should write you into an *Oz* book!" the bad witch sneered. "I don't need self-help! I don't need self-improvement—"

"You certainly do!" Hilda thundered past the castle, which Essex had mentioned to Helga might make a good hideout, if ever the bad witch discovered their cave. Of course, they couldn't stop there now, as the bad witch was on their tail, but hopefully they would circle back once Hilda got them to safety.

If Hilda got them to safety.

"I need that baby!"

An ice blast grazed the bristles of Hilda's broom, knocking them off course and down, straight into the path of a thick tree branch . . .

Which made way for them.

Essex stared at the tree as they flew past. Was it friends with the birch? The maple? The holly? Her heart warmed. Even in the midst of turmoil, there was always something to be thankful for.

They kept to the helpful trees and passed a wide expanse of snow to the east . . . a great lawn. They flew over the pines. The reservoir loomed ahead. The bad witch was gaining, as the sisters had to keep swerving to dodge her blasts.

Weaving between the trees, zipping in and out at extreme angles, Mabel felt a sudden absence, the disappearance of a long-term burden, a great weight off her shoulders.

She looked down, to see her ~~frog~~ husband falling to the snow below, too far gone to reach without abandoning her quest for the baby.

Eh. Frogs landed on their feet. Or was that cats?

She turned her gaze forward, and maintained pursuit.

"Oh, for crying out loud!"

Hilda had seemingly had enough. Essex glanced over her shoulder, just in time to see Hilda pull out her wand and shoot a fireball at the bad witch's broom. Essex turned back to watch, for as frightening as it was, it was even more exciting than watching the TV.

The enemy broom exploded into a thousand tiny pieces—the bad witch falling, falling to the snow below.

"I'll get you, Hagglebottoms! Don't think I'll forget! Ever! Not in this lifetime, not the next ... I'll get you, if it takes me a thousand yeeeeeeaaaaaaaa—"

Whatever other threats she may have made were drowned out, swallowed as she was by the snow, the flaming broom fragments melting around her.

"Hilda! You could have killed her!"

"Good riddance!" Hilda zipped ahead of her sister and Olaf. She banked hard to the left, swerving in between the pines, then doubled back.

The turret of the castle loomed ahead.

Harvey limped along, hobbling and sliding with his sprained leg through the slush and snow.

He could just *stay* here. Mabel would never find him. She'd never be able to pick him out from all the other frogs populating the park. This was his chance to finally be rid of her.

She was, to quote the Bard, a most notable coward, an infinite and endless liar, an hourly promise breaker, the owner of no one good quality.

And if she couldn't turn him back into a man, what good was she anyway? He could subsist on . . . on flies, and worms, and—

No, he couldn't. Gross!

In their other hideout on the West Side—as their East Side home was now certainly a crime scene—Mabel would at least feed him the people food he was used to, at least when she was in a good mood. Although, there was that devil cat to escape from on an almost hourly basis. Here, he wouldn't have to be afr—

Something flashed in the moonlight.

He barely sprang out of the way as huge fangs snapped. He looked up—and stared into the jaws of a hideously large, immensely long snake. Which, had he been human, he would have considered a tiny, harmless snake, and stepped on.

The snake grinned, slithered closer, and opened its maw wide . . .

And writhed in pain, ensnared in the talons of a hawk.

As the hawk flew off with its next meal, Harvey hopped on his good leg to get to the West Side faster. Who knew how many snakes were lying in wait? Weren't they supposed to be hibernating?

Home, to Mabel. Better the devil (and the devil cat) you knew.

TWENTY FIVE

They landed.

Essex was again smushed against the side of the diaper bag as Baby scrabbled to get out and back on firm ground. Finally, she was able to poke her head out. Olaf carefully dismounted, rocking and cooing to Football, who'd begun crying during the turbulent ride.

Hilda shook off the diaper bag—just as Essex was stepping out, making her drop back to the bottom. Then she was unceremoniously turned upside down. She slid out of the bag, the newspapers cascading onto her head and to the snowy ground.

"I'll take the baby to the fire station in the morning," said Helga. "They'll alert the Chief Detector."

"Over my drowned and bloated body, you will! That baby is an amplifier! What do you think that tyrant will do, once he finds out? Unleash her on all the anti-magic devices they've already developed, and whatever they think up next. That baby is the means of our demise, and you're practically dropping her into our enemy's lap!"

"Mistrust and antagonism breed more of the same," said Helga. "This is the right thing to do, no question. I'll write the Chief Detector a nice little note. We need more understanding and compassion between the Conflict Resolution Professionals and the people."

"Yes, you do that," said Hilda. "I'm sure the Chief Detector will have lots of compassion for us, after he's locked us up."

Helga sighed. She headed toward the stairs leading to the castle grounds, chanting strange syllables and waving her wand.

"Are you setting up shielding charms?" called Essex, thinking about what Snarky would do.

Helga turned around. "Yes, but don't worry. Even if she's clawing her way out of the snow at this very moment, the bad witch probably won't even *think* to look for us here. She saw

us fly past. She'll assume we kept going. Besides, she knows witches wouldn't be caught dead in a castle. Well, they *would* be dead in a castle. Or soon to become so."

Essex finished taking care of important business and looked back at Helga. "But what if she suspects we turned back and all came back together?"

"She'd never think that," said Hilda. "You stink. And I don't mean that as an insult. Well, yes. I do. But I mean, you *stink*. What's with peeing on the wall and all?"

Essex looked to where she'd just marked their territory. "So other animals will know to stay away. That this is our space." Was this not normal?

Hilda threw open the broken-glass-and-metal door and stormed inside the castle. "I'm not staying here, if they're going to act like animals."

"But, they *are* animals," said Helga. The door slammed shut, just barely missing crushing Baby and the gray cat as they darted inside.

Through the broken glass, Essex watched the Truly Mean One go, resolving, once they were all settled down for the night, to pee on her shoes.

Hilda marched through the tiny stone castle, searching for the room farthest away from all the others. If she was going to have to stay here awhile, she might as well make it the least worst experience possible.

Some castle! It didn't even have a working kitchen. How was she supposed to brew her potions?

Of course, it had been built specifically as a "folly," a place to waste time staring idly out over the park's grounds neglecting one's responsibilities, and later turned into a weather station and finally, a visitor center. Still, a castle ought not call itself a castle if it was lacking even the basics.

The windows had been broken. The geothermal heating system had obviously fallen into disuse. The light fixtures had been smashed. There weren't even any interior doors, just archways, and the glass main and side doors were cracked.

Nowhere would afford her any privacy. The "dungeon" should remain accessible to all, as it was the best place to house a new refrigerator. (An old, busted fridge, as well as an empty space on the counter where a microwave had probably been situated, indicated where the hard-working Conservancy staff had taken their well-deserved breaks from dealing with the annoying public.) A metal door led to a path around Turtle Pond; it would serve as an escape route. The second floor was nothing more than a room with an arch that led to a terrace; that would work for landings and takeoffs. The main floor was a small foyer with narrow stairwells and an archway to a slightly larger room with small glass windows and three side doors. Hilda could easily replace the broken glass—she was well-versed in elemental magic—but if Blackthornudder or the CRPs came by, they would realize someone other than the struggling Conservancy had been engaged in repairs.

Hilda peered out a side window at the pond below. Well, while she was inconvenienced here, she was going to enjoy some turtle soup.

She couldn't have just given in and taken her chances with the fire people, could she? *Nooooooo.* She had to be her usual, stubborn self, and *now* look what—

A loud, complaining *meow* sounded behind her. That darn cat of her sister's was following her. Hilda ignored it. Why was it that cats always seemed to like those who didn't like *them*? Hilda much preferred crows. They were smart, and they brought her things. True, most of it was shiny, useless junk. But reciprocation was important in any relationship.

One arrived right now, flying through a broken window, carrying something in its beak. It landed and set a bottle cap at her feet.

"Wonderful. Marvelous. Best thing ever." Hilda reached into her pocket, drew out some breadcrumbs, and fed them to the crow. "Good work! Thank you. I mean that sincerely."

A working flashlight would have been more useful. Just saying. Although, those were perhaps a bit heavy for a tiny crow to carry.

The crow flew off, doubtless to look for a drained battery or something just as helpful. Hilda sighed. Crows just didn't spend enough time in human company to pick up the language. They were always flying off somewhere. They knew just enough, like a dog knew *No!* and *Good boy!* and *Fetch!* And a cat knew … nothing.

The cat meowed again. Loudly. Complainingly. One would think it would have put some effort into learning human language, considering how many years (lifetimes!) it had been mooching off her sister.

It wouldn't have had a chance to eat breakfast, though. Hilda dug into her pocket. She drew out a Girl Scout cookie she'd been saving for leaner times and set it on the floor.

"That's all I've got. You're welcome."

The cat set right to eating, no thanks or anything. Not even for a yummy bit of flour and sugar totally devoid of the nutrients needed to sustain life.

Essex lay down for the night with her friends, feeling lighter now they were all safe and she had relieved herself in a novel spot. Baby was already dreaming of chasing something—the bad witch, perhaps—curled up in the corner, legs churning.

"This is right by where we saw that play." Out of Football's mouth, Olaf pulled a spiky seed pod she had snatched up from somewhere, and nestled her in a bed of leaves he'd carried in from outside and wiped dry. He lay down by her and Essex. "Remember, where that human was chased by a bear?"

"That wasn't a real bear. That was a human wearing a bear costume."

"Still." He rested his head between his paws. "I wish he'd caught him."

"I've seen more than one." Essex licked her fur flat, envisioning the amphitheater across from the castle. All those characters deceiving each other, manipulating each other, betraying each other . . . "My mother used to take me, and then I took Bolton. I think they're by that Bard fellow the holly mentioned. Not all of them had happy endings."

"The mean characters don't get happy endings."

"Not even some of the good characters. The plays are supposed to be like real life that way."

"Were there other bears in those plays?"

"No. But there was a king who wanted to trade all he had for a horse."

Olaf nodded. "A sensible wish. What did the Even Meaner One mean, that Football belongs to . . ."

"Chief Detector Something? Maybe . . ." She lowered her voice, as if that would soften the blow. "That he's Football's father?"

"She couldn't be." He gently placed a paw over the baby's outstretched hand, keeping his claws out of her reach. She curled her fingers around him. "Could she?"

Essex stared at their little hand and paw, intertwined. The holly had warned that Olaf would betray her. But surely he wouldn't keep Football from her real father?

"The wind was terribly noisy. Perhaps I was mistaken." There was no need to upset him right before bed.

He grunted. "Good characters deserve happy endings."

She watched as he slowly fell asleep, then closed her eyes. Olaf was a *good* character. The holly had been mistaken.

TWENTY SIX

Hilda threw the morning paper on the dungeon counter, where her sister would see it.

WITCH CONFESSES
CRITICALLY INJURES CRPs

A mugshot of Blackthornudder underneath. Not a flatter-ing one, but you couldn't make chicken salad from chicken poop. And to the right, a picture of several bloodied "Professionals" on the floor. Staged, obviously. No witch would use a spell drawing blood, when there were so many cleaner alternatives.

Helga finally deigned to descend the narrow stone stairwell. (Hilda had already been out while everyone was lazily lying about and bought them a refrigerator. How the non-magical "help" at the store had scoffed when she'd insisted she didn't need it to be delivered.)

Helga smiled "good morning," then glanced at the paper. She stood in shock, staring at the pictures. Then she folded up the paper and stuck her head inside.

Hilda waited while her sister absorbed the information in her own way. Finally, Helga pulled her head out again, unfolded the paper, and smoothed out its wrinkles. She laid it back on the table, her shoulders shaking ever so slightly.

"Well?" Hilda set her fists on her hips.

"Two wrongs don't make a right."

"It's your funeral." Hilda let her hands fall limply to her sides. "Well, your funeral, my funeral, every magic-competent-in-the-city's funeral . . ."

To top off an all-around pleasant morning, her sister reached for the refrigerator as if it had always been there, without even a "thank you." The gray cat was rubbing off on her at last.

"I'll tell the animals. We'll bring the baby back tomorrow morning, before the fire station opens its door."

Hilda shook her head. "Wait till just before. Who knows what that dumb bear will go off and do."

"It's not like he would run off with the baby."

"Just saying."

"They need time to say goodbye."

"Bye! It takes less than a second to say."

"You know what I mean."

"It's a baby. It won't miss him. Soon enough it won't even remember him."

A distinctly non-frightening growl announced the entrance of that big, dumb bear, holding, what else, the baby. "What are you talking about?"

"Nothing. Go away." Hilda opened the refrigerator and

took out the eggs she'd bought to make *her* breakfast. It wasn't like she was everyone's servant around here.

"You were talking about Football. I heard you."

Hilda smirked. "Leavesdropping, were you?"

The none-too-clever fox appeared in the archway, too. "The stone echoes."

Helga patted the bear on the head, as if he were another stupid cat of hers. "It might be a good idea for us all to sit down and talk."

The bear and fox lowered their rumps and stared up at her expectantly.

Helga sighed almost imperceptibly, and drew up a chair. She sat and plastered a smile on her face, trying to look upbeat for everyone's benefit. Someday she would collapse from all that effort.

"The baby . . . She's the daughter of the city's Chief Magic Detector. How wonderful!" She pumped her fists in the air in an attempt to seem happy. "We've solved the Mystery of the Stolen Baby! Just like we set out to. If only indirectly."

"Just like Snarky," said the fox, but it looked worriedly at the bear.

The bear pulled the baby tighter to him. The stupid baby, not old enough to know better, sighed and snuggled against him.

Hilda had had just about enough. "Listen here, dumb-dumb. Just because the baby loves you best, doesn't mean you're what's best for it. Get that through your tiny bird brain."

The bear brightened.

"It's not a compliment!"

Helga gently touched the bear's shoulder. "I know it's hard

to want the best for someone else, without regard for your own happiness."

The bear hugged the baby even tighter. "I *do* want the best for her."

Hilda snorted and turned back to her eggs. "Then don't crush her."

TWENTY SEVEN

In the safety of her hideout on the West Side, Mabel put on a fancy hat like all the uptight society mavens were wearing, snooty designer-frame sunglasses, and that most convenient accessory for hiding one's true identity: a face mask.

Wearing a fur coat that was totally unnecessary as well as ridiculously expensive in this era of synthetic fabrics, holding under her arm a pen and clipboard with fake signatures on a fake petition, *and*—in an inspired, if she did say so herself, last touch—decked out in a sandwich board declaring *SAVE OUR SCHOOLS*, she was thoroughly disguised.

She'd thought she'd made a huge mistake, offering to join forces with the Hagglebottoms. Of *course* that drip Helga would never go along with any scheme that wasn't totally on the up-and-up. But now that Helga knew to *whom* the baby belonged, she would insist on returning it. And inadvertently bring it right back to Mabel.

Mabel probably had a day to prepare. The younger

Hagglebottom was a sentimental sort. The bear had seemed attached to the baby, the way it was clinging to it, and Helga wouldn't heartlessly tear them apart. She would indulge it another day.

Mabel took out her wand and zapped the clipboard. While it still *looked* like a regular clipboard, it was, in reality, a weapon. Still not too heavy to carry, but one wouldn't want to get hit over the head with it.

Ha!

With Harvey on her shoulder and her tools in her handbag, carrying her broom in its case, and a surprise for Harvey in another case that had slits for air to get through ("to air out the herbs," she'd told him), Mabel made her way to her car . . .

Which sat sunken to the ground. The right front tire had been slashed. Dozens of tiny little cuts were visible, made by tiny little claws.

She was annoyed for a good, long second, then smirked. Those dumb squirrels thought they'd gotten one over on Mabel Blackthornudder! But the joke was on them, as she had a spare in the trunk and, like any female driver worth her salt, knew how to swap it out. She made her way to the back . . .

And stared. Both rear tires had been slashed as well. She walked a little farther and . . . so had the front left. She clenched her fists. The squirrels would pay.

Not like she would be able to distinguish them from any other random squirrels in this rodent-infested city, but no matter! They would *all* pay, once she had time to get ahold of them. Right now she had to focus on "becoming" Brenda. And she did not fancy using mass transit, with all those horrid people. And it was a long walk to—

Something *sharp* dropped onto her head. The hat fell to the ground but the sharpness moved around. She screamed, dropped her cases and scrabbled at her hair. A squirrel dropped to the sidewalk and darted away—just as another small, dark shape fell from the tree branch overhead. Mabel jumped to the side. Claws scraped at the sandwich board.

The second squirrel landed, just as a squadron of birds appeared in the sky. A liquid missile dropped. And another, and—

Mabel grabbed her cases and hat and ran, dodging left and right, all the way to the park and down the 86th Street sunken transverse road. These sorts of things always seemed to happen *just* after you'd washed your hair.

*

Huffing and puffing, Mabel set both cases on top of Brenda's stoop and waited to catch her breath. Luckily she remembered to hunch down, as her seven-foot frame would give her away. And good thing she thought to grab Harvey and stuff him inside her bag. Uptight Brenda would never allow anyone inside her pristine home carrying a slimy amphibian.

She closed the flap to muffle outraged ribbiting and rang the doorbell. A few moments later, footsteps sounded, and Brenda's six-foot frame and ~~sophisticated~~ snobby, perfectly coiffed hair appeared behind the wood-and-glass door.

"*Oh,*" she clearly said, then ...

"*Alexa. Open the door.*"

A light blinked. Tumblers unlocked. The door opened.

Mabel grimaced. She'd have to figure out how to disable Alexa, too.

"Good day! I don't normally encourage soliciting, but I do support your cause." Brenda cocked her head. "What is that sound?"

"Nothing." Mabel pulled the cord of her bag, shutting the flap tighter, and gave the contents a menacing squeeze. "I have some initiatives for you to look at and a petition to sign, if you'd be so kind."

She motioned to enter, and her sister stupidly stepped aside. Rich ladies were easily fooled by seemingly-rich ladies. Mabel subtly noted the locations of security cameras as she stepped inside, and once safely in a blind spot, as Brenda shut the door, she raised her magically-hefty clipboard—

And plunked her sister over the head.

Brenda made a satisfying *THUD* as she hit the beautifully polished oak.

*

The potions were coming along swimmingly, bubbling in Brenda's designer Italian cookware in her fancy modern kitchen. Harvey hopped about, placated slightly by the filet mignon Mabel had found in the fridge, as well as the absence of Fluffy.

Or, so he thought.

She didn't relish using potions. They were effective, yes— but only in the short term, so you had to keep taking them. And they often came with *bonus* consequences, reminding her of those ghastly pharmaceutical commercials on TV ...

Side effects will probably include but are not limited to: Itching, burping, swelling, nausea, hair loss, ingrown toenails, hideous red bumps in places you can't hide without arousing suspicion, nasal hair growth, nasal growth, disgusting goo oozing from any and all orifices, new orifices, and . . . eventually . . . death. If you're lucky.

Mabel hadn't even taken so much as an aspirin in what seemed like millennia. But any side effects would be negated, once she had that baby.

She *was* dreading the bone and tissue compression, however. She and Brenda looked nothing alike, so it wouldn't be a simple matter for the potion to temporarily rearrange her features. And Mabel was a full foot taller.

Brenda was considered tall, in normal human terms. She had been the tallest in grade school. Lording her tallness over Mabel. Her popularity. Mabel had prayed every night to grow taller, by a good few inches, at least.

She had prayed too hard, apparently.

No matter. Height was an advantage in life. Just not when one had to shapeshift. But she would have to endure it. All seven feet of her.

She stirred the brews awhile, then added devil's tongue, which non-magical people knew as "konjac" and sometimes used in weight-loss supplements. And had no idea how *much* weight—and shapes and height!—could be lost, and *transfigured*, if one only knew how to prepare and mix it properly. She stirred, sighed with satisfaction, and reached over to cut off a lock of her sister's hair, just as Brenda, trussed up on one of her fancy barstools at the counter, regained consciousness.

In Brenda's foggy haze, she didn't notice her perfectly coiffed hair was now missing a great big chunk in a very

noticeable place. Mabel might have gone a bit overboard.

Brenda's vision seemed to finally clear. "*You* ... You have a lot of nerve showing up here. If you've harmed my daughter in *any* way—"

"Oh, chill." Mabel was aware no one cool said "chill" anymore, but one didn't need to be cool in the eyes of the world when one specialized in cold ~~and evil~~ magic. "I'm not planning on hurting her—or you. I'm not cruel." Except, perhaps, to Harvey, who deserved it.

Mabel added Brenda's hair to one potion and stirred. Brenda's eyes narrowed, and reflected awareness of a hair styling appointment in her indeterminate future.

"I just want you to know," she said in her haughty manner, "I never told my husband or any of his colleagues about you. If you hadn't kidnapped our baby, no one would be the wiser."

"It would have just been a matter of time before someone found out. Besides, I didn't steal your baby to hurt you. Only to get the authorities to drop their persecution of my kind."

Brenda paled. She recovered—but not soon enough to fool Mabel.

"You know, don't you? That your daughter is a magic-competent?"

"Madison? You're out of your mind. She's a normal baby. *My* baby."

"Just think what your husband would do with that information." Mabel sneered. "He'd weaponize her. Her life would never be her own."

"You would never tell. He would use her against you." Brenda drew herself up to her full sitting-height. "My daughter will use her gifts in service. *True* service. Not persecuting relatively harmless cranks with their little tricks. She will be a doctor, or an engineer, or—"

"Engineers developed the new technology used to persecute us. And, 'little tricks'? We're much more powerful than you know."

"You may as well return her to me. My husband would rather sacrifice his own daughter than give up this ridiculous vendetta. He treats his elder daughter abominably. I do what I can to make up for it, but it's too late. This obsession of his, it's a distraction from dealing with more pressing issues. All these photoshopped photos, witches *flying*, as if that were really possible, those bloody photos—"

"*That* was staged." Mabel's heart thumped as she envisioned the morning paper she'd seen as she passed the newsstand. "But I assure you, any witch worth her salt can fly."

Brenda laughed, her tone dripping with scorn. "Of course you can." She looked at Harvey as he hopped optimistically by. "And I suppose this frog is your husband, whom you turned in a fit of pique?"

Listen to that pretentious snob, using *whom* correctly all on her own. "More like years of anger and frustration, culminating in a fiery explosion. But yes."

Brenda rolled her eyes. "All right. I'm a reasonably open-minded person. Prove me wrong. Fly."

Mabel huffed. "I don't mean I flap my arms. That would be ridiculous. I ride my broom. I doubt you want me flying indoors and damaging your precious furniture. Besides, right now these potions require all my attention."

"Right. To turn *me* into a frog?"

Fantastic idea. Her sister wouldn't think her so crazy, once Mabel turned her into a frog and dumped her in the park. Perhaps, along with Harvey . . .

That reminded her. It was time to bring Fluffy's carrying case in from outside. He was probably hungry.

*

Finally, sometime in the middle of the night, the potions were ready. Perhaps Chief Detector Thomas wouldn't give in to ransom. But with Mabel's powers amplified, she wouldn't need to use the baby as a bargaining chip.

She was not looking forward to shrinking to her sister's height. The compression of the bones, tendons, ligaments and other delicate tissues of the body was rumored to be extremely painful.

Well. It had to be done. She set the poisoned chalice to her own lips, grimaced, and downed the draught. The height difference was only a foot. A measly twelve inches. It wouldn't be so

baaaaaaaahhhhaaaad!

After several torturous minutes, it was worth it to see the look on her sister's face, witnessing an exact replica of herself standing before her. (Well, leaning painfully against a barstool.)

"All right," panted Mabel. "Your turn." She dipped a new cup into the second potion, into which she'd stirred a carefully, artfully snipped-off lock of her own hair. "Bottoms up!"

TWENTY EIGHT

"**A**re you sure you want to come with me?"

Olaf nodded.

The Nice One patted his shoulder. She was being her usual nice self. She knew he felt miserable about giving the baby away. But she didn't know *why* he was coming.

"Even though it's not quite light yet and you're wearing your disguise, we shouldn't take chances. I'll take you as far as the park wall. Then you'll need to say goodbye for ..."

"I know. The last time."

The Nice One gave him a one-armed hug, careful not to smush the baby nestled in the carrier under her cloak. "I'm sorry, Olaf. I know it's hard to let go. But know you're doing the right thing."

Olaf *was* going to do the right thing. He was going to tail the fire people to see where they brought Football. Snoop on the real parents to make sure they were loving and kind. Not like the Even Meaner One.

"Good thing we're going early. It's supposed to snow again."

The Nice One carefully lifted a sleeping Football from the carrier and handed her to Olaf. "Why don't you carry her one last time?"

They lifted off on the Nice One's broom—by now used to Olaf's heft and determinedly pretending it had carried heavier loads. They headed out over the park.

Olaf looked back. Essex watched from the turret. She waved a paw in a final farewell. She'd formally said goodbye to Football earlier, nuzzling and gently tickling her.

The Mean One hadn't even bothered to say goodbye. ("I'll run into her when she's a working witch, so what's the point?") Neither had Baby.

The Nice One alighted behind an elm on the inside edge of the park wall. They dismounted, Olaf staring all the while. They'd passed the dilapidated zoo. The clock with the fake animals playing their fake instruments. Here was where Wendy had been leading him the night the enclosures had been broken into. Where Essex had run up to cut them off.

The shelter where Wendy's girlfriend worked, where she'd meant to bring him, must be around here somewhere. She wouldn't have taken him too far into the city. She wouldn't have risked someone seeing them and taking him from her.

Why had he never thought of that? He would need to search for the shelter, for Wendy, once he was sure Football was safe.

"Ready, Olaf?"

He looked at the Nice One, who was finishing tucking her broom into her bassoon case. She'd bought her own pair of shiny silver eyeglasses that showed you your snout when you looked at them. And she wore an extra-large face mask (although it did little to hide her naturally lovely nose). Still, he could tell she was smiling kindly.

He looked down at the baby. She was awake, smiling at him as she always did. He pulled her to him in a gentle hug. To say goodbye. At least, for now. Tearing up, he handed her to the Nice One, who'd been politely looking away on the pretense of examining the elm's leaves, as if she could really see that high. ("Good, good, no sign of Dutch elm disease. Whew!") Even though this was not *really* goodbye, it was still a separation, and those were always hard.

The Nice One carefully took Football from him and tucked her safely in the carrier.

"Well then, we're off. Chin up, Olaf."

Olaf lifted his chin, not exactly sure why, but the Nice One undoubtedly knew why it was important. He watched as she walked off holding her baby bump with one paw and her bassoon case with the other.

She looked over her shoulder. He waved a paw, turned, and continued on—

And hid behind a bush. She'd turned forward, assured he was on his way back to the castle.

He stalked her out of the park and down the cobblestone sidewalk. The old snow had been pushed into piles at the curb. The street adjacent wasn't busy, as it was still early. He kept an eye out for the shelter. For Wendy. If he should see her, he could come back, once he was sure Football was in good paws. He took care to avoid humans on the sidewalk, in case they looked too closely at his disguise.

Just ahead, loomed the fire station's big red door. He crouched behind a motorcycle and poked his head out.

The Nice One strolled by, bending and laying Football and the teddy bear down in one quick motion. Swaddled in a blanket Olaf had borrowed from the baby store, a note attached. He wasn't sure exactly what the Nice One had written, but Essex had suggested adding, *Keep a bazillion body-lengths from flame.*

Football turned her head to watch the Nice One go. Once she disappeared around the corner, Football looked all over and waved her paws. She began to cry.

Olaf stifled a roar. All he wanted was to rush over and comfort her.

A loud *screeeeeech*, and the red door rolled up. A human female wearing a shirt and pants the color of blueberries and boots the color of blackberries ducked underneath. She knelt and picked up Football.

Olaf jerked his head behind the motorcycle. Carefully, he peeked out again.

The fire person read the note. She looked up and around.

He ducked again. The next time he poked his head out, she was gone.

And so was Football.

*

It began to snow.

Olaf waited for what seemed like all day. Ducking behind the motorcycle. Darting behind a car when the human who belonged to the bike came to ride it away.

More cars arrived. Humans in yellow. They nodded at the humans in blueberry who came out to greet them. One of the yellow humans took off his hat and scratched his furless head. He shook hands with one of the blueberry humans, and they all disappeared inside the station.

Olaf waited, wishing he'd brought a snack. He didn't want to leave his post even to rummage through the rubbish bins. He couldn't take the chance.

Finally, the yellow humans returned. The furless male carried Football. She looked around and waved her tiny paws. Maybe she thought Olaf would be back to collect her. As if the humans had only been babysitting.

He could easily rush over, grab her and outrun them. At least make it to the park wall. From there they couldn't follow in their cars; they'd have to ride around to get to the road that cut through the park.

But he was going to do the right thing.

The humans brought Football into their car. The engine roared and the car rolled away.

*

Olaf followed, up the sunken road through the park. Surely from a distance he looked like any other huge human jogging while oddly dressed. The car exited the park, drove on a few blocks, and stopped.

Cars and vans sat parked in front of a brownstone. A crowd of humans waited, frantically waving and calling. They carried hunks of metal they held forward and made *click*. Others held what looked like metal ice cream cones. The furless human took off his hat and waved it, lifting Football in his other paw as if she were a trophy.

He brought her up the stoop. The brownstone had barred ground floor windows, and second floor windows that were shut and possibly locked. Not in and of itself a problem, as Olaf's snout was strong enough to push through glass. Except that might wake a human, or cause an alarm to go off. If, of course, Football should need rescuing.

The door opened. A human female emerged. Not quite as tall as the Even Meaner One, but taller than most. She exclaimed with joy and held out her arms. Football was placed in them and began to cry.

Watching from behind the nearest car, Olaf dug his claws into the snow.

"She was taken from me so soon, we didn't have time to bond," said the tall female. She started to cry as well. "Tears of joy!"

But Olaf did not believe her.

The tall female and the furless male nuzzled. They turned to the crowd and smiled as the hunks of metal clicked away.

Everyone had told Olaf he could trust the fire people. That they would call the yellow people. Who the Nice One had called Conflict Resolution Professionals. The Mean One had called them pigs. Olaf grunted. They did not look like any pigs *he* had ever met.

Still, he did not trust these pigs. And he did not trust Football's mother. He couldn't put his paw on why. All he could go on were his animal instincts, and they screamed something was wrong.

Mabel suppressed a smirk. It had been stupid of her sister to leave her cell phone out. Ah, the wonders of technology, that plunking an unconscious person's fingertip on a screen would unlock all their private discourse.

The CRPs had arrived to find "Mabel Blackthornudder" unconscious, a large bump on her head, tied up on Brenda's barstool. They took "Brenda's" statement and "Mabel" away.

Brenda's husband hadn't bothered to call. Of course, he showed for the photo op. Mabel had to kiss him for the reporters. Ugh. She'd never understood the appeal of bald men. She'd always liked hers hairy. Of course, this had led directly to the poor life decision of marrying Harvey. Who, in the end, had turned out bald all over.

As the fuss and ballyhoo waned, her sister's husband grunted that he'd be in touch. Mabel entered the house with the magic baby. Finally, her ordeal was over!

Olaf waited till the yellow humans left and the crowd dispersed. Waited, till the sun went down.

He looked left and right, then hurried up the stoop, clambered over the banister, carefully balanced on an ornamental ledge slippery with snow, and toed his way to the window.

It was locked. He heard Football crying through the open window on the third floor, and the mother hissing, "Shut up, you. I'll feed you soon enough."

It was all Olaf could do to wait, as Football cried and cried, and the mother didn't seem to care one bit. But it was difficult staying inconspicuous in broad daylight, even behind a nearby shrub. He did slink away, just for a moment, to inspect the trash cans. They were "locked." He flipped one over and the lid sprang open. He had his dinner.

Finally, the sun and day parted ways. The wind and snow rested. The street grew quiet. The mother stopped cursing and moaning, "Why won't it work?"

The last light in the house flicked out.

*

Sometime during the evening, the window had become unlocked. Olaf lifted it and heaved himself through, taking care not to fall on the floor.

It was dark. He took off the shiny silver eyeglasses that showed you your snout when you looked at them. And the face mask, the scarf and hat, the glove and mitten. Running back on all threes, no one who noticed him would think he was human. He stuffed everything in his coat pockets and took a look around.

Now the moon was enough to light his way through the house. He smelled a cat. Hopefully it was sleeping.

He crept upstairs and passed the mother's room. She snored

loudly. Funny, he'd smelled her somewhere before. Perhaps one day he'd encountered her in the park.

He entered the baby's room. At least the mother had everything set up. A crib, with wooden animals rotating at the top. A llama, a bunny, and . . . a bear.

Football slept. Carefully, he picked her up. She opened her eyes and smiled, as if she'd always known he was coming back. The teddy bear fell out of her paw. It was noseless now and even more charred—had she set off another fireball?

Nestling her against his chest, he picked up the teddy, his claw hooking into the fabric. He handed it to her. Her tiny paw curled around it.

She was wet. He quickly inspected the cabinet. It was orderly, with everything she needed tucked neatly inside the drawers. He didn't have the diaper bag and might not have much time. But he quickly changed her—ooh, baby powder!—and dressed her in a warm onesie. Holding her carefully, he left the room and padded down the hall, and—since they both deserved some relief after the tumult of the past couple days—slid down the banister.

He found the kitchen. A half-empty bottle of formula sat in the fridge. He took that, too, in case Football got hungry before they reached the castle. He could tuck it under his arm on the way.

He was tempted to leave by the front door, as so far human locks hadn't even been a challenge. But a tiny light flashed, and a beep *meeped*, and it was safer not to chance it. He returned to the window and left the way he'd come. The mother and cat slept through everything. A pet frog—they must be getting popular—silently watched them go.

*

They stopped off at the cave, as Football began crying and Olaf didn't want to wait to feed her.

The lighter sat on the earthen floor, as if it had been waiting for them. One of the treasures he'd overlooked in their hurry to escape. He surveyed their surroundings as Football contentedly slurped from her bottle. The cave had sheltered them for many seasons. It would make a good hideout again, for someone who needed it.

"Glrg," she said, a milk bubble forming at her lips. She dropped the empty bottle and held out her paws.

"That's right." He gently popped the bubble and picked her up. "We're going home, to rejoin Mama."

He wrapped her in another trash bag from the Pile of Human Garbage. Now that she was extra warm, they set on their way. A new snow fell, and Olaf stuck out his tongue to catch the falling flakes. Football opened her mouth to try but missed each time, the snow running down her cheeks. Which made her laugh, and him, and helped make it seem everything would be all right.

They neared the castle. Essex watched them approach from the turret. Olaf couldn't make out her expression, but it was probably one of disappointment.

But she would soon be on his side.

The sisters had yet to return for the night. Back down in the foyer, Essex pawed at the cold stone floor. She was not looking forward to this conversation.

Olaf appeared through the glass, holding the baby securely against his chest. He fit his other paw under the metal handle and pulled open the door.

Football *was* content, not seeming to miss her real mother at all. Laughing and moving about, a hopefully only slightly-used trash bag cackling along with her.

Olaf shut the door against the wind. "Before you say

anything, let me tell you what I saw and heard."

Essex listened to tales of Football crying. Understandably, given she'd been snatched from her mother at such a young age, probably didn't even recognize her, and had become attached to Essex and Olaf.

She listened to tales of the "bad mother." Neglecting to feed her baby. Cursing under her breath.

It wasn't that Essex thought her friend would lie about something so important. Something that could hurt someone so. He just couldn't see the park for the trees. A new mother and stolen baby, who hadn't been able to bond, of course wouldn't be in sync. The mother couldn't correctly interpret Football's cries. And surely she'd been cursing at herself. Feeling inadequate, or perhaps overwhelmed.

"Olaf," Essex said gently, when he'd finished and looked imploringly at her. "You're seeing in the mother what you *want* to see. Not what's real."

"You weren't there," said Olaf. "You don't know."

"I know *you*." She laid a paw on his leg. The baby reached for her. But Olaf moved away so Football couldn't touch her. And so Essex couldn't touch him.

Hurt tore through her heart. But she composed herself and continued. "We all love Football, Olaf."

He didn't look convinced.

"That is, you and I and Helga love her. But Olaf, Football's not ours. She never was."

"I was right about the Even Meaner One."

"That doesn't mean—"

"You always think you know what's right, just because you watch the TV. And because you talk to the Nice One a lot. I know I'm not the sharpest bulb in the shed—"

"Sharpest tool. Or brightest—" Essex held her snout in her paws. Using human expressions correctly wasn't important now.

She placed her paws on the floor and looked at her dear friend. "This has nothing to do with how smart you are. It's that you're letting your heart talk so loud it can't hear your head."

"Just because you thought Bolton should have stayed home that night and he got killed doesn't mean you're right about every—"

He broke off, his bark-colored eyes suddenly sad. "I didn't mean—"

Something hot spiked in her belly. "If Bolton *had* listened to me, he might still be alive. He would still be with me. I wouldn't . . ."

She couldn't finish that sentence.

He looked mournfully at the floor, just as if she had. "You wouldn't have to be with me."

She reached out a paw. "That isn't what I meant."

"Isn't it?"

Her tail drooped. As much as she loved Olaf and cherished the time she'd spent with him and Baby . . . Football . . . Helga . . . Hilda, not so much . . . If she were being honest, a part of her wished life had taken a different turn. That the car that had struck her mate had taken a different turn, down a different street.

She shook her head. This wasn't about Bolton, nor her. This was about what was best for the baby.

"Football doesn't belong here. She doesn't belong to us. She doesn't belong in a park, or in a castle, even. She belongs with her mother. In the human world, no matter how difficult or troubling that world can be. It can also be wonderful. Beautiful. We're depriving her of all she could be, and is *meant* to experience."

Olaf gazed down at Football. He looked back at Essex, and his eyes turned hard. He'd never looked at her that way before.

Essex lifted her chin, sure of this. "We would be taking her from her path. Her destiny. Just like Bolton. He should have been mine for longer. He shouldn't have been on the streets that night. He *should* have listened to me. I *am* smart, and I *do* know better than—"

She stopped, realizing what she'd been about to say. It was the truth, but it wouldn't be kind. Instead she said, "I knew better than him."

But Olaf knew what she'd meant.

"I have to put Football to bed. I already fed and changed her."

He lumbered past her without another look and disappeared up the staircase, even as Football cried out and reached for her.

Essex stood as if stuck to the stone, her heart heavy. That had gone so wrong.

*

She wasn't sure how much time passed. Upstairs, Olaf lumbered about, then seemed to settle down for sleep. Finally, she dragged herself up the stairs, but didn't stop at the next floor. Olaf wouldn't want to see her now. She kept on toward the tower and sat in the turret, looking out over the vast fields of snow.

She would let him enjoy this last night. Helga would take Football back in the morning. Once the baby was gone, things would slowly get back to normal.

Olaf waited till everyone fell asleep.

The sisters snored, their thunderous rumblings echoing up the stairwell. The Nice One had been kind to him, but it was clear she was on Essex's side. The Mean One had, as usual, said mean things. The gray cat ignored him.

Baby said nothing. She just noted his presence, stretched, and went back to sleep.

Essex had waited awhile to come to bed. Maybe she thought he wouldn't want to see her. He shouldn't have left like that, when she surely meant well. She kept getting up, turning around in a circle, and lying down again. Perhaps she felt bad about what she'd said, just like him.

But now all was quiet.

Very softly and carefully, he got up. Silently, he packed the diaper bag with the few supplies he had left. He looped the straps over his shoulders. Gently, he picked up Football. Her eyes opened and she smiled. He rested her against his chest, and tiptoed toward the stairs.

He looked back at his best friend.

He couldn't do it. He couldn't leave Essex. She was getting older, and foxes didn't live as long as bears. He might never see her again.

The baby nuzzled against his heart. Which hurt, as he turned and padded down the steps. He just couldn't keep them both.

Football reached out a paw, wanting Essex to follow, and grunted with frustration when she didn't.

"Shh, sweetheart," he whispered. "Mama will join us later."

Which was true. Even if only, once they were on the Other Side.

*

They'd look for him elsewhere in the park. Or in one of the other parks in the city. They'd never think to look where they'd just left.

Olaf tucked Football under his arm, and ran.

Loping through the snow, he could pretend for just a moment nothing had changed. He was running to get back home, where his friends were waiting. He could even go so far as to pretend that so was his mother.

She'd never seen him grown. She'd always protected *him*. He had never been a protector, while she was with him.

He could almost feel her watching him. She would be proud. She would agree, the baby's real mother didn't act like a mother should. She would say Olaf had done the right thing.

The moon shone brightly overhead. But there were no birds to tweet hello. To enquire, what was so important, he was carrying it so carefully. All his bird friends had flown south for the winter.

Normally, he would sleep right through it and not miss them. But now he had a baby to care for. And he needed new friends to help him. As he'd just run out on those he could count on.

TWENTY NINE

Olaf had never noticed how small the cave was. How dark. How cold.

Football slept soundly on her smooth-rock-and-magazine bed, as if she and Bearington had never left. But Essex's spot was empty. So was Baby's.

Olaf sat on his rock and moaned. Quietly, so as not to wake Football. He had once thought he would choose his best friend Essex over anything. Over all his bunny friends. Even over a baby bird, if he ever got to have one.

He just couldn't give up Football. His mother would have wanted him to protect her, no matter what.

He looked around. He still had baby supplies, and there were plenty of things that might prove useful in the Pile of Human Garbage. But they only had the formula left over from before Essex had started to nurse. And he needed to eat. And you didn't leave a baby all alone in a cave. Everyone knew that.

*

As night traded places with the day, Olaf held his sleeping baby and waited at the entrance to the rabbit den. It wasn't long before one of his bunny friends emerged.

"What you got there, Olaf, hmm? Oh, your human baby. I heard tell you had one."

"I need help taking care of her."

A second bunny Olaf didn't know emerged from the tunnel, apparently decided he was harmless and dashed off to begin its day. Olaf turned back to his friend.

"Would you mind watching her, just for a bit? I need to find food."

Bert shook his head. "Sorry, no room down here for a baby. Won't fit at all."

Olaf looked closely at the entrance to the burrow. It *was* rather small. "Can you wait with her in my cave? It won't take long."

Bert recoiled. "Your friend, the fox—"

"She's not there. She won't be back"—he pulled Football closer to him—"ever. Which is why I need you . . . why I'm asking—"

"Sorry, no can do. What if a snake should enter your cave? I'd be cornered. Sorry! Go ask one of your bird friends, surely they can help you."

Something churned in Olaf's stomach, which was odd, because it was empty. "They all left for the winter."

"Good time to make new friends, then, hey? Must run now. Sorry!"

Bert raced off. A movement caught Olaf's eye. Another

bunny he knew! Another friend. "Please, can you—"

"Sorry, heard you ask Bert. No can do. Sorry!" His other friend ran off, too.

Olaf stroked the fur on Football's head as he padded around the park, searching for food. Essex or Baby had always looked after her before. And he wasn't used to snow. Normally he'd sleep right through winter.

But things were not too terrible. He couldn't hunt with the baby, but he could forage. Berries, he'd heard, were scarce in winter, but he found a few still clinging to thin branches, dusted with snow.

Olaf thanked the berries before shoving them in his mouth. He thanked the bushes for saving them for him. Then he and Football made their way to the lake. He needed to drink his fill before preparing her formula. The water flowed almost to the edge of the cave, but if they went farther out they might encounter a duck.

He drank, then snatched a surprised fish and stuffed it in his mouth. He scanned the water, looking for another.

A duck he'd never met swam serenely just ahead. He restrained his instinct to run, not wanting to frighten it. Slowly he waded till they were close enough, so he didn't have to shout.

"Excuse me . . . Hello? I don't mean to bother you—"

The duck squawked, flapped its wings, and flew off.

"Wait! I only want to ask you—" Olaf splashed through the water, and was careful not to jostle Football as he clambered up the embankment and over the fencing.

But the duck was gone.

Football laughed and squealed with joy, thinking they were playing a game. Olaf pretended to laugh, too. He didn't want her to sense him worrying. Besides, maybe they would come across another duck on the way home.

He trudged on. Football kept giggling and tickling his side with her paw. He couldn't help smiling, and soon neither could his heart.

Rising on his hind legs, he carried her the rest of the way with both arms, tossing her in the air (only a tiny bit!) and catching her on the way down. She screamed with laughter. He held her securely against his chest and clambered over the iron railing. As they descended the stairs to the cave, he thought things through. (Football squealed, demanding more tosses, but he had to take care not to slip on the snowy steps.)

He only had a bit of formula and a few water bottles left. If only he could bring Football with him to get more. Hide her under his coat perhaps. If only he'd brought home one of those baby carriers from the baby store. (He would have, but the sales clerk was already eyeing him suspiciously.) Or snuck in the Nice One's room and borrowed hers. Really, what would she need it for anymore?

He stopped short. He smelled something—some*one*. Someone had entered their cave! Someone …

… he knew. And loved. And felt such gratitude for, like he'd never felt before.

Baby sat waiting for him, a nice big fat dead rat at her feet.

*

Olaf heated Football's formula over the log pile. The rat could wait till he'd fed her. "Remember, don't make her laugh," he reminded Baby, who scrunched up her nose in reply.

He extinguished the fire, throwing an old blanket over it and stomping on it. Then he held Football as she slurped down her breakfast.

He shouldn't suspect his friend of selling him out, but he had to ask. "Did you tell them—"

"That I was off to find my Betty. I'm no snitch." She licked her paw and smoothed down her fur. "Speaking of which . . . We need to shield ourselves, so the bad witch won't know we're here. Or anyone else, for that matter."

"You mean with magic?" His shoulders slumped. "We haven't been taught enough. I only understand that little squiggle."

"We know enough."

"We do?"

"What's important is our intent. And aligning with the Everything." Baby narrowed her eyes. "I pay attention to the sisters, too. And other random weirdos I happen across."

As Olaf burped Football, Baby purposely dragged her bum leg in a wide circle, so it drew a line in the dirt.

"You want to protect the baby. And I want to pro—not be bothered by all this anymore."

She stepped into the circle, and kicked dirt into a little mound. "We acknowledge the Elements and their power to protect us. Here we have plenty of Earth." She nosed over one of the water bottles. "We have Water." She waved a paw. "Air is all around us."

A nearby twig, she pulled into the pile. "Wood." She pawed through the Pile of Human Garbage, and emerged with a bottle cap. After batting it around awhile—she was, after all, a cat—she added it to the clump of dirt, twig and bottle. "Metal.

Now where's that lighter?"

Olaf laid Football on her bed with her teddy bear to sleep. He pressed the lighter between his paw pads and brought it into the circle. Holding it under his arm, he banged on the button. "Fire!"

Baby looked up at the craggy ceiling and slitted her eyes. "Byyyyyy the miiiiiiight of the Elementsssss . . . I caaaaaaaall on the Aaaaaaall and the Evvvv'rythinnnng . . ."

Olaf wished his paws were free so he could cover his ears, as Baby's "calling" sounded more like caterwauling. But surely she knew what she was doing.

". . . to shieeeeeeeeeeld us from the pryyyyyyyying eyes and waaaaaaarped miiiiiiind of the baaaaaaaaad witch!!! *And* any other human scum."

Olaf smiled. Baby had recently learned that synonym for garbage and was quite pleased with herself.

She sighed and closed her eyes, like cats do when they're content.

"That's all we need to do?" Olaf couldn't help thinking there was more.

"That's all." She opened her eyes. "Except, the sisters aren't scum. Well, one of them isn't." She focused on the mound of dirt. The bottle cap and water. The twig and flame. "Sacred Elementsssss . . . the Evvvv'rythinnnng . . . pleeeeeeease also shieeeeeeeeeld us from the witch sisterssssssss! *And* anyone who would separate us, regardless of their intentions."

Olaf stared as the air shimmered. "I . . . I think I just saw my mother. Smiling at me. I'm not sure, though. She *was* rather fuzzy."

"Not surprising. We're acknowledging Spirit. It makes it

easier for individual spirits to connect with us. Or, rather, for us to see *them*. We're always connected."

She turned in a circle, settled on the floor, and wrapped her tail around her.

It was time for Olaf to finish his breakfast. He banged on the button to extinguish the lighter, and chewed the rat slowly, thinking things through. As kind and helpful as Baby was (although he'd never offend her by telling her so), surely she disapproved. "You think I should bring Football back, don't you."

"What would it matter if I did? Everyone thinks I should give up searching for my Betty. How could I? I love her, like the Everything meant me to." She looked over at Football with perhaps a smidge less disdain than usual. "Do what your heart tells you. Don't listen to anyone else. You're the one who has to live with your decision."

Olaf finished his rat. He lay down and gazed at Football. She was warm and dry. No one was neglecting to feed her. No one was telling her to shut up. He had made the right decision.

Except, he couldn't help wondering what Essex was doing now. Was she out looking for him?

Or rather, for the baby. Doing the right thing—at least, what *she* thought was right—was more important to his friend than, well, friendship.

Maybe they'd never really been friends. Essex had told him, the trees had told her to wait for him by the clock that night, under the fake animals playing their fake instruments. Maybe their friendship had been fake, too. Maybe all along, she'd just wanted to do the right thing.

Olaf rested his head on his paws, and closed his eyes.

In the "dungeon" of the castle, Helga stared at her dark mirror. Her intent was clear. To find the bear and bring back the baby. But the spirits, apparently, were unwilling to assist her.

"Will you look at that?" Her sister peered over her shoulder, into the void. "Looks like dumb-dumb learned a trick or two."

THIRTY

Mabel slept late, to make up for a late start. That darn baby had cried forever, and she hadn't thought to bring earplugs.

She perused the morning paper. She had time. No one would believe Brenda, that she was actually Brenda. Not until she changed back in approximately six hours.

Ha! Splashed on the front page was a picture of the clueless Chief Detective, holding his trophy high. Next to a snapshot in a pub, one of the CRPs she'd supposedly critically injured. *Interesting* . . .

She smirked, relishing the brouhaha to come, her delicious brunch of croissants and gourmet coffee, and the laughable sight of Harvey waiting by his food bowl with an eye out for Fluffy.

Mabel narrowed her eyes. It was probably her imagination, but Harvey looked . . . smug, somehow. Not that frogs could really look any specific way, other than alive or dead, awake or asleep, eyes bulging in a disgusting fashion or not. Still, she could swear he knew something she didn't.

Eh. It was probably just her imagination. She savored her sister's ridiculously expensive coffee and kept reading.

Odd that the baby was still sleeping.

Finally Mabel got up and put out some cat food for Harvey, before spooning the rest into Fluffy's bowl.

Harvey made a quick exit.

From his perch high up on an ornamental molding where Fluffy couldn't reach him, Harvey hopped with glee as screams of outrage emanated from the baby's room. Along with threats to the bear.

It was obvious. The M.O. was the same. Cabinet drawers thrown open, baby clothes in disarray. Big wet paw prints all over the floor. So much more evident this time, thanks to the elements. A window left wide open to said elements. (Good thing Harvey had flipped the lock open after Mabel had gone to bed. Not that he could have foreseen the bear would be by, of course, but it was important to always hold hope in one's heart.)

It had been the last straw, watching Mabel attempt to turn Fluffy into a frog, instead of trying to turn him back. It was only a matter of time before she succeeded in aligning her energy with the baby's. Then she would be consumed with lust for power, and leave him behind.

Out of the corner of his bulging frog eye, he spied Fluffy

crouching, attempting once again to jump from the top of the mahogany table to the molding. Harvey ignored him. Fluffy had yet to make a successful leap.

Mabel's clogs *thump* *thump* *thumped* as they took her from the baby's room, down the stairs and to the hall where she'd stashed her bag of tools. Harvey watched while she dug out her scrying mirror and candles, set up in the parlor, and drew the curtains.

She stared at her black mirror, clawing at her hair because it showed her absolutely nothing. Harvey smirked at the void, then down at Fluffy, who sat at Mabel's feet, waiting for her to finish and give him a treat. Or at least, leave the room so he could again harass Harvey.

Mabel screamed and cursed the spirits. (Not a bright move, to be honest.) She jumped up and ran out of the room. ***Thump thump*** *thump* went her clogs. *Eh Eh Ehh* went the punching of buttons on Brenda's cell phone.

WAAWAAWAA WAAWAA.

"Yes, I'd like to report a stolen baby."

WAA WAA WAAWAA, WAA WAA WAAWAAWAA WAAWAA?

"Yes, I'm perfectly aware this is Animal Control. It was a bear that took my baby."

WAA WAAWAA WAA WAA WAAWAA?

"No, not a dingo, a bear. A bear took my—why are you laughing?"

WAA WAA WAA WAAWAA WAA WAAWAA WAAWAAWAA WAAWAAWAAWAA.

"No. I do not want the Conflict Resolution Professionals involved. They would just be wasting my—*their*—time. A bear took my baby, it's obvious. Big slushy paw prints all over my floor. The window thrown wide open—"

WAA WAA WAA WAAWAA WAAWAA WAA WAA WAA WAAWAA?

"No! I did not leave my window open during a snowstorm. In fact, I made sure it was locked before I went to bed. In any case, here's my address—"

CLAshhhhhhhhhh! Claws frantically scraped at the edge of the molding, scrabbling to find purchase.

THUMP!

Harvey smirked as Fluffy got back on his feet, arched his neck in what he apparently believed was a dignified manner, and slunk away, as if he'd meant to miss.

"Yes, that address is correct. I *am* Dr. Brenda Blackthorne, wife of Chief Detector Damon Thomas."

WAA WAA WAA WAA WAA—

"*No*, I do not want him involved—don't you see, there's no need to trouble him."

WAA WAA WAA WAAAAAA WAAWAA WAAWAA?

"Of *course* this is the real Brenda Blackthorne, who else would it be? I just need all your resources at my beck and call for a few hours."

. . .

"Hello? Hello?"

THIRTY ONE

Essex sat on her haunches high atop the castle, looking out at the beautiful view. At the pond and snowy grounds below, the human dwellings visible above the trees in the distance. But her heart was with her friend. Wherever he might be. Helga had gone out looking for him.

She settled on the cold stone floor and tried to sleep in the sun. She hadn't gotten much rest last night.

Her heart tugged at her, egging on the thoughts coursing through her head. Why did she always have to be such a goody two-shoes? Why couldn't she for once do something she knew was wrong, but right for Olaf? Was she only sad her kits had grown and gone, and projected that onto the baby's mother? She didn't even know the mother, or anything about her. Maybe she truly was unkind, like Olaf had said.

But chances were, he was wrong. And he'd hurt her feelings, saying what he had about Bolton. About her. She didn't *need* to be right. It was just ... she usually was. Bolton *would* be alive if he hadn't gone out that night. And Football *did* belong with her

mother. Essex did know what was right, and so did Olaf, even though he didn't want to admit it. He'd betrayed her, just like the holly had said.

Sleep would not come. Time and time again she unfurled her tail, got up and turned in a circle, lay back down and tucked her tail under her muzzle. Why was life so complicated? Everything had seemed so simple when she was a cub.

*

She did the only thing she knew to do. She returned to the trees.

She focused and let go of her thoughts as best she could,

ignoring a mouse that darted across the field. She thanked the Three profusely, and asked what they should surely know.

"Where did my friend Olaf go?"

She waited, while the wind blew patterns in the snow. Waited, while the holly's leaves whistled sad notes. Waited, while all manner of fears arose in her soul.

Finally, she heard again, what seemed so much like words, and yet like the wind.

We cannot know all, said the holly. *That is only for the Everything.*

Essex stared at the holly and tried not to sound accusatory. "How can you not know? You knew he would betray me. You said so."

Did I?

He says so many things, said the birch.

Too many things, said the maple.

Can't shut him up, said the birch.

We've tried, said the maple.

"Olaf's my best friend. And he's left me, all for a baby that's not ours. That we were meant to return."

You need not worry, said the birch.

This too shall pass, said the maple.

"My life will pass," said Essex. "That doesn't help me *now.* How can I get my friend back? And still do the right thing?"

Danger! said the holly. *If you go after your friend, it will not end well for you. Be—*

"—ware, yes, I know," said Essex. "Please stop being dramatic and tell me what I need to know."

The Three were silent.

Oh no. Essex lowered her head. She had offended them.

The birch snickered. The maple giggled. Or maybe, that was just her imagination.

Have you been reading the Bard? said the holly. *Therein will you find all wisdom.*

"I can read 'I'm,' and 'a,' and 'dumb,' and 'fox.' That's all I've been taught so far."

I see, said the holly. *Well, let us skip ahead. The Bard famously said, 'There is nothing either good or bad, but thinking makes it so.' What about this situation with your friend makes you think he betrayed you?*

"*You* said—"

Eh, I say so many things. Feel into yourself, and answer.

Essex thought back, dumbfounded. Ever since the holly had said Olaf would betray her, the thought had been lurking in the back of her head. Hadn't he? "He knew we were supposed to return the baby."

Is it a betrayal, for one to do what he thinks is right, when you do not agree?

"Well, no, not generally. But he *knew* this was right. We'd discussed it many times. Just because he's so attached—"

Why is he attached?

Essex sat there, the world silent around her, remembering the grieving bear she'd first met. The sad tale he'd told her, once he trusted her. Because, he did trust her.

"He believes, deep down, if he protects the baby . . ."

She saw him losing his mother, just as if she'd been there. Instinctively she pawed at the air, trying to comfort him. She looked at the holly. "It's like he's protecting his mother. Whom he couldn't protect when he was little."

What good would it do your friend, if you made him return the baby?

Essex looked to the birch. The maple. Surely they would help her out. They were always putting the holly in its place.

They didn't. They waited patiently.

She closed her eyes, and saw her friend grieving, still. Her heart hurt at the memory.

"He might never heal from the loss of his mother." She opened her eyes, and gazed again at the Three. "But aren't I hurting the baby's mother, if I don't try to make him ...convince him ...influence him ..."

What if your friend is right, and the mother is wrong for the baby?

"Do you know? Do you know if she—"

We cannot know all.

Essex snorted. She did not mean to be disrespectful, but it seemed awfully convenient for the trees, what they knew and what they didn't.

What is it, to truly know a thing? Is there not just belief?'There is nothing either good or bad, but thinking makes it so.''Life's but a walking shadow, a poor—'

All right, said the birch.

That's enough, said the maple.

Don't overwhelm the poor fox, said the birch, while the maple rolled its eyes.

Essex shook her head. She had definitely imagined that, as trees did not have eyes. Only branch scars.

Perhaps she was imagining this entire conversation.

For a moment, she saw the world as it had appeared to her, before her mother had shown it to her in a different light. The wind caressing the snow. The bare birch and maple, waiting for new leaves to grow. The brilliant moon. A beetle scuttling to safety. Three trees huddled together—appearing to conspire—but only because they'd been planted so.

And yet... the humans who couldn't understand her vocalizations, could not because they did not believe. The witches believed, and they understood. And the witches believed in the trees. Even Hilda, though she disliked them, respected them in her own way.

Do actors feel betrayed, when one amongst them plays his part well?

"Of course not. They're all in the play together."

Are we not all in this life together?

Essex stared down at the snow as the wind howled.

How wonderful that your friend has played his role with such heart and allowed you to play yours. That you may both learn and grow.

The wind blew patterns in the snow... seemingly random, yet beautiful to behold.

What do you believe in? said the birch. *What do you want?* said the maple. *What, what, what?* chanted the Three, finally in solidarity.

Essex stilled, and the world fell away.

She wanted Olaf.

THIRTY TWO

The snow slowly melted, then fell again, like icing on the cake the Nice One had baked on Olaf's last night with his friends.

Grief gnawed at his heart, insisting on reminding him what he'd lost. Thankfully, he had many distractions. He needed to "shop" for Football. He now had his own baby carrier. She had onesies, booties, and a real hat, which didn't get soggy when it rained (but didn't smell quite as tasty). He was able to stock up on formula and bottled water, as the bored checkout teenager left the exact items he'd taken his previous visit on the counter—and still never looked up from her nails. He managed to find a few of his bird friends who hadn't flown south after all. They introduced him to a few of *their* friends, as well as a few ducks.

One evening, one of his new friends, Louise, flew into the cave to warn him: a human in gray, wielding a large net and rifle, was searching nearby. Olaf extinguished his fire, rocked Football so she wouldn't fuss, and hid with her. They huddled in the far corner, Louise perched on his shoulder.

Footsteps sounded from above. He tensed. Louise flexed her beak, ready to defend them all.

But the footfalls never descended the steps, and eventually faded away. The humans truly had forgotten about the cave. Just like his mother had said.

Louise lightly poked his shoulder in farewell, before flying off. He finished preparing Football's formula, fed and burped her, and set her down for the night with her teddy bear. Which could now more accurately be described as a lump of black-and-brown fuzz. He lay next to her and waited for sleep, thinking happy thoughts. Baby birds. Slushies. Lollipops.

But his head and heart always brought him back to Essex. His head and heart didn't want him to be happy.

Essex looked out over the castle grounds.

Hilda had said she couldn't care less what Olaf did, but Essex suspected she was secretly glad the baby was out of the pigs' hands, since she now hummed while stirring her potions. Helga still searched for Olaf on her broom. Sometimes she took Essex with her, tucked in her handbag, the gray cat riding the bristles.

Olaf and the baby weren't in any of the city's other parks. They weren't still here, hunkered down under a bridge or arch. They weren't in one of the yellow brick houses, under one of the wooden shelters, or in the wooden house where the puppets used to perform. Nor were they under the humongous terrace—with ready access to the fountain, the fake angel watching over them.

Baby came and went. Essex couldn't help suspect she knew more than she let on. Baby had friends all over the city. Quite likely, some dog or cat—or even a bearded dragon—was now sheltering a bear and baby, its humans oblivious.

"Good try today!" Helga would say, back at the castle grounds. "Want some dinner?"

The gray cat would leap off the bristles and race to the door. Helga would dutifully follow. Essex would endure her hunger awhile longer and ascend the staircase. Up in the tower, she gazed out over the park and pondered again where her friend might be.

Her sorrow wasn't quite like before, when Bolton had been ripped from her life, their kits already gone. She wasn't alone. She had friends. She had Baby, if only some of the time. She had Helga. She even had Hilda…sort of. But no one could replace Olaf. Just like no one could replace Bolton.

But Olaf hadn't gone to be One with the Everything. He was still here, somewhere in the city. And it was Essex who had driven him away.

Keeping Football wouldn't bring his mother back. Football did belong with her mother. But Essex could understand now. This was something he was going to have to figure out on his own. But she could stand by him.

And what if he was right? What if something was terribly wrong with the mother? What if they'd all just assumed Olaf couldn't see clearly? What if his heart knew more than all their heads put together?

She should have trusted him. He was so connected to the baby, surely he could sense something the rest of them couldn't. She should have supported him. Defended him. Even gone with him, if it came to that.

She was at an age now, considered advanced among foxes. Lucky, even, to have escaped this long all the dangers of urban living. She might never see Olaf again. At least, until they met on the Other Side.

And she did not want to wait that long.

Olaf galloped through the park in his coat and hat, the diaper bag flapping against his back. Full of diapers and formula, and a few new baby toys Football absolutely needed to have.

He had started venturing out to other food palaces, not wanting the bored checkout teenager to get in trouble. Today he'd gone all the way to the East Side, where the Nice One had taken him not long ago.

He entered the deserted, dilapidated zoo, and padded down the cobblestone path, up the stone steps to look over the remnants of his enclosure. The moonlight glinted off the broken glass. Graffiti had been sprayed onto the stone façades. The waterfall was no longer falling, the stream no longer streaming. Not much of the devastation had been cleared, and it was overgrown with weeds.

He lumbered through the rest of the zoo, looking over the abandoned enclosures. He'd only ever seen his own, and heard the rushing water below. The night Wendy had led him outside, he'd been too frightened to really look. He'd heard rather than seen the seals, the sea lions *Uh*-ing and *Urk*-ing, as scared and confused as everyone else.

He sat on a wooden bench, and thought of Wendy. Where had she gone? Where was she now? Did she have a new bear cub to look after?

Maybe in the spring, once he had more birds to help him watch over the baby, he could look for the shelter where Wendy's girlfriend worked. Maybe Wendy would be there. Surely she'd want to see him as much as he wanted to see her.

He wandered out the old gate hanging off its hinges, to the clock with the fake animals playing their fake instruments. Where Essex had waited for him. The fake monkeys pretended to strike a bell. The hippo played a violin. The goat piped. The penguin drummed. But where was the bear? He was sure he'd spied it that night.

He passed under the arch and looked up. There it was, playing its tambourine.

How were humans able to worship bears, so much so they erected statues of them, and then turn around and steal a mother's only cub? And then …

He didn't want to remember that night. Dreaming about it was difficult enough.

He gave his old home a last look, then turned his back and lumbered off. The past was gone. Life went on for everyone, including him. He had to get back to the little being that depended on him.

~ THIRTY THREE ~

Now was the winter of Mabel's discontent.
    She had been taking more care moving about the city,
as CRP surveillance had increased. She continued scrying, but
neither the spirits nor her subconscious seemed willing to assist
her. She searched the entire park and fanned out to the rest of
the city. It seemed every winged, clawed, and beady-eyed in-
habitant of not only each and every park, but every shrub and
tree, knew who she was and was conspiring against her. More
than once she'd had to magick bird poop out of her hair. But the
bear and baby were not to be found. (Getting bird-pooped on
wasn't good luck after all.) She may have taken her frustrations
out on Harvey. ~~She may have felt somewhat bad about that.~~

(Couldn't Harvey just stop, already, harping on the past?!?
You couldn't reverse a spell once it'd been cast; you didn't need
to be wicked to know that.)

She meant to search the initial hideout, the cave, but it
had been commandeered by a big, nasty bird, which pecked

at Mabel all the way up the slippery steps and halfway across the Ramble, so hard and fast she couldn't even get her wand out. She checked Belvedere Castle. The Hagglebottoms were surely squatting there, now that their cottage had been roped off as "evidence." (Mabel may have anonymously tipped off the CRPs.) Only an aesthetically-challenged witch would leave such a huge imprint in a memory foam pillow.

For now, she would leave the Hagglebottoms be. Had they known the baby's whereabouts, that drip Helga would have insisted on returning it. But Mabel would keep the castle on her radar, in case the fox and bear came back for help.

She had time to ponder, could Helga Hagglebottom possibly have been right? *Could* she turn ~~Harvey back~~ someone *else*

into a frog, all on her own? Did she not need an amplifier, after all?

What would it hurt to see what she could accomplish on her own? Perhaps all she had to do was focus. Practice. *Whom* could she practice on? *Whom* would no one miss if they disappeared from existence?

*

Behind the cover of a tree, Mabel waited for her quarry in the parking lot of the all-night food market.

As expected, the morning manager arrived promptly. Several minutes later, the surly checkout girl who'd been rude to Mabel one time too many emerged. Mabel stalked her to the bus stop, which was still deserted this early. She'd already knocked out the nearby CCTVs. The girl sat and opened her purse. Perhaps to take out her phone?

Before she could, Mabel drew her wand and pounced!

And tripped over a squirrel that darted out from underneath the bench.

"Ohmigod, are you okay?" The girl jumped up and hastened to her.

Mabel protested, while surreptitiously shoving her wand in her pocket. The girl helped her up and onto the bench. The squirrel nattered on about how Mabel was a no-good, rotten, evil piece of poop—and not to help! But too bad, the girl obviously wasn't a witch and couldn't understand.

Mabel's ankle had already started to swell. The bus arrived. The girl insisted on assisting her up the steps, and snapped at someone to *move* so Mabel could sit. The bump had already

grown to the size of a melted candle, and with witnesses around, Mabel couldn't magically heal it.

The girl encouraged her to go to the emergency room for an X-ray. "Better safe than sorry, y'know?"

Mabel insisted she was fine, seething internally. How was she supposed to turn the girl into a frog *now*, when she'd slipped off Mabel's hit list?

"Well, make sure to put your foot up as soon as you get home. Alternate hot and cold packs—do you have those? I could run to the pharmacy and—"

This was getting worse and worse.

The girl offered to accompany her home. Mabel insisted she and her husband had a sort of telepathic connection going on, they were so close. He would surely intuit something was wrong and be waiting for her at her stop. The girl insisted Mabel use her phone.

"It says you're low on minutes," said Mabel, frowning at the display.

"I'm on a limited plan. Saving for college 'n' stuff."

"Well. In that case, I certainly couldn't—" said Mabel, glad to have an excuse not to.

"I *want* you to."

Mabel left a voicemail for the frog.

Finally, the girl left her at her stop, and even smiled and waved goodbye to her and the bus driver, who had seemed bored the entire time but now smiled and waved back.

The bus resumed its route. Mabel hobbled off at the next stop and hid behind a dumpster to take care of her ankle.

This would not do. No liking people!

THIRTY FOUR

Winter hung on, then resigned itself to spring, with all its warmth and sweet scents. The wind stopped squalling, instead gently rustling brand new leaves, humming kind tunes and promising new beginnings. Baby bunnies abounded, their mothers keeping careful watch.

All life was precious.

But Essex needed to eat, and the humans couldn't be counted upon to throw out leftovers in accessible places on a regular basis.

She slunk low to the ground, stalking a bunny on the edge of a clearing. It paused to nibble at some weeds. She crouched, readying her muscles to spring ... and stumbled, as if some unseen force had shoved her aside. The bunny startled and ran off. Essex stared after it. She was normally so sure-footed.

Not that bunny. This one.

She pricked up her ears. Had she really heard that? A voice that sounded just like Bolton! Or had it been it a trick of the wind, like she often wondered while conversing with the Three?

A twig snapped in the distance. She swung her head, narrowing her eyes. A second bunny loped across the field.

Silently, she followed, keeping downwind. Patiently, she waited, till the bunny stilled. She readied herself to pounce and quickly gave thanks.

Thank you, Spirit of Bunny, for sacrificing yourself so I may eat and live another day. Thank you, Everything, for making me so much bigger than a bunny, so they may be food and I may live another day.

With that, she sprang.

The bunny leapt away. But Essex didn't miss by much. She had it by the tail—she pulled it to her with her claws—

"Don't eat me!" Instinctively it spread its legs as if playing dead, even though it clearly wasn't. Yet. "I have information on Olaf!"

Essex's grip slipped slightly. But she kept her cool and didn't let go. "You know where Olaf is?"

"That's what I said, isn't it? Let me go, and promise to leave me alone forever—or as long as I live, whichever comes first—and I'll tell you where your friend is."

Essex slowly disengaged her claws, but kept her eyes on the bunny, lest it bolt. "Isn't he your friend, too? You would sell him out?"

"Wouldn't you?"

She should eat this bunny, just for betraying Olaf. But hadn't she, also?

The bunny seemed to think so, too, the way it narrowed its eyes. "Isn't that why you're not with him now?"

Essex sighed, but didn't relax quite yet. "Go on, tell me what you know."

*

From the castle turret high atop the park, Essex stared across the treetops, trying to ascertain the location of the cave.

She turned her head toward the amphitheater where she'd seen the Bard's plays. Stories abounding with betrayal. Humans didn't seem to think twice about stabbing each other in the back.

In her mind, she saw herself go to Olaf. A deep calm took over. It was almost like it had already happened. The play had been written, and Essex was performing her role.

She looked to the stairs. She didn't have a diaper bag, or any possessions, really. There had been no reason to return. Surely she would see Baby at the cave, at least until Baby found her little girl. But Essex couldn't leave without seeing Helga one last time. The helpful sister had been so good to her. (The not-so-helpful one had been, too, in a mean sort of way. Still, Essex suspected Hilda wouldn't mind if she vanished, forever.)

She trotted down the narrow spiral staircase. An awful odor emanated from the kitchen. She slunk inside. A bird was keeping Helga company on the counter, as she brewed a potion in a small black cauldron she'd bought at the "Halloween store," using the battery-powered hotplate Hilda had procured at the pharmacy. Hilda had been teaching her sister, along with keeping up Essex's reading lessons. (Hilda would surely be glad to be done with those, too.)

Helga looked over. "There you are. What do you think, does this smell too terrible?"

Essex sniffed, trying to discern a difference since—

"It's a little less bad than last time."

Helga heaved a sigh of relief. "My sister said no more lessons for the foreseeable future. Said I have to learn for myself. I've relied too much on spells; I'm rusty with potions."

Essex pawed at the stone floor. Couldn't she hint where she was going, so Helga wouldn't worry she'd been run over by a car, or carried away by a hawk, or any of the myriad of terrible things that could befall a small animal in the big city?

Helga lifted her spoon to her lips and took a taste. "Ugh. This is truly terrible. It would take an entire dispenser of sugar to get this down. I'm going to have to start over."

She turned off the hotplate and withdrew her wand.

Waving it over the cauldron, she chanted an invocation that lilted just like a song. A lovely song she played on repeat on the CD player she'd bought at the pharmacy and kept in her bedroom, which annoyed Hilda to no end. The bird fluttered its wings in appreciation and joined in. The bubbling brew turned into vapor and dispersed into the air, as if it had never been.

Helga *had* been important in Essex's life. But Essex couldn't say anything to give Olaf away. Softly, she leaned against Helga's shin. Hopefully Helga would remember this moment in the coming days and realize Essex had meant farewell.

Helga reached down and patted her head. The bird sang a beautiful, bittersweet song, that Essex somehow knew was about friends coming together, then parting forever.

Life *was* bittersweet. But maybe that was why it was so precious.

With Football in the carrier under his coat, Olaf lumbered through the food palace, looking for anything she might need besides the supplies the bored checkout teenager had left out.

Finding nothing—she'd thought of everything—he slipped out the doors, feeling gratitude, yet still fear. How did she know so much without ever looking up from her nails?

He made his way across the park, Football awake now and babbling. He opened his coat to let her look up at the stars, which shone down brightly, full of joy to see her.

As perfect as she was now, wouldn't it be even more wonderful when she got older and could talk to him? They could have deep philosophical discussions about life and death. Why, for instance, did Essex's mate Bolton have to die? Or why . . .

Don't think about Mama.

And when she got older, they could—

"Look, sweetheart!" He knelt and picked up a red rubber ball some other child had lost. He handed it to Football. "Won't it be fun when we can play ball togeth—"

She promptly stuffed it into her mouth.

"No, it's not an *apple*." He booped her cheeks together and the ball popped out. "Although, good idea. I'm hungry, too."

They continued on, with Football reaching for the ball, Olaf snatching it away at the last moment, both of them laughing. Finally he let her have it—"But no eating, okay?"—and had to pluck it out of her mouth anew. She was a stubborn little thing. How would he parent her alone?

Distracting her insistent lunges with his cold, wet nose, he got her laughing again, and stuck the ball in his coat pocket before hopping the iron railing.

Halfway down the steps to the cave, he froze. He smelled a scent he'd thought he would never smell again. Half of him wanted to run away . . . and half wanted to run toward his best friend.

But she was only here to take back the baby. He stood, unable to move, not knowing what to do.

Essex emerged from the cave, having smelled him, too.

Football cried out with joy and held out her tiny paws. Olaf clutched her tighter. "I can't, Essex. I can't give her up."

"I love you, Olaf." Essex lifted her chin, in that way she did when she was sure of something. "I'm here, with you, no matter what."

Olaf's heart hurt at how unloving he'd been. "I'm sorry for what I said. I didn't mean—"

"I know. I'm sorry, too." She padded over and leaned against his leg.

Something in him released. He sank to the ground. Football squealed and reached for Essex. Olaf held them both tight, like he'd thought he'd never do again.

They were a family. They had always been a family.

Along with Baby, the crotchety old auntie.

THIRTY FIVE

The seasons passed.

Essex was getting older, grayer around the muzzle—which was apparent when she looked into the shiny silver eyeglasses that showed you your snout when you looked at them. The trees whispered, the bad witch was searching; it was not wise to get too comfortable. Still, it was necessary to teach Football to talk like a normal human, not one raised by wolves . . . or by a fox and bear. The baby carrier saw a lot of use. Essex got to watch the shows she'd been missing, and Olaf got to experience, for the first time, the brilliance of Snarky and her buds.

Time spent solely among "wild" animals hadn't seemed to have a negative effect on a developing human. Even Baby had to grumpily acknowledge that Football wouldn't grow up to be "garbage" and dump a poor cat out of a moving car. On family outings in the park, Football would toddle ahead upon spying a stray dog, eager to make its acquaintance.

Thankfully, none of the dogs ever tried to bite her. Instead they lolled at her feet, basking in her tummy rubs. Football also loved to stroke Essex's fur—her muzzle, sides and head—and of course, to boop the snoot. Essex would screech with pleasure, momentarily forgetting *she* was the mama—er, caregiver—in this relationship. Essex often forgot she was a canine, who liked to jump and play. She had been consumed with worries for far too long.

They jumped and played a lot more now.

Olaf would toss a bright yellow ball. Football would squeal and jump to catch it, but it always sailed over her head.

Essex would leap, snag it in her jaws, and land. She'd dodge her young charge and dart to the corner of the cave. Football would laugh and run to catch her, but Essex always swerved and sprinted back to Olaf. She'd drop the ball at his feet, then dash back as he lobbed it in the air.

It was difficult, in such moments, to resist the natural urge to think of Football as one of her own. At others, as when Olaf tried to help Football learn to control her powers, the oddity of their pack came into sharp focus.

He'd bang on the lighter—sparking a tiny flame—and growl, "Fire!" Football would scream, "Haaaaaaaaaaaaaaaaaah!" Aiming her eyes, directing the explosion of flame at her intended target. For now, the log pile. Perhaps, someday, the bad witch.

Someday, she would return to the humans. Someday, she'd be ready. For now, they were happy. Careful. The birds and ducks and Baby helped them.

Except, Essex could tell Olaf's mind and heart sometimes wandered to the past. He would go "shopping" for Football, and be gone all morning. Or he'd leave after lunch, and return only with the stars.

He never said, and Essex never asked. But she knew he was searching for the human who had been like a mother to him.

Sometimes, while Football was sleeping, he would borrow her teddy bear, tuck it under his arm, and wait. Wait to dream. Perhaps anticipating the day he would again see Wendy.

*

Baby kept up their makeshift magic lessons, and Essex continued to teach herself to read, trying to include everyone. Baby turned up her nose at the idea. Olaf also resisted.

"I'm not any good at it," he said.

"But maybe you'll want to read a newspaper," said Essex.

"Why?"

Baby sighed. "To find the parents of the next baby you bring us."

They would stare at puddles of water.

"I see bunnies," said Essex, licking her muzzle.

"Lollipops," said Olaf, drooling into his puddle.

"Focus!" screeched Baby.

They progressed to where Essex and Olaf could see themselves wandering the food palace, which seemed a step up from desiring treats for themselves. But Baby would sit, forlorn, as the puddles only ever showed her the animal shelter.

*

"Look, the next letter is the first letter of lollipops," said Essex one night as they slunk through the candy aisle.

Olaf stopped at a section of brightly-colored packages. Essex leaned farther out of the diaper bag and read, "Dumb-Dumbs."

He grunted. "Couldn't they have been named, 'Hoo-Mans'?"

They shared a good laugh. Softly, so as not to attract the attention of tonight's checkout human. This human had also not looked up at their entrance, and instead continued to sullenly organize the products that had been left on the counter by shoppers who'd changed their minds. The bored teenager was not here tonight. Hopefully she hadn't quit. They'd gotten used to her leaving them supplies.

"How does she always know what we need?" said Olaf. "She *must* be a witch."

"What if she is?" said Essex. "The Nice One is a witch."

"A *nice* witch."

"It's pretty nice of the checkout teenager to leave things out for us."

"Yeah," said Olaf. "Nice and scary."

*

"Mama?"

Sitting by the mouth of the cave, Football paused in the serious work of making mud pies and stared into Essex's eyes.

"Essex," said Essex gently, for the gazillionth time.

"*Mama*," said Football, and Essex sighed. "Why Bolton died?"

Essex laid her head between her paws. This was not an appropriate story just before bedtime. But she didn't want to squash her young charge's curiosity, especially about the natural world.

"Why did Bolton die? It was his time."

"Papa said . . . he was ran over."

"*Olaf* said he was *run* over. Technically, that's true. But that doesn't take away from the order of the Everything. A car and Bolton occupied the same space at the same time. And it was not the car's time."

Football did not seem satisfied by this answer.

"It's a great mystery, how the workings of the fur-and-flesh-beings fit into the plan of the Everything. I will be with Bolton again. When it is my time."

Football clenched her tiny fists, squirting mud out of the spaces between her fingers. "Don't *want* . . . you and Papa . . . die."

Essex stretched and nuzzled Football's cheek. "Everyone dies, sweetheart. I'm not certain about . . . Papa." Now was not the time to insist on calling Olaf, Olaf. "I've seen some very old bears. But I've never heard of a fox living two dozen seasons."

Football started to cry. Essex sighed. She had again said a wrong thing. How did any human grow up sane, with their caregivers constantly making mistakes?

"Sweetheart, don't cry. I *do* hope very much to die before you. That would make me very sad, if you died and I still—"

"No," said Football, tears rolling down her cheeks, perhaps trying to outrun the oncoming temper tantrum. "*You,* never die."

Even before Football had started talking, Essex had learned from spying on the humans how exceedingly difficult it was to reason with a toddler. She tried a different tack. "That's right, sweetheart. I won't ever die. Not really. My body will, but my spirit will always be with you. I will always be with you, in your heart."

"No!" screamed Football at the top of her tiny lungs. She jumped up and stomped her feet, splashing mud. "*You*, never die! Always be here! Never die, ever! *Ever!*"

"Yeah," said Olaf, from where he'd woken up from a nap, propped against the cave wall—exhausted from the endless questions Football asked, now that she was older and could talk to him. "I don't want to live without you ever again."

Essex's heart gave a sharp pang. She was not a magic fox. She'd always known her time would come, many seasons before Olaf's. And now they had Football to worry about.

Baby looked down on them from the top of the steps, scowled at the screaming toddler and mopey bear, and slunk away again.

THIRTY SIX

Damon Thomas leaned back in his chair, staring at a new piece of equipment the Chief Engineer had laid on his desk.

His position as Chief Detector was coming up for reappointment. Which was looking more and more unlikely, given all that had transpired.

He had become the laughingstock of the city, once the "captured witch" turned into his own wife before his very eyes. Said wife quickly and efficiently divorced him. The real witch was still at large. Newspapers routinely ran editorials questioning how good a detector he could be, when he couldn't even detect the whereabouts of his own baby.

A number of witches and other magic-competents had escaped during the faked system malfunction, a fact he couldn't keep quiet. They'd sold their stories to opportunistic journalists, which had resulted in an investigation into departmental procedures. And to top it all off, Stempniewicz—one of the supposedly critically injured Conflict Resolution Professionals, his visage clearly visible in the doctored photo—had been spotted relaxing with a beer in a bar that very night. The resulting photos had gone viral on social media, even before the morning's newspapers came out.

His elder daughter had too much class to speak to the media, apparently, but had been photographed displaying a "**C**hronic **R**otten **P**roblems" badge on her jacket. He couldn't help but suspect she was behind the production and distribution of the popular badges throughout the five boroughs, and even New Jersey.

He'd surely only managed to escape dismissal through all the years of dirt he'd accumulated on his superiors. The Commissioner, the Mayor ... the *moneyed*, who really ran the city. But even that could hold sway only so much longer.

"I know it seems a bit barbaric," said Chief Engineer 'Two Bits' Masseus, bringing Chief Detector Thomas back to the present. "Building a machine to permanently rob a witch of her speech."

"That's not what I was thinking." Chief Detector Thomas eyed the prototype on his desk. It should soon be a fully functional Vocal Cord Eradicator. He looked back over at his colleague with the mockingly tall afro. "It works using frequency?"

"Yes. If we alter the vibration of the vocal cords, we can render them useless."

"Hmm." Chief Detector Thomas drummed his fingers against his head. "It won't *completely* take care of our witch problem, will it?"

"Well, no," said Chief Engineer Masseus, a bit bemusedly. "You *do* know witches use wands, sometimes even their fingers, to direct energy?"

"Of course I know." Chief Detector Thomas banged his chair back on the floor. "I don't suppose we can rig a machine to break their wrists, too?"

"Sir…" Although they were both chiefs, technically Detection presided over Engineering. "Most witches *are* healers."

"Chop them off, then?"

Chief Engineer Masseus steepled his fingers, staring over them at Chief Detector Thomas.

"No, I suppose not." Chief Detector Thomas sighed. "It'd be too noticeable."

Chief Engineer Masseus's barrel-like body slumped ever so slightly, and Chief Detector Thomas could almost swear he heard him mumble, "They don't pay me enough."

But he must have been mistaken, which had never happened before. He gazed at the prototype once more. "It's a start." He picked up the papers on his desk to signal dismissal. "Use all the resources at your disposal to finish it."

THIRTY SEVEN

Mabel was but a shell of her former self.

She had meditated and scryed and lost herself to the point she could feel her eyeballs fuse to her brain, *and* she'd put in the grunt work. She'd continued her systematic search of the Ramble, the North Woods, the Nature Sanctuary and all the fields. She had frightened off scores of squirrels, birds and chipmunks, and been bitten by a raccoon.

She brushed away a persistent fly, shushed Harvey as he nervously nattered on about the recent explosion in the red-tailed hawk population, and continued squeezing through the bushes.

There was only one bright patch in all this mess. Her scrying sessions were growing ever more powerful. She could *feel* the spirits taking over. Images grew clearer. Voices emanated from the black mirror. *Soon . . . soon . . . Patience is required . . .*

Mabel sighed. She had been so very patient, for so very long.

*

Soon . . . the voice said as she sat in the darkened attic, trying not to scratch the rash from the poison ivy that had proved immune to magic. *The bear feels guilt. It will return the child. Wait. Do nothing.*

"What?!?" Mabel almost jolted out of her trance and repelled the helping spirits. She refocused and recentered, then enquired again, from a very calm and non-desperate place, "Why would the bear feel guilty? Why would it return the child?"

It learns and grows. Do nothing. Don't screw it up!

The vague images in the mirror grew sharper. The bear grieving. Leaving the toddler at Brenda's doorstep.

Mabel leapt from her chair and jumped for joy, remembering this time to spring to the side, as her second home also featured a low-hanging chandelier. Of course, she would once again need to finagle her way inside her sister's house and knock her unconscious. But she'd only need to brew one potion, as her sister's divorce had come through. It had been headline news.

She still had some hairs left over from her sister. She'd brew the potion here; it would save a lot of bother.

But wait—a new image was taking shape in the mirror. The elder Hagglebottom sister, drawing her wand . . . firing at Mabel!

Mabel *would* be patient. She would do nothing. She would wait for the bear.

But first, she was going to take care of those infernal Hagglebottoms, once and for all.

From his perch high up in the corner where Fluffy couldn't reach him, Harvey watched and listened in.

He had had enough. He was not a frog, he was a man! Temporarily housed in an inconvenient body. It *wasn't* easy being green, nor tiny.

He waited. Mabel went off, presumably to prepare a new potion, totally forgetting to feed him yet again.

He waited, till Fluffy tired of waiting for him to come down and went to go nap on Mabel's bed.

He waited longer, to make sure Fluffy wasn't just pretending to sleep and lurking behind the door.

Then he made his move.

Mabel staggered down the hallway, enduring the pain of possibly the last physical transformation she'd have to undergo. Before changing back into herself, of course.

She should feed Harvey before they left. She dug out a forkful of leftover meatloaf and plopped it into his dish, which she'd placed next to Fluffy's food bowl to her endless amusement.

"Harvey?" she called in a near whisper. "Come out. We need to go soon, and Fluffy's asleep." Or, so she assumed. Fluffy had been chewing in his sleep as Mabel packed her bag of tools. Dreaming of eating Harvey, probably.

She waited, tapping her foot, and called again. And again. Each time a little bit louder and more impatient.

"Harvey? Where the doggone—"

She huffed and strode into the den—where Fluffy sat, chewing on something. Mabel peered closer, and gasped. A *frog leg* stuck out of his mouth.

Fluffy sucked in the leg, chewed once more, and swallowed.

And shot her a satisfied grin.

A painful sensation tore through Mabel's heart. Images of a younger Harvey surfaced in her mind. A thoughtful Harvey. A kind Harvey. A loving Harvey.

She sighed, and shoved those memories down. That Harvey had left her long ago.

Harvey hopped down the sidewalk, feeling exceedingly bad for the poor female frog he'd tricked into leaping up the steps, hopping over the banister, balancing on the ornamental ledge, and springing through the window—all for the promise of some amphibian affection. Then luring her straight into Fluffy's jaws.

Still, better her than him.

He hopped as fast as his little frog legs would carry him, to warn the fox and bear. This was his chance to redeem himself. And get back at Mabel.

Finally, after what seemed like interminable hops, he spied the entrance to the park. All he had to do was find the younger Hagglebottom sister. She had, at least until recently, been squatting at the castle. Surely she'd be able to—

Something flashed in the air. Oh no, was that a—

Harvey was lifted into the air, carried away by a hawk.

Harvey's spirit floated up into the ether. He watched the hawk eating his lifeless body. His frog body, which he was finally free of. The hawk regurgitated it and fed it to its little hawk babies. Gross!

Still, Harvey's spirit was glad to be done with this lifetime. Harvey had been a bit of a chump.

A heavenly white light opened above, beckoning to him. He rose, and wished good luck to the fox and bear. And the baby.

THIRTY EIGHT

Olaf peeked out from the back of the parked car.

A human had just taken his little dog inside the shelter. Olaf had checked this shelter many times, as it was nearest the park. He still searched for others, but the city stretched far. He'd realized, maybe Wendy owned a car. Maybe the shelter she'd meant to take him to, all those moons ago, was far away after all.

He'd figured he'd find her. Surely she was visiting her girlfriend regularly. She was probably constantly finding birds that had fallen off a branch and had broken a wing. Baby squirrels that had lost their mothers and needed someone to find them. Frogs someone had stepped on (accidentally, of course), that might only need a miniature set of crutches to be set right. All of which, Wendy could do. Wendy *would* do.

He leaned his head against the rubber tire. What if Wendy had left her girlfriend? Like Olaf's father had left his mother? He would never find her.

Unless … He could ask Baby if she'd ever seen Wendy.

Why had he never thought of that? He'd ask Baby if she'd seen the most beautiful human ever. Definitely not sad. Well, maybe sad over her girlfriend. Not pathetic at all.

The doorbell chimed. The human left. Olaf watched him waltz down the sidewalk, secure in his heart that Wendy's girl-friend—or whoever's girlfriend she was—would take good care of his little dog.

Olaf moved away from the car and toward the shelter window. Even though he was unrecognizable in the coat and floppy hat, with all the other accoutrements—Essex had taught him that word—actual humans still looked at him funny. So he tried to keep out of sight, out of the range of their nosy stares.

He looked in, over the cats in their little makeshift houses. The girlfriend-of-whoever was holding the little dog. She looked upset. She spoke animatedly to another human, who was . . .

Wendy.

Olaf blinked. She was just as beautiful as he remembered. With her gentle manner, even when she was arguing. Arguing with her indeed-girlfriend. Holding . . .

What must be their little boy.

Wendy bounced him up and down. Olaf could hear his laughter through the window. It sounded like the chirping of baby birds, even sweeter than blueberries.

Olaf turned, and ran.

*

He sat on a bench in the old zoo grounds and stared at the

remnants of his enclosure, at all the weeds growing like they belonged there.

Something touched his foot. Like Essex had, when she'd asked him, *What would you think if the humans heard us arguing and assumed we were bad parents? What would you think if they stole MY cubs away?*

He'd always thought Wendy would be proud of him for caring for Football, just as she'd cared for him after he'd lost his mother. If Wendy knew he'd stolen Football from the real mother, maybe she *wouldn't* be proud. Maybe...maybe she'd be disappointed. Maybe he'd only assumed the real mother was bad.

Maybe his mother would be disappointed in him, too.

Maybe everyone had been right. Maybe he loved Football *too* much. Maybe he'd seen what he wanted to see. Heard what he wanted to hear.

He sat there on the bench, and didn't even feel better when an adolescent bird alighted on his shoulder.

Had Football's real mother really mistreated her? He tried to think back to that day, to what he'd really seen and heard. Had she *really* told Football to shut up? Or had he just imagined it? Had she truly neglected to feed her? Maybe Essex had been right. A mother and baby, separated for so long, wouldn't be in sync.

It was hard to think clearly, when one felt so deeply.

He looked down. A big bug crawled off his foot, onto the ground. He bent and plucked it from the dirt. Normally he would tuck it in his diaper bag and bring it home for the whole family to share. Now he held it for the bird, which promptly ate it.

★ 284 ✿

He'd always thought *he* was what was best for Football. He and Essex. But they had Football eating bugs, and liking it! She couldn't stay in the cave with them forever. He'd always known that. Once she rejoined human society, all the other humans would make fun of her for eating bugs. And worms, fried or otherwise.

He slowly reached out his paw and gently patted the bird on the head. He was grateful it was here. It would help give him the strength he needed to do the right thing, once and for all.

*

Essex and Football were play-wrestling when he got back. Football was laughing. But Essex had remembered to put away the lighter.

Olaf took off his coat, his hat, his scarf and mask. All the human accoutrements that had clouded his mind to the fact he was not a human. He was not what was best for Football. He had never been.

The not-real-after-all family shared the dinner he'd brought. A fruit, vegetable, and hummus plate from the deli section. Not-chocolate milk from the dairy section (chocolate was poisonous to animals). Bread from the lumpy section. Dumb-Dumbs from the best section.

Football giggled as Essex read her a bedtime story—the "funnies" from the newspaper. Essex was quite proud she could read enough words for the funnies to, well, be funny.

Afterward, Football demanded more. Olaf made up a scary story about a human child who would not go to sleep and the big bad bear who gobbled down the stubborn child, then burped really loud and went to sleep himself.

Football merely laughed, not finding this story at all realistic. Finally, after an exhausting tickle session, she fell asleep.

"What's wrong?" said Essex, who'd been looking at him worriedly all through dinner.

Olaf hung his head. "I did a bad thing. I think I was wrong about Football's mother. Maybe I really saw what I wanted to see. Heard what I wanted to hear."

Essex tilted her head, the way she did when she didn't really understand.

"I found Wendy today."

Essex's golden eyes widened. "Isn't that what you wanted?"

"She has a cub of her own."

Essex laid her head on her paws. "And you think . . ."

"If someone were to come by and hear Wendy and her girlfriend arguing and assume they were bad parents . . ."

"But you were right about the first set of supposed parents. They were the bad witch and her frog."

Olaf reached for the remnants of the teddy bear. "I was right then. But I was wrong about Football's mother." He hid his face behind the lowest lump. "Maybe I just *wanted* her to be a bad mother. So I could keep Football. I did a bad thing."

Essex reached out a paw, and gently touched his. "No, Olaf. Just . . . misguided, maybe."

He looked out from behind Bearington. There was no judgment in his best friend's eyes. Only love and care.

For a while, there was only the sound of breathing and Football's soft, sleepy murmuring.

Essex glanced at Football in the corner. She seemed to be fast asleep. Just in case, Essex whispered, "We'll have to wait to tell her till just before. Otherwise, she won't leave us."

Olaf nodded. Essex wanted to close her eyes, so she wouldn't have to see the pain in his. But she forced herself to stay with him, till he fell asleep.

THIRTY NINE

"When shall we three meet again? In thunder, lightning, or in rain?"

Mabel glanced at the ceiling, at the magical ice floe slowly melting. She smirked at her captives, bound and gagged, trussed up on the chairs in the downstairs makeshift kitchen.

"In rain, it seems."

A "raindrop" fell from the ceiling onto her head. She turned up the battery-powered space heater, in this tiny room in a fake castle surprisingly similar to the ones she and the Hagglebottoms had been shackled in over the centuries.

The water was already up to their ankles.

Mabel rubbed her palms together. "Unlike on *Snarky* every week, I haven't accidentally left you any recourse. Yes, the One energy is everywhere. Right at your fingertips. But good luck directing it to loosen those ropes without your wands, without even sacred sound. I've taken everything from you, and soon, I'll have your very lives, too."

She turned to the elder Hagglebottom. The one she hated so

much, she almost didn't want to kill her, in hopes of not having to meet her again in the next life. "Add one more drowning to your tally."

"Mmpfh mmpppppfh mmm mm𝐦𝐦𝐦 mmm mpfh."

Mabel looked over as the younger sister struggled to speak through her gag.

"I *am* getting away with it, actually. The bear is practically on his way to return the child to me as we speak. Or, as *I* speak. Ha!"

She glanced over her shoulder, at the wands she'd so tantalizingly placed right there on the counter. So near, yet so far.

"As much as I'd enjoy staying and watching the proceedings, I mustn't miss the bear. See you in the next life, Hagglebottoms. Unfortunately."

FORTY

As dawn broke, Olaf zipped up Football's poofy jacket. The jacket the baby store had so kindly, unknowingly donated. Carefully, he stuck the tip of his claw into the tiny hole and pulled up the metal. It was extra cold when night was just turning into day.

"Say goodbye to Baby, sweetheart. We never know if we'll see her again, right? Today could be the day she finds her Betty."

Football hugged Baby—gently, like Essex had taught her—while Baby grimaced and endured it like she always did. It was easy to tell that Football expected Baby would always be here, no matter what they said.

Essex jumped into a brand new rucksack Olaf had "borrowed." He pulled the flap over her—allowing for enough air—picked up Football, and slung the sack over his shoulders. Bursting at the seams with a donated car seat and Football's things, which he'd packed during the night. She reached out a paw, pulled his mask and let it snap back, laughing at her reflection in the shiny silver eyeglasses that showed her her nose when she looked at them.

They started on their way out the cave, like almost any other family outing. Football had no way of knowing she wasn't coming back.

"Good riddance," hissed Baby, but once they were gone she seemed to meow sadly.

*

In front of the real mother's door, Olaf arranged Football in the car seat, just so. With the seat belt that locked her in. It had been hard enough to figure out how to fasten it last night; she wouldn't be able to get free. His throat tightening, he leaned the rucksack against the door with the rest of Football's things. Though Essex could read, she unfortunately couldn't write a note, at least not legibly. Still, the real mother would understand somehow. Olaf hoped she would understand, too, that he was sorry.

"Visit?" Football looked curiously at the door. "Papa's Mama?"

Olaf and Essex looked at each other.

Essex sat on her haunches. She touched Football's knee with her paw. "Sweetheart, you know Olaf and I love you. That's why we have to leave you now. We're not your real parents. We were never meant to keep you."

Football stared blankly back.

Essex sighed. She leaned in and nuzzled Football's neck.

Football squealed with laughter, surely not understanding.

Olaf couldn't bear it. But he had to, just a little longer. He knelt in front of the only child he'd ever known. The only child he'd ever have.

"This isn't goodbye," he said, holding Football's tiny face carefully in his paws. "Not for good. We'll come visit. We promise."

He nuzzled her nose. She screamed with laughter, as his nose was probably cold.

"I love you," he said, and refrained from adding, *more than anyone, more than any human ever will.* It was true, but probably not helpful in this situation.

He let go, rose on his hind legs, and rang the bell. And pounded on the door for good measure. He and Essex ran down the stoop, Football screaming after them.

This time, not with laughter.

*

They waited, and watched behind the nearest car.

Football shrieked, kicking her little legs, scrabbling at the seat belt with both paws. She dropped the teddy bear.

Olaf couldn't stand it. He rose—

"We can't." Essex gently touched his leg, knowing how badly he wanted—needed—to rush to Football's side. To comfort her. Even if he had to say goodbye all over again. "We can't, Olaf."

He sank down and dug his claws into the rubber tire. He had failed. Failed Football. Failed as a fake father. She would have been better off without him, all along.

The door swung open. The mother emerged, a look on her face like she'd been expecting Football all along, but had perhaps been caught momentarily in the bathroom. She shiftily looked about. (Essex whispered to Olaf, this was understandable, as the mother was surely wondering how her child had mysteriously appeared on her doorstep.)

The mother lugged Football inside in her car seat, ignoring the screaming. She came back for the rucksack and shut the door. Muffling Football's frenzied cries of "Papa! Mama!"

Essex leaned against Olaf's leg, as the tire decompressed and the car sank even lower. "I know it's hard now. But it'll get better. We *will* come visit. Just, not right away. We have to give her time to get used to her mother."

Olaf nodded and leaned his head against the tire. A few moments later, Essex nudged him with her nose. It was time to go. They trudged back home.

Why anyone ever wanted to love anyone was a great mystery. Everyone always got taken away, without you being ready.

FORTY ONE

Once again, aligning her energies to the child's was proving exceedingly difficult. But not impossible. Fluffy now sported one bulging frog eye. He went tearing through the house, screeching. Mabel couldn't help but chuckle.

The doorbell rang. That would be the pizza delivery boy. She strode to the hallway.

"Alexa! Open the door."

The security system flashed and beeped. The locks rattled. The door opened.

"Al ... ex? Alex ... ah?"

Darn toddlers ... repeating everything everyone said ... Mabel shoved the little brat into the closet, where it continued its babbling, and reached for her pocketbook.

Or, Brenda's pocketbook. Ha!

FORTY TWO

Baby waited at Jack's door, her head hanging limply. Her limbs ached—but worse, hurt her heart. She just wanted to crawl onto his bed and fall asleep. And fall into a dream where she finally had her Betty, and never wake.

Danger...

She swiveled her head, and pricked up her ears. Had that sound—*word?*—really come from the beech in the grate?

She stared, then swung around as the doorknob turned and Jack's nose appeared just underneath. Barking emanated from within. It was a *Guard Dogs of New York* night.

The sound from the tree grate had only been her imagination. She squeezed into the small space. Jack nosed the door shut.

FORTY THREE

Hilda gazed at their wands lying right there on the coun-
tertop, just out of reach. The water was up to their belly
buttons. The magic ice floe was melting exponentially.

Soon they were going to drown.

She looked at her sister, trying to express all the love she'd
never verbalized. Asking for forgiveness for her own extremely
tiny share of the blame for their often-contentious relationship.
This would be the last time they ever saw each other. In this
lifetime.

Her sister's kind eyes smiled back. She knew. She'd always
been able to see past Hilda's gruff exterior, into her very soul.

A sudden movement caught Hilda's eye. She turned her
head.

A crow flew in through the stairwell, something shiny in
its beak.

*

Hilda finished cutting through the ropes that bound her sister with the very useful piece of broken glass. She fished a soggy biscuit out of her pocket and held it out to the crow on her shoulder.

"I never doubted you."

The gray cat, of course, was nowhere in sight. It had surely run off to save itself and find a new sucker to mooch off of.

Her sister waded to the counter and took up her wand. A moment later, the rising water turned into vapor, then dissipated into the air. Hilda did the same with the ice floe, changing its form before the melted water could even hit the ground.

She turned to her sister. "Let's go get Blackthornudder."

Finally, they agreed on something. They ran up the narrow stairwell and grabbed their brooms.

"She's disguised herself as her sister. Brenda, I think her name was?"

"Who cares? She must be at the sister's. Let's move!"

Her own sister smiled, wasting precious time. "Isn't this wonderful? Maybe in our next life we won't have such a contentious relationship, now that you've acknowledged—"

"Nothing. I acknowledge nothing." Hilda mounted her broom.

Her sister's eyes twinkled. "Yes, while we were tied up and you looked so very sad …"

"Oh, go stick your head in a newspaper, why don't you?"

They flew off through the window, the crow following.

FORTY FOUR

*D*anger...
Olaf opened his eyes. Something had woken him, something that sounded just like the wind. Except the wind was telling him something was wrong.

Football needed him.

He looked to the corner, where Essex had moved sometime during the night. To sleep where Baby usually slept. Maybe she, too, felt their little family falling apart.

He rose, lumbered over, and shook his best friend.

Essex woke with a start. "What—what's wrong, Olaf?"

"I don't know. I just know we have to go. To get Football."

Essex stared at him. Her gold eyes flashed. She was going to argue with him again, say—

"I trust you, Olaf. Let's go get her back."

FORTY FIVE

Mabel screamed.

The front door was open. The child was gone. Fluffy, who had woken her by pouncing on her head for no reason at all, had gone back to bed, unconcerned.

That infernal bear!

It was after hours. Animal Control would be closed. But the officer had, stupidly, given her his card.

She stomped to the phone in the bedroom. He sleepily picked up. She proceeded to give him a piece of her mind, while getting dressed and grabbing her broom and wand. She hung up, and remembered to shut and lock the front door. How in blazes had the bear gotten it to open from outside?

Had it been a mistake to call Animal Control? What if the officer felt inspired to get up and go hunt for the bear, and they crossed paths? He would just get in the way.

She already felt the pangs and ripples inside her body, the start of the slow and terrible transformation back to her true self. But she couldn't wait to ride it out. She had to get the child.

She needed strength. She closed her eyes, opened her arms wide—Brenda had a six-foot wingspan, after all—and called the evil spirits to her. It was dangerous, but she did not need to keep them. She only needed to borrow them awhile.

The spirits happily complied. Their darkness filled her energy body . . . moved on to and through her physical body . . . her energy centers, organs, tendons and ligaments, to her very cells. She could *feel* the last vestiges of her sanity slowly spooling down the cesspool of her mind. Just like Lady Macbeth. Except, Mabel's husband was already dead.

She snapped her eyes open and mounted her broom. Wait—she could use a cat to go after the fox while she took care of the bear. Finally, Fluffy would earn his keep.

"Come, Fluffy!"

. . .

"Fluffy, come!"

. . .

"Fluffy! Come here this instant!"

. . .

"Fluf—" Eh, what was the use? She really needed a new familiar. Perhaps, next time, a toad.

FORTY SIX

Olaf and Essex raced through the woods. Birds they knew enquired, what was so important that they were in such a hurry? But they had no time to stop and answer questions.

The birds followed them anyway.

Stray dogs Football had comforted came running out of nowhere, and squirrels, and birds Olaf didn't even know. Even his bunny friend Bert poked his head out from his den, thumped his tail, and scampered to catch up. A duck woke as they passed over the bridge, squawked and flapped its wings, and fell in with them. Angry geese, too. (Geese were always angry about something.) Sleepy bats emerged from under the bridge and swarmed over.

And somehow Olaf knew, his mother was with them, too.

Mabel flew with a burning rage through the black and purple sky. If the fox and bear thought they were going to stand in the way of her getting that child back, they had another think coming!

Think? Thing? Eh, who cared?! Harvey was no longer around to correct her.

Olaf's pounding heart skipped a beat.

Football ran toward them down the human footpath, as fast as her little legs would carry her. Which was not fast at all. The half-moon shone as brightly as if it were full, lighting her way so she wouldn't trip over the cobblestone edge and—

Fall.

She pushed herself back up off the ground, as Olaf pushed himself to run even faster, faster than he'd ever run before. To reach her before—

Mabel swooped into the park, so close to the child she could almost reach down and—

"Aaaaaaiiiiiiiiiiiiiiiiiiiiiiiiiiiiiiiiiii!"

Sharp beaks pecked at her head, her ears, her eyes! A swarm of birds surrounded her—a duck, angry geese, and *bats*, on top of everything else! She struggled to control her broom, keep her balance and not—

Fall.

Into the road, skidding to a stop as her traitorous broom traveled on without her.

She rolled onto her back, drew her wand, and fired. *Fired!* She didn't care who or whom she struck. She fired wildly, her arms flailing as the birds and bats insisted on braving her attacks and homed in on her head.

Olaf pulled Football into his arms. She was *his* to protect. His and Essex's. He turned his back, so whatever awful things shooting from the magic stick of the—*real mother?*—wouldn't hit her.

Something sharp pierced his shoulder. He kept steady, even as Football yelled to let go so she could help fight Strange Lady. All around him animals went flying—stray dogs, bats, birds, squirrels . . . even Bert. Some frozen solid. Some—

Essex screeched and was thrown all the way across the road, her torn ear shot clean off.

"Papa! Leggo! Mama need help!"

If only he'd thought to bring the lighter!

He gazed at friends lying prone on the ground, pinned by daggers of ice. He turned and stared as Strange Lady twirled her magic stick.

He looked at Football, and an idea struck. Just because they'd never tried her powers on ice, didn't mean they wouldn't work.

"Football," he whispered. "Fire!"

He swung her around. She screamed.

"Haaaaaaaaaaaaaaaaaaaaaaaaaaaaaaaaaaaaaah!"

The ice darts halted in mid-air.

They seemed to collectively decide something, turned—and like a formation of birds in the sky, attacked as one, amplified.

Mabel gasped, as the only dependable minions she'd ever had—not Harvey, not Fluffy, *no one*, just the powers at her command—*turned* on her.

There was only one thing to do.

She thrust her wand in the air, and channeled Lady Macbeth. "Come, you spirits that tend on mortal thoughts ... Fill me from the crown to the toe top-full of direst cruelty!" (She left out the "unsex me" because ... have you *done* an internet search on evil women throughout history?!?)

The ice darts exploded into harmless flurries. Invigorated, she fired at the wind. It buffeted the bear and made him lose hold of the child. Mabel pulled it to her. It clung to the bear's paw.

But Mabel was stronger.

Hilda and her sister flew over the treetops, the real Brenda perched precariously on the back of Helga's broom—and from the looks of it, trying not to lose her lunch. (That is, if Blackthornudder had even bothered to feed her.)

After they'd discovered the panic room, Helga had worried Brenda needed to lie down. Rest. But Brenda insisted on coming along. Hilda reluctantly agreed. After all, the child *was* hers. And no one deserved revenge on Blackthornudder more than—well, Hilda, actually. But Brenda came in a close second.

"Incoming!" called Helga, swerving out of the way of a

horrendous gust of wind. Brenda lost her balance and fell—

Helga reached out and grabbed her. She was slowing them down!

Another gale thundered at them. Helga banked hard to the left, with Brenda *again* not pulling her weight, slipping off the broom and having to be saved.

"Come *on!*" Hilda glared at her sister. Helga nodded and shot toward the ground. As Helga helped a green-faced Brenda (*not* a sign of latent magical ability, mind you, just inner weakness) dismount, Hilda harrumphed and turned forward—

Only to be thrown back with the force of a hurricane.

Olaf ground his teeth as Football clung to his paw, the wind whirling and howling around them. She kept slowly slipping. He couldn't dislodge his other paw's claws from the tree root, or they would both be sucked right at Strange Lady.

Without opposable thumbs, he couldn't hold onto Football. *She* needed to hold onto *him*, and she wasn't that strong. He was going to lose her.

A tremendous din sounded over the wind. Olaf looked past Strange Lady, toward the gap in the park wall.

In ran dogs—dozens of dogs. Ducking under the wind blasts. Swerving to the sides. Or simply jumping over each incoming gale. All led by a Golden Retriever.

And riding his back, Baby, yowling at the garbage human who was going to get hers.

Strange Lady twirled madly, directing the furious gusts of wind while desperately attempting to evade the bats and birds that pecked at her relentlessly, the squirrels that clawed, the stray dogs that bit (and even peed on her a little bit). Olaf's winged and furry friends got thrown all the way across the road, but determinedly turned back and attacked again and again.

The wind pulling at him weakened, then vanished altogether. Essex ran off, Strange Lady's magic stick in her jaws. Olaf let go of the tree and tugged Football to safety.

The Golden Retriever neared. He wore a blue collar and brown harness, which strangely, seemed to be wriggling.

Baby leapt off Jack's back and hurled herself into the melee, along with the Guard Dogs of New York. Good thing Jack had heard the talking beech, too, or she would have missed out on helping her friends. Missed out on vengeance!

The top of her head tickled. Earl was crouching, getting ready . . .

Olaf's heart leapt at Essex's victory. At Baby clawing at Strange Lady's hair. At Strange Lady screeching. At—

A tiny roach leaping off Baby's head?

It flew up Strange Lady's nose and she screamed like she was dying. Arms flailing, almost tripping over the curb, she half-blindly tottered under the nearest tree, where squirrels dropped onto her hair. Or, what was left of it.

Strange Lady shrieked even louder. She pulled something out of her pocket—

A knife!

Olaf needed to help—but he couldn't put Football in danger. If he set her down, she would run to help.

Strange Lady wildly slashed and hacked. The dogs launched themselves onto her, braving the thrusts of the knife, biting, biting, biting—

Screaming—slashing—screaming—slashing—

Football struggled in Olaf's arms. He hung on harder, keeping her safe, his heart crying out at the slaughter of his friends, even the ones he hadn't yet met.

The Golden Retriever's harness broke apart—

It wasn't a harness at all.

Hundreds of tiny roaches clinging to the dog's fur let go. They jumped onto Strange Lady, slithering into her ears, crawling up her curls, sliding into—

Olaf had never heard a living being scream so loud. What could be worse than dying?

Strange Lady broke free and ran up the road leading out of the park.

Everyone still alive fell to the ground. They watched the evil human go. They turned to each other and cheered. They had done it!

Jack lowered himself onto the gravel and gently nuzzled Earl. His friend was tiny, but not to be underestimated. Not to be dismissed.

FORTY SEVEN

Mabel ran, swiping at the birds-from-hell that pecked at her relentlessly, the cheering of the vermin and other woodland pests reverberating through the air.

Something wriggled in her cleavage. She pulled out a roach, shrieked, and threw it to the ground. She resumed defending herself against the winged assaults—which mingled with the building pain inside her. The transformation back to her real self wasn't far off.

A gray van veered off Central Park West and roared down the road into the park, scattering birds. It screeched to a stop so as not to hit Mabel. That incompetent Animal Control officer hopped out, brandishing his net and rifle, neither of which had done any good whatsoever in the two years he'd been searching for the bear.

He opened his mouth to say something useless as usual—but Mabel grabbed him by his collar and jerked him to the ground. Even being only her sister's height had its advantages.

She jumped in the van, pulled the door shut—just *try*, birds, to get at her now!—and turned the key Animal Control had so helpfully left in the ignition.

Olaf looked to the bend in the road. Strange Lady had truly vanished. He and his friends were safe. He loosened his hold on Football. She broke free and ran to help a stray dog that had collapsed onto the ground.

He teared up as he gazed at the dead bodies all around him. He would need to bury his friends, who had given their very lives to help him.

A *ROAR* sounded in the distance. He looked up. A van sped down the road toward them, Strange Lady at the wheel.

He ran. He had time—the road turned, heading away from them. He could grab Football before—

The van jumped the curb, heading straight for her.

"Leave the dog! Football!"

She didn't hear, so focused on comforting the dog that was going to die anyway. But not Football—she couldn't—

A blur of orange—a screech of pain—

Essex flew through the air for the second time ... this time slowly. This time hurt worse, she thought idly ... not just her ear, but her entire body.

Strange Lady skidded and veered back onto the road—then plowed right onto the footpath leading into the woods. Possibly aware of Hilda and Helga swooping in on their brooms, hot on her tail.

Football lay a few body-lengths away, safe. The stray dog had been knocked to the side, still breathing. Essex must have hit the ground a few moments ago, but she couldn't remember. She couldn't feel anything.

"Mama?" Football got up on her hands and knees, and

crawled toward her. Just as Olaf's big feet pounded the gravel and stopped in front of them.

Olaf knelt and closed his arms around Football, staring down at his fallen friend. She was just as still as his mother had been.

His best friend feebly stretched out a paw. Her gold eyes dimmed. Then the light went out altogether.

Essex's spirit floated up into the ether, toward the shining light. It was so bright. Everything felt peaceful. The pain was gone.

She heard crying below and looked down. At Olaf and Football.

Don't cry—I'm right here, she rushed to reassure them. Her paws scrabbled in the air—

Except, they didn't. She had no paws anymore. Her paws were with her still body, which her friends were crying over.

"Don't!" said a human voice. "You could hit the child!" said another.

"Back off, Jackson. Gardner," said a third. "This one's mine."

Olaf looked up from the body of his dead friend—and froze.

Two humans in yellow were staring at a human in gray. Who was holding a rifle.

Who had shot his mother.

Run, Olaf! cried Essex. But he could not hear her.

Baby hissed. She recognized the human in gray. He had never caught her with that stupid net. And he never would.

He aimed his rifle. Two humans in yellow had screeched to a halt and gotten out of their car, yelling at him to stop.

"Run, Olaf!" she screamed.

Her friend did not move. It was as if he were frozen to the ground.

And Baby knew she would never see her Betty again. Because Olaf needed her.

She leapt at her friend and that horrible little human, who couldn't be that bad, really, because Olaf loved her.

CRACK!

Olaf lost his balance as his little friend crashed into him. He kept one arm tight around Football, steadied himself with a paw on the ground, and slowly stood.

He stared at Baby, lying still on the gravel. No—he couldn't have lost them both—

Run, Olaf!

A bevy of voices called to him. He couldn't tell where they were coming from. But he obeyed.

~ FORTY EIGHT ~

Essex's spirit watched as her best friend tucked Football under his arm, and ran.

Football cried out and reached for Essex's motionless body. "Papa! Leggo! Mama need help!"

Essex screeched, *I don't need help—I can help YOU! I—why can't they hear me?*

They will, said a voice she knew. And loved. And had missed. Bolton.

More accurately, a ball of light. A ball of light within the brighter light. But she knew it was him. And not far behind him …

Cubby? she cried. She hadn't known—

Car, said Bolton. He smiled. Or, the ball of light smiled, somehow. *It seems the berry really doesn't fall far from the tree.*

Apple, said Essex.

What?

Nothing, she said. *I'm so happy to be with you again.*

They nuzzled, and it felt just like it had on Earth, except . . . more intense.

Essex looked past Bolton. There were her mother and father, her grandmother, and . . . Olaf's mother.

Sounds below made her look down. The humans in yellow—now she knew what was truly yellow, and that truly, there was no yellow—ran after Olaf, into the woods. But humans were slow. They wouldn't catch him.

The human in gray shoved Baby's body into a sack and slung it over his shoulder. He muttered, "Got one, at least," and took her away.

But Baby would be okay; Essex just knew it. She understood now, about the trees.

Hilda and her sister swooped under the canopy of leaves, right on Blackthornudder's tail as the van plowed through the twisting footpaths of the Ramble. Hilda fired her wand. Blackthornudder swerved, then tore into the shrubbery and black iron fencing, before righting and veering back onto the path. She lunged out the driver's side window and fired.

Hilda swung out of the way of the ice blast. Her sister rose through a break in the leaves.

Blackthornudder fired again, before turning her eyes back to the road.

A tiny clearing loomed up ahead. Hilda banked right and fired—just as Blackthornudder aimed, taking her eyes off the road.

The blast hit her wrist. Her wand shot out of her hand and she jerked. The van jumped the cobblestone curb and careened onto a dirt path, heading straight for Muggers' Woods.

Hilda's sister swooped down into the van's path.

Blackthornudder stepped on the gas to try to run her over. But Helga shot out of the way. The van plowed through the iron fencing, through the shrubs—

CRASH!

Hilda and her sister alighted, leapt off their brooms and ran through the dense brush. They came upon the van, its engine idling, having smashed into the great black tupelo. Blackthornudder must have jumped out in transit like an idiot and hit her head. She lay on her back, in obvious pain. Moaning pathetically, an embarrassment to witches everywhere.

The crow sat on Blackthornudder's shoulder, doing its finest impression of a woodpecker on her big blockhead. (Even if she did still look like the less stupid sister.) The black tupelo stared down at them with satisfaction.

Hilda sighed. Small pleasures couldn't last forever. Blackthornudder had tried to kill her and her sister. And reciprocation was important in any relationship. She aimed her wand.

"No, dear sister, don't!" Helga held out a pleading hand. "Think of your next life—yet another wrong you'll have to right."

Hilda clenched her teeth. Of *course* her sister would worry for her. For her very soul, should she take a life. Which she'd done in other, more satisfying lifetimes, when her sister hadn't stuck her big nose into Hilda's business.

Maybe that was why this lifetime had burned so.

"Gaaaaaaaaaaaaaaaaaaaaaaaaah!"

She switched the intention in her heart. The sacred syllables on her tongue. She chanted—the wand reacted—Blackthornudder cringed—

And was bound by ropes, just waiting for the pigs to find her.

"Have fun in prison, Blackthornudder. Orange is not your color. Come, sister."

Her not-totally-annoying-after-all sister beamed and touched her arm. "*Dear* sister."

"Don't push it."

Mabel smirked as the Hagglebottoms strolled away as if they didn't have a care in the world, the elder Hagglebottom's wand hanging loosely from her fingertips. Mabel was already turning back into herself. An entire foot taller. Her bones expanded—she gritted her teeth to keep from screaming—the ropes strained—

And snapped. She sprang up and forward, and lunged for the unprotected wand. Before the Hagglebottoms could even turn around, Mabel had it.

She aimed. She would do what the elder sister didn't have the strength of character to do—*finish* her opponent.

The wand fell from her hand.

Mabel no longer had fingers! At least, not the ones she was used to.

Ribbit!

Mabel hopped about, horrified to suddenly find herself so much shorter than everyone and everything else.

"I knew it!" said Hilda. "I *knew* you were holding out on me!"

Her sister picked up the wand and handed it to her. "I

suppose it had to be done. But I don't feel good about it."

"Poetic justice, is what it is. You've got to teach me to do that!"

"I don't think it's something you *can* teach. I just sort of winged it."

"*Come* on! Er, dear sister . . ."

Helga smiled, a nauseating twinkle in her eye. "Trying to bribe me now, hmm?"

"Oh, go stick your head in a computer, why don't you?"

FORTY NINE

What was worse than dying, was being left behind.

Olaf stared at where his best friend had given up her life for them. Only blood marked the ground now. He was too late to bury her. A hawk had already carried her off, or maybe a coyote.

He sat on the curb and hung his head. He had failed his friend yet again.

The shadows moved, reminding him there was more to be done. He heaved himself up, and lumbered to the remaining bodies of the dogs. The squirrels. The birds and bats. Bert, his bunny friend. Everyone who had helped him last night, in ways he could never repay.

There had been so many bodies. Too many, even, for the hawks and coyotes. He dug graves by the trees. He set flowers he had plucked along the way to mark them. He said prayers to the Everything.

The teddy bear lay on the ground where Football had dropped it. Olaf knelt and picked it up. It had been through too much with them to be left behind, even if it was now not much more than a dirt-encrusted ball of fuzz.

He sighed, and set off to find Baby.

*

Gently nudging an inquisitive squirrel back under his coat, Olaf pushed open the door of the seventh animal shelter he'd visited today.

Surely he looked like a human about to hibernate for two winters straight, with all the squirrels that had wanted to come along to help spring Baby. But so far, they'd had no luck. Of course, he'd visited Wendy's girlfriend's shelter first. But no one he loved had been there.

The door tinkled like baby birds, announcing his presence. But no one inside looked up. Everyone was looking at a little girl, and ...

Baby.

She lay curled over the little girl's shoulder, her eyes squeezed shut. Happy. For the first time Olaf had ever seen her.

Smiling humans hovered over the little girl. The shelter human grinned. "That's the great thing about chips. Every pet should have one."

Olaf tilted his head. *One?* One could certainly not stop at one potato chip. Especially if there was a great big bag of them available.

The adult male and female watching the little girl squeezed each other's paws. "I'm so glad we thought to get in touch and update the contact information," said the female. "Anything for our new little girl."

Baby gently thumped her tail against Betty's back. *Her* Betty, at last!

And the horrible humans were gone. Betty was being taken care of by two other humans, who had not yet exhibited any horrible behavior. Humans who even had the courage to smile at Baby, and pet her, too.

Where had the horrible parents gone?

Baby purred, her heart warming even more. Perhaps Betty had *eaten* them.

She opened her eyes, sensing Betty and her new parents moving toward the door.

Olaf stood there, wearing the floppy hat. The stupid silver eyeglasses that blew up your nose when you looked at them. Who did he think he was fooling, with all those lumps under his coat? That was one misshapen "human" right there.

Of course, the real humans were too dumb to notice. Except for Betty. And Betty only had eyes for Baby right now.

Baby rubbed against Betty's neck. As they neared the exit, Baby looked back at Olaf. He waved a mittened paw.

And there was Essex, smiling, shimmering over his shoulder.

Baby smiled and flicked her tail in farewell. She would miss them. But she had her Betty now, and all was right with the world.

FIFTY

Essex's spirit watched as Football slept peacefully in Olaf's arms, having screamed and cried till she'd tuckered herself out.

Olaf had finally fallen asleep. Exhausted from being strong for Football, unable to cry for Essex, too.

Essex nuzzled Football's cheek. *Sweetheart, I would have died soon anyway, and now you are safe.*

"Safe …" murmured Football.

Whenever you need me, I will be here. You only need call.

"Call …" Football opened her eyes, saw Essex and smiled. She reached out her tiny fingers. Essex laid her "muzzle" inside Football's little palm. Football sighed, and fell back asleep.

Hopefully, she would remember.

Essex moved to Olaf and nuzzled his shoulder. *Olaf, it was just a body on a road. You haven't let me down.*

Olaf swatted her away, thinking she was a flea, or a fly.

She would keep trying.

FIFTY ONE

"So we've discovered, if we make the machine a bit too strong, the resulting physical damage to a witch's vocal cords could be proven in court to—"

"It could be from smoking," said Chief Detector Thomas, leaning back in his chair. He stared at the prototype back on his desk, unfinished, even after all the money the department had poured into it.

"That excuse would never fly." Chief Engineer Masseus ran his hand over his afro unnecessarily. "Nicotine remains in the system longer than a person can quit cold turkey, and it could be proven—"

"Chronic acid reflux," suggested Chief Detector Thomas, drumming his fingers against his head.

"No, no, no." Chief Engineer Masseus rubbed his sideburns, which he'd been ostentatiously growing. "No one would believe a proper witch couldn't cure her own acid reflux."

"Improper singing technique, then! Everyone knows witches are terrible singers!"

"Au contraire. Some of the most celebrated sopranos of our time—"

"That's neither here nor there." Chief Detector Thomas brought his chair down with a *bang*. "What do you need to get the machine's vocal-sapping strength to the point it will be both effective and untraceable to this department?"

"It could work through resonance to another's perfectly tuned vibration." Chief Engineer Masseus sighed. "This isn't what you want to hear, but we'd need to hook it to an amplifier."

"Not a problem," said Chief Detector Thomas. "I play a bit of bass on the side. Just a hobby, really. My stuff is too highbrow for the masses, you understand."

"I . . . do?"

"I'll just bring in my amp and—"

"Oh no, no." Chief Engineer Masseus chuckled, as if Chief Detector Thomas had just told a joke. "A human amplifier."

"Excuse me?"

"We've had reports of the prisoners discussing it. Some magic-competents are born 'amplifiers.' They can enhance another user's magic, also through vocalization. They instinctively operate on the same subatomic principles science has—"

"Where do we *acquire* such an amplifier?"

"That's the problem, *sir*. We've only heard of it as an abstraction. Whether an actual living amplifier exists now or will in the near future—"

"Get out of my office, and don't come back till you're not a complete waste of time and funding."

Chief Detector Thomas turned back to the monitor on his desk and resumed playback of the surveillance footage from last night's disturbance in Central Park. A number of witches *and* his kidnapped daughter had been spotted—but not, as one would assume with all the resources at the department's disposal, apprehended.

Chief Engineer Masseus sighed, got up from his chair, and left, this time *definitely* mumbling, "They don't pay me enough."

Chief Detector Thomas dismissed from his mind this excuse-for-a-chief, who obviously cared more about other things than ridding the city of human vermin. And who had, unfairly, been blessed with a full head of hair.

He stared at his screen, drumming his head as his daughter was held aloft by the bear, which had managed to elude not only his Professionals, but that incompetent Animal Control officer as well. (Animal Control was severely underfunded.) *Where to get such an amplifier?* His daughter opened her mouth and screamed … *Where, where, where* … The witch's ice blasts halted in mid-air and reversed course. *Where, where*—

He leapt to his feet, dashed out of his office, and raced after the Chief Engineer—glad there was no need to apologize, as he was technically superior.

FIFTY TWO

The sun shone through the mouth of the cave. A crow flew in, carrying something in its beak.

Olaf gently set Football and her teddy bear to the side, and crept softly toward the crow. It laid a lighter at his feet. Olaf picked it up. It felt half-full, and should last him and Football many seasons, unlike the old one that was now barely sparking. They might need to fight Strange Lady—or the Even Meaner One—again, someday.

The crow cawed, and left them.

Olaf found it hard to decipher crow language, but it seemed the crow had said Strange Lady *was* the Even Meaner One. That she was gone for good. And that Football's mother—the *real* Strange Lady—was heartbroken without her.

Olaf's own heart hurt, because he knew what that meant.

"*No.*" Football raised her head from fake-sleeping, and wiped away a tear. "*Mama* is Mama. Not Strange Lady."

Olaf dug his claws into the dirt floor. He could run off with

Football and keep her hidden. Keep her for himself.

But that wouldn't be doing the right thing.

He padded to her, knelt, and stared into her pond-algae eyes, so fierce and determined. "Mama will always be Mama," he said.

What could he say, to get her to agree to leave him? He thought ahead, to what might happen.

"Maybe someday the humans will come for *me*, like they did *my* mama. And I'll need you to know all about them. Things I could never teach you. So you can protect me."

The color drained from Football's little face as she seemed to ponder this possibility. She got to her feet, and wrapped her arms around his belly. Or, tried to.

"I protect you, Papa."

*

The crow sat in a window high in the back of the castle. Black smoke spewed from the slightly open kitchen door. The Mean One, at least, was probably home. The opening music of *Snarky Bravewand and Her Spookalicious Buds* emanated from within.

Olaf looked up at an annoying fluttering, which had been disturbing the natural sounds of the park on and off since morning. One of the human flying machines was hovering, but so many tree-lengths above him, surely it couldn't see him. Besides, he was wearing his disguise, with Football tucked safely under his coat.

"Should we go in, sir? Could be just a homeless woman."

Chief Detector Thomas watched the helicopter feed from the Situation Room. "Homeless woman, my head. That's how the bear has been evading Animal Control all this time. Lower troops to follow on foot, but keep your distance. Use handheld fans to waft away your scents. The bear's gone to the witches for help—we can kill two birds with one stone."

"Er, Chief? I'm an avid birder, and I take offense at that expression," piped up Detector Kinney. "Could you maybe find a new way of saying that."

At his glare, she mumbled, "Or not."

Still, he made a mental note never to have her fetch his coffee, just in case.

Olaf politely banged on the door, as he no longer belonged here. No one heard him above the fluttering and the frolicking of Snarky and her friends. He reached in, pulled the door open wider, and entered.

Once inside, he opened his coat. Under the floofy scarf, Football let go of his neck. He set her on the floor. She smiled and reached out, calling, "Nice Lady!"

The Nice One smiled, wiped off her hands from where she'd been rolling dough, and strolled over, revealing the gray cat lolling on the counter, and in the corner, the Mean One stirring a potion.

Football scowled. "Mean Lady."

The Mean One threw up her hands. Potion batter flew off her spoon and stuck to the ceiling. "You were in my presence *one* day! *Maybe* two. You couldn't possibly remember me!"

She craned her neck to see what everyone was staring at, and emitted a great long sigh as if the entire world was, unfairly, descending upon her. "I'll need to remember to clean that later."

The Nice One knelt to Football's level. "Sweetheart, Olaf and I and Hilda—"

The Mean One snorted.

"—we will always be here for you. We're your family. But you have other family, too. You have a mother who loves you and misses you. It's wonderful you're giving her a chance. It'll be another defeat for—" The Nice One looked up at Olaf.

"Strange Lady."

The Nice One nodded, and gave Football a big smile. "Strange Lady is your mother's sister. Your mother is . . . let's call her, maybe, *Kind* Lady."

Football scrunched up her nose.

"Or not." The Nice One winked. "You can figure that out on your own."

Football stomped her tiny foot. "Want Mama. Want Papa."

"You'll always have your papa. And I'm sure your mama, wherever she is, wants you to give your human mother a try, at least." The Nice One smiled at Olaf. "Right, Olaf?"

Wrong, thought Olaf.

But he gently squeezed Football's tiny paw in both his own.

*

He peeked out from behind a parked car as the Nice One held onto Football's paw and knocked on the real mother's door. Football stared stubbornly at him. He smiled to encourage her. He had promised he would visit. She only needed to keep her window slightly ajar.

She looked over his shoulder suddenly, smiled, and waved her free paw. Olaf glanced behind him. No one was there. One of their new squirrel friends must have come to see Football off, and darted away again.

He turned back just as the door opened. The real mother came out. She exclaimed with joy and knelt to hug Football. Football refused to look at her, fixing her eyes on Olaf, frowning and enduring.

The Nice One and the real mother led Football inside the house. Football sent Olaf another quick smile and subtly waved her fingers, already expert at keeping secrets. The real mother shut the door, and Olaf was all alone.

He rested his head against the tire, not wanting to go home.

FIFTY THREE

Mabel hopped through the park.

The hideous shrieks of wild beasts reverberated through the air. Animals she had—armed with her wand—never before feared.

There was a flutter of wings, and she lunged to the side, barely escaping the talons of a hawk. It was the third winged thing that had tried to grab her so far.

She hid in a hollowed-out tree. After sufficient time passed, she peeked out. The coast was clear. She hopped off, making her way through the jungle of the Ramble, toward the park exit.

If anyone thought she was down for the count, they had another stinking think coming. It was absurd to even consider. Her! Mabel Blackthornudder, the most powerful ~~witch~~ frog in New York City.

FIFTY FOUR

Olaf padded slowly to the cave, his heart heavy and hurting. Something *squelched* underneath his foot. He lifted his paw to look. Oops. He had accidentally trod on another poor frog. This one looked like it had been angry in its last moments. Or maybe that was just his imagination.

That was the thing about frogs. They were always getting underfoot.

He wiped his paw on the grass and continued on, into the cave.

Harvey's spirit floated "down," to meet the spirit of his wife.

The souls of loved ones often waited for them at the moment of death, to greet them in their transition, to reunite, to reassure them all was all right, that death was not the end.

Only another beginning.

Mabel's spirit floated out of her frog body and ascended to the light.

Harvey's heart warmed—even more than was a spirit's natural wont. He and Mabel would forgive each other for their Earthly mistakes, their occasional tendency to be cruel, their inability in the material world to recognize each other for the Love they truly were.

Mabel turned her "head," saw him, squinted, and recognized him.

Harvey waved, his heart jumping for joy.

Loser! Mabel sneered. *See you in the next life . . . NOT!*

Harvey sighed. With that attitude, she probably would.

Not all souls had the capacity to forgive, not even in the light. It was hard even for souls, sometimes, to let go of the adrenaline rushes of anger and resentment, and relax into the softer energies of understanding and compassion.

Inevitably, his thoughts turned back to the Bard. "What fools these mortals be!" Although, once shuffling off this mortal coil, we all discover, we go on for eternity.

Mabel floated up, up, up . . . and disappeared from sight. Soon, she would meet with her main guide and discuss her accomplishments—failures, more like—from this life.

Harvey followed. It was time to prepare, to quote Macbeth, for "the life to come."

FIFTY FIVE

Olaf sat on his rock and cried. He was now truly alone.

He had done the right thing, and what had it got him? Football was gone. To her real mother, who loved her. Baby was gone. To her little girl, who loved her. Even Essex had gone. To again be with her mate, who loved her.

Nobody loved Olaf anymore.

He would visit Football every day, but soon she would become enmeshed in the human world, with its human concerns. She might in time not even want him to come around anymore. She might forget him. Essex had said humans were good at forgetting. At least, about the good things.

He still had other friends. The birds. The ducks. The squirrels. Jack and Earl, and Earl's many,

many, many, many, many, many, many, many, many, many, many,
many, many, many, many, many, many, many, many, many, many,
many, many, many, many, many, many, many, many, many, many,
many, many, many, many, many, many, many, many, many, many,
many, many, many, many, many, many, many, many, many, many,
many, many, many, many, many, many, many, many, many, many,
many, many, many, many, many, many, many, many, many, many,
many, many, many, many, many, many, many, many, many, many,
many, many, many, many, many, many, many, many, many, many,
many, many, many, many, many, many, many, many, many, many,
many, many, many, many, many, many, many, many, many, many,
many, many, many, many, many, many, many, many, many, many,
many, many, many, many, many, many, many, many, many, many,
many, many, many, many, many, many, many, many, many, many,
many, many, many, many, many, many, many, many, many, many
friends. More friends than Olaf had known any one being could
have.

But it wasn't the same. He wasn't even sure Wendy would
want to see him anymore. She had her own cub now.

Still, he had done the right thing. Essex would be proud of
him. So would his mother. Maybe Wendy, too. And Football
would be grateful, at least someday, to be with her real mother.

He got up, and lay down on his bed of soft leaves. He closed
his eyes. Was it too early to go to sleep for the winter? It wasn't
particularly cold out. And anyway, he hadn't prepared. His belly
had not again grown big and round.

But he did not want to keep waking up, just to face this
loneliness.

Life *was*, as Essex had relayed after her last visit with the
trees, "a poor player, that struts and frets his hour upon the stage,

and then is heard no more ... a tale ... signifying nothing."

Olaf *had* nothing, *was* nothing, was—

Something nudged his nose. He opened his eyes. Perhaps a baby bird had flown in?

His mother smiled down at him.

Olaf stared. Was it really her? She was fuzzier than he remembered. He reached out to touch her, and felt ... *something*.

And over her shoulder—was that ... Essex? Smiling at him?

There was a shimmer, and the air seemed to open for him. Tentatively, he reached out. His paw disappeared, though he could still feel it. He thrust his arm farther in.

He left the cave behind.

Berry. I love you. I am always with you.

Olaf—Berry!—exploded with a happiness he'd never known. It was fuzzy and warm. There was no grief, no fear ... there was nothing but love. His mother hugged him, and he clung to her. Essex leaned against his leg. If only he could stay here forever.

You can't stay, Olaf, said Essex.

"Why?"

Because Football's in danger.

Instantly, he was back in the cave. The fuzzy, warm feeling was gone.

Not bothering to don his disguise, he bolted out of the cave, through the woods, out of the park ... to the real mother's house. Football's screams reverberated through the night, along with the shouting of other humans. Olaf pushed himself to run even faster, his lungs on fire.

He bounded up the stairs, climbed over the banister, carefully balanced on the narrow, ornamental ledge and pawed his

way to the slightly-ajar window. He stared at the humans in yellow. Two held the arms of the real mother and the Nice One behind their backs. One had a paw over the real mother's mouth. Some kind of metal contraption encased the Nice One's jaws. Wires extended to a little metal cap . . . which sat on Football's head.

"No!" she screamed over and over, as the furless, spaghetti-colored human held her aloft and yelled, "Do it! Say haaaaaaaaaaaaaaaaaaaaaah!"

And then, he *shook* her—her fragile little body, her fragile little brain—

"They don't pay me enough!"

The big bark-colored human dropped the hunk of metal he held. He put his large hands around Football and pulled her out of the Furless One's grasp. Before the Furless One could react, he tucked her against his broad chest, yanked off the metal cap, and slugged the Furless One in the face.

CRACK!

Olaf flinched at the sound of a gun. The big human fell to the floor.

Football landed on her feet, like Baby had taught her, and made a break for the door—where she was corralled by the Furless One, who had regained his balance and rushed to intercept her. He dragged her to the center of the room and forced the metal cap back on her head.

Olaf could push in the window pane with his snout. But the humans would hear him. See him. Shoot. He would be no help to Football dead.

He carefully made his way back to the banister and bounded down the steps to the sidewalk. He had spotted a large rain puddle on his way here.

He stared down at it, like Baby had made him practice, willing it to connect him to his mother and best friend. To ask them, what could he do? How could he help Football?

Miraculously, an image formed. Or was he imagining it? Himself and Essex, skulking through the food palace. Approaching ... the bored checkout teenager?

Was he just seeing in the puddle what he wanted to see, his best friend alive? Like he'd seen the lollipops while practicing? But then, why would he see the bored checkout teenager? Who he found rather scary, and would rather not approach. No, it had to be a message from Essex.

He broke into a run, ignoring his burning lungs. Before he knew it, he made it to the food palace.

Huffing and puffing, he burst through the sliding doors. As usual, the bored checkout teenager didn't even look up. He stared at the diapers she'd laid on the counter for him, and the newest baby toys.

She would be able to understand him, if she really was a witch. "Help me, *please*."

She looked up at him with surprise. "Are you trying to talk to me?"

He nodded.

She smiled slightly. "I've always known you're a bear. Your tail sticks out."

Olaf looked where she pointed, in front of her knees. Under the counter, a hunk of glass and metal showed black-and-white images of the entire food palace. Oh! The Scary One had never been scary at all.

"But I'm not good at understanding animal vocalizations. My teacher says I need to relax and not try so hard. If you want something else in the store, go ahead and grab it. I'll futz with the recording like I always do."

How to tell her what he needed? He looked down at the counter, at the abandoned items. Among them, a pack of paper. A carton of crayons.

He ran his paws down the pack, ripping the plastic. He tore off the carton cover and dumped the crayons onto the counter. Holding the red crayon between his paw pads, he drew lines on the top paper.

The not-bored checkout teenager craned her neck at the upside-down letters.

"H—" she read aloud. "E . . . L . . ."

That was all he knew. Essex had last taught him L, for lollipops.

"It *is* hell working here, that's for sure." Her eyes widened. "Oh! You mean *help!*"

From the handbag at her feet, she pulled out . . . a magic stick! She straightened and leapt over the counter.

"Gertrude!"

A door behind the counter banged opened, and a wide face with blazing eyes, a warty nose, and wild hair poked out, as well as a hand shaking a funny-looking gun. "I'm not even done pricing the green beans yet, Abigail!"

"Forget all that!" snapped Abigail. "Hold down the fort! Unless you want to go back to jail."

"Fine." Gertrude heaved a sigh. "I'll work the register. Anything but go back to that hellhole."

A thoughtful look crossed Abigail's face. "Ah, screw it. Come along, and bring your wand. We may need backup."

Gertrude let out a triumphant grunt and threw the funny-looking gun to the floor. She ran into the secret room and rushed back out holding a broom, her wand sticking out of her robe pocket. They all dashed out of the food palace. Gertrude straddled her broom. Abigail got on behind. They turned their heads to look expectantly at Olaf.

He threw a leg over the broomstick and sat. The broomstick sagged, also not accustomed to his weight, then bucked, trying to pitch him off.

"Quit it," said Gertrude. The broomstick settled, heaved itself up, and Gertrude kicked them off into the night.

With Olaf navigating, they soon reached the real mother's house. Shouts and Football's screams punctuated the night. The broom let them off—dumped, in Olaf's case—at the top of the stoop. Gertrude aimed her magic stick at the door.

"And give up the element of surprise?" Abigail took two small somethings out of her jeans pocket. "My stepmother gave me a key and the security fob." She clicked the longer metal stick, and a light outside the door flashed. She slid the small silver stick into the door slot.

"Wait a sec." She climbed up onto the banister, carefully stepped onto the narrow ledge and toed her way to the window, before retracing her steps. "Dad's holding Madison. It's too dangerous to attack him. Focus on the others. Maybe in the confusion, Madison can bite him, drop to the floor and get away."

Pulling her magic stick from her pocket, and taking hold of the small silver stick in the door slot, she locked eyes with Gertrude. "One . . . two . . . three!"

She turned the silver stick and flung the door open. Gertrude had barely stepped inside to aim before green light coursed through the entranceway. She and Abigail ran inside.

Olaf peeked in the doorway—just as a humongous wire net enveloped them.

A yellow human pressed buttons on a hunk of metal, and the netting hummed ominously. Abigail and Gertrude screamed.

"I knew it!" The Furless One shook Football even harder. "Both my daughters have chosen the side of evil!"

In the din and confusion, no one noticed Olaf peeking

around the foyer. Still, the Furless One had the upper paw. Olaf looked on in despair. What could *he* do, when all the humans who were good at magic had failed? He was just a big, dumb bear. And he had already asked the puddle of water for help.

His gaze wandered to the banister he'd slid down with Football when she was just a baby. His heart warmed. Yes, he was dumb. But he was also *big*.

Warily, he crept forward, keeping to the sides of the room. None of the humans noticed him. Maybe because he moved so slowly, so unthreateningly. He reached the stairs and began the climb, one by one, as the Furless One shouted louder, and

Football screamed, "Bad Man!" While the real mother, the Nice One, Abigail, and Gertrude helplessly looked on.

Olaf reached the landing, rose, and threw a leg over the banister. He looked down, marking the body that was just far enough from long arms that held Football aloft. He swung his other leg over, slid off and—

SPLAT!

Squashed the Furless One flat.

"Ooh," said Gertrude. "That must've hurt."

The Nice One and the real mother yanked their arms out of the yellow humans' grasps, and—as they stared at their fallen, flat leader—turned, and socked them in their shocked faces.

Football, having landed just like a cat, squirmed out of the Furless One's still hands and jerked her head out of the metal cap. She ran to Olaf and threw her arms around his leg. He caressed her head with his paw, keeping his eyes on the room in case the danger hadn't passed.

The Nice One grabbed her magic stick from where her captor had dropped it. She waved it around the room.

The yellow humans set down any weapons they held and stuck their hands in the air. One punched buttons on the metal box. The netting quieted. Abigail and Gertrude managed to untangle themselves and emerge. The Nice One motioned to the contraption around her jaws, and one of the yellow humans worked it open for her.

The real mother ran to Football, knelt, and threw her arms around her. She stared at Football's arms around Olaf's leg, looked up at him—seemed to finally register he was a bear, not a human wearing a "swat team" costume—and fainted.

The Nice One bent to revive her. "For a doctor, she sure has a queasy disposition." She smiled up at Olaf. "Magic can do a lot of things. So can guns. But have a bear land on you, it's all over."

Olaf looked down at Football holding him tight. And just above her ... Essex and his mother shimmered and smiled. Then they faded into the ether. But he knew he would see them again. Be with them again.

Life was *not* a tale signifying nothing. He loved other beings, and they loved him. *That* was something.

That was neverending.

Thank you so much for reading my book. Times sure have changed since humans lived in caves and relied on Uncle Groog's enthralling tales of hunting saber-toothed tigers (or Aunt Boomba's tales of saving Uncle Groog from the tigers) for something to occupy the time. There are a plethora of things you could have been doing—for fun or necessity—instead of reading this story and sticking with it till the end, and I feel honored that you did.

If you enjoyed it, please tell other eager readers about it, and please consider leaving me a review.

Read on for a preview of the sequel . . .

Hilda

and

Helga

PREVIEW

Over the edge of what appeared to be a long table in a big, bright room, Mabel Blackthornudder—or, more accurately, her soul—peered through the somewhat fuzzy dimensions at the Earth.

She couldn't help snarling at two of her three still-living-on-the-physical-plane nemeses: the elder Hagglebottom sister (Hilda), and that dumb bear. The bear that was about to break yet another set of playground swings. Lucky for the toddler (Football, what a dumb name!) she had a propensity for soft landings.

So, said Groh, Mabel's main guide, tapping his "pen" against his "notebook." (Solidity in this dimension was, of course, an illusion, just like on Earth.) *Now that you've had time to rest and recover from your latest Earthly adventure, as well as your journey Home . . .*

(At least Groh hadn't started off this life review like the last: *So, Mabel . . . screwed up again, didn't you?*)

He flipped a few pages back in his book, reviewed his notes, and again rhythmically tapped his pen. *During which you once again failed to accomplish any of the objectives we agreed upon . . .*

So, not *too* different from last time.

That dumb bear pushed the swing higher and higher. The toddler hung on and laughed. The lamppost got so bright it almost caught on fire.

Fingertips drummed against the table. Mabel looked up from the Earth, back at Groh. *Sorry, but no, not true at all. I had more self-doubt last go-round. Less certainty. Less self-righteousness.*

Even now, she recognized she shouldn't have such mean thoughts about her fellow Earthly beings, especially as she currently had such a wider point of view.

It was just so easy to carry over lingering resentments. People on Earth thought when you died and went to "Heaven," you became just like an angel, innocent and pure. Loving everyone and everything. And some did. But they were usually the simple-minded, already-easygoing ones, like that insufferable Helga

Hagglebottom, who had been offered the position of alternate dimension guide ever since completing her very first Earthly lifetime—but kept turning it down, believing she could do more good for her fellow beings in yet another Earthly incarnation.

Groh looked unconvinced, so Mabel continued, *I changed my mind about Surly Checkout Girl. I mean*—she peered at the Earth down below—*Abigail*. Yes. The rude checkout teenager at the large West Side all-night food market, who had turned out to be not only a witch-in-training, schooled by Helga Hagglebottom herself, but also, the Chief Magic Detector's elder daughter.

Yet you held on tight to resentments. Groh was holding on right now, to his need to minutely examine Mabel's every little flub from last lifetime. *Fixated on things outside yourself. Took out your frustrations on others . . .*

Mabel shrugged. Best to let him ramble on.

How is Harvey doing, by the way?

Who knows, who cares? At Groh's disapproving glance, she clarified, *I haven't seen him, except for a few moments in passing.*

Groh's fingers paused in mid-drum. *Usually, souls meet their loved ones on the way back. To talk through their*

Earthly experiences together.

Mabel snorted. *As if I'd want to spend time with that loser.*

Groh's eyebrows rose. Oops. Mabel had again said a wrong thing. Not only *said*, but *felt* it, too. Objectively, she could admit it wasn't *really* Harvey's fault that everything had gone wrong last lifetime. At least, not *all* his fault.

She really ought to let go of all this accumulated animosity. She could work on that here, in the space between Earthly lives. She certainly didn't want to deal with his incompetent self in yet another incarnation.

Oops! Yet again had she thought a wrong thing. Wrong, but true.

Groh scribbled something, most likely uncomplimentary, in the unused section of his notebook. Mabel surreptitiously leaned over to look.

WILL SUGGEST . . . MABEL AND HARVEY . . . TOGETHER AGAIN, NEXT—

Whaaaaaaat?

Mabel jerked her head away and stared at him. *Are you cra—I mean, I respectfully disag—*

Mabel. Groh sighed, put down his pen and notebook, and looked at her. At least *somewhat* kindly.

Wouldn't you like to finally get over your blocks and make a huge leap forward in your evolution?

Sure. Whatever.

And who better to give you those opportunities than—

Fine! Yes! Let's get on with it. Mabel knew from talking to other souls, most guides were not as hard on them. And Groh hadn't always been. At least, not when Mabel had been a young soul, *expected* to make mistakes. *Does it HAVE to be Harvey, though? Couldn't I maybe just skip right to having a frog familiar, and NAME him Harvey?*

Groh ran his hand through his long black hair. A part of his soul was simultaneously living on Earth right now, as a musician (of horrendously loud "music," Mabel was sorry to say). His Earthly mannerisms were carrying over. *I've never had such a difficult case*, he mumbled, apparently forgetting they were not human here, and she could hear him perfectly.

—asked to be reassigned again and again—

Perhaps his simultaneous Earthly lifetime was getting in the way. Mabel nudged his elbow to remind him where the greater part of his soul lay. *Come now, Groh. You LOVE me.*

We ALL love each other here. Or at least, we're supposed to. He narrowed his eyes at her, his goatee seeming to narrow disapprovingly as well. *But you annoy me greatly.*

See! Mabel slapped the table with her palm. *NOW can you see how I feel about Harvey?*

Groh sighed and laid his head down on his book, his long black hair splaying out on the table in a sign of defeat. Or so, Mabel hoped.

ACKNOWLEDGMENTS

Instead of repeating "Thank you for your encouragement and emotional support" umpteen times, I wish to include all the following in that thanks.

Louise Ma, thank you for proposing we do *The Artist's Way* "Morning Pages" together, and when I tried to beg off, citing it would aggravate my carpal tunnel symptoms, for suggesting that I talk nonstop into a recorder. It was 2019, I was just starting this story with no idea where it was going and was trying out different beginnings. Thank you for laughing so hard at the "I had a husband, but he croaked" joke. It made me realize how much I enjoyed writing Mabel and Harvey, and that I should combine a couple of the versions and get them back into the cast.

Thank you to my early readers for your precious time and feedback: Tandy Grubbs, Sophia Chang, Colleen DeTroy, Alisha Wielfaert, and Victoria Key.

Thank you to my editor, Jennifer Rees, for your attention to detail, your sense of humor, your kindness, and for valiantly trying to rein in my excesses.

(Readers, any grammatical or punctuation irregularities are my own. I changed some things back to fit my own rhythm and quirks . . . like my loathing of four-dot ellipses.)

Xiao, thank you for your beautiful illustrations. Jennifer Kyte, thank you for designing such a lovely cover and interior. Thank you both for being such wonderful creative partners, for your keen eyes and great ideas, your sense of fun, your hard work, and for dealing with my quirks. I so appreciate you both.

Thank you to my writing buddy, Alicia J. Novo, for all your helpful comments, suggestions, and information, and for making my journey to publication much more enjoyable. Thank you, Andrew Colarusso and Diana Cruz at Taylor & Co. Books in Brooklyn. If it weren't for you, I might still be reworking my synopsis and query letter. Thank you to all my writer friends from New York Write to Pitch. Our WhatsApp chats are a continual source of . . . encouragement . . . but also information and fun. Thank you, Cathy Dipierro, for all your helpful suggestions and advice, and for building me a fantastic website via Unreal Creative. Thank you, Alisha Wielfaert, for helping me to think more positively about the business side of writing. Thank you, Ashton Gooding, for your lovely photography.

Thank you to friends who have helped to buoy me through this long journey through self-doubt: Tandy Grubbs and Sue Ryan, Peter O'Brien, Imelda Siocheng, Daniel Sosa, Kristine

Johnson, Paolo Visentin, Aneta Key, Sandhya Dhage Kaurwar and your family, Phyllis Marcia Goldberg, Colleen DeTroy, Richard Cruz, Louise Ma, Alena, Nell, Kimberly, Benjamin Cheung, Heidi Cain, and Isaac Omar Reyes. Thank you, Benjamin Cheung and Heidi Cain, for agreeing to lend your vocal talents to my promo videos. And thank you, Serika Douglas, for helping me think of the right word that was eluding me.

Thank you, Michael Moon, for your guidance when I didn't know how to move forward. Thank you, Glenda—things you told me kept coming true, and kept me believing. I hope to meet you again in our next lives, or on the Other Side.

Thank you to the wonderful Central Park Conservancy guides for giving such interesting, informative, fun tours. And special thanks to tour guide Juan and Melissa at the castle for being so kind and helpful.

Thank you to my relatives in Germany and Austria. A special shout-out to my cousin Ralf Maier for suggesting I incorporate goat tickle torture.

Thank you to my Onkel Ed and Tante Margot McCarthy for encouragement and emotional support over my entire life.

And to my brother, Chris—thank you for being my first comedic inspiration, and for all your and your family's help over the years.

I also have a whole slew of "no thank you"s, but that list shall remain private. ;)

ABOUT THE AUTHOR

As a child, Patti Calkosz would have loved to have been rescued by a talking fox and bear. Like many kids, she grew up in an environment where it didn't feel safe to be her authentic self. She created a protective shell in which to hide, which led to deep unhappiness, social isolation, a self-perception of being "dull," and escalating health problems.

Employing "alternative" healing practices later in life, Patti's energy began to open up, unleashing her creativity. She loves making people laugh and writing about important social issues in an entertaining way.

Find her online at www.patticalkosz.com or patticalkosz on Instagram.